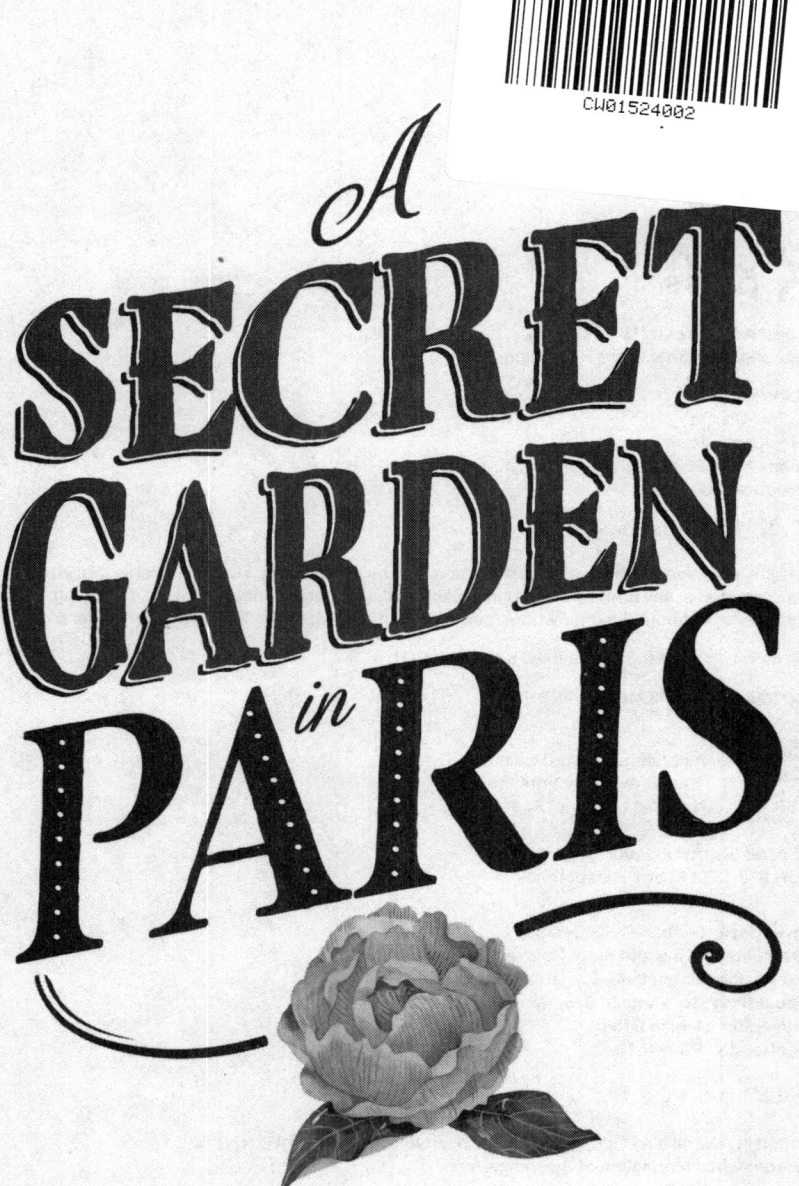

A Secret Garden in Paris

SOPHIE BEAUMONT

ultimo press

Published in 2024 by Ultimo Press,
an imprint of Hardie Grant Publishing

Ultimo Press
Gadigal Country
7, 45 Jones Street
Ultimo, NSW 2007
ultimopress.com.au

  ultimopress

All rights reserved. No part of this publication may be reproduced, stored in a retrieval system or transmitted in any form by any means, electronic, mechanical, photocopying, recording or otherwise, without the prior written permission of the publishers and copyright holders.

The moral rights of the author have been asserted.

Copyright © Sophie Masson 2024

 A catalogue record for this book is available from the National Library of Australia

A Secret Garden in Paris
ISBN 978 1 76115 361 7 (paperback)

Cover design Christabella Designs
Cover illustrations and map Courtesy of Cheryl Orsini
Text design Simon Paterson | Bookhouse, Sydney
Typesetting Bookhouse, Sydney
Copyeditor Deonie Fiford
Proofreader Pamela Dunne

10 9 8 7 6 5 4 3 2 1

Printed in Australia by Opus Group Pty Ltd, an Accredited ISO AS/NZS 14001 Environmental Management System printer.

 The paper this book is printed on is certified against the Forest Stewardship Council® Standards. Griffin Press – a member of the Opus Group – holds chain of custody certification SCS-COC-001185. FSC® promotes environmentally responsible, socially beneficial and economically viable management of the world's forests.

Ultimo Press acknowledges the Traditional Owners of the Country on which we work, the Gadigal People of the Eora Nation and the Wurundjeri People of the Kulin Nation, and recognises their continuing connection to the land, waters and culture. We pay our respects to their Elders past and present.

Also by Sophie Beaumont

The Paris Cooking School

La fleur est courte, mais la joie qu'elle a donnée une minute, n'est pas des ces choses qui ont commencement et fin.

The flower blooms briefly, but the joy it gave to a minute has no beginning and no end.

PAUL CLAUDEL

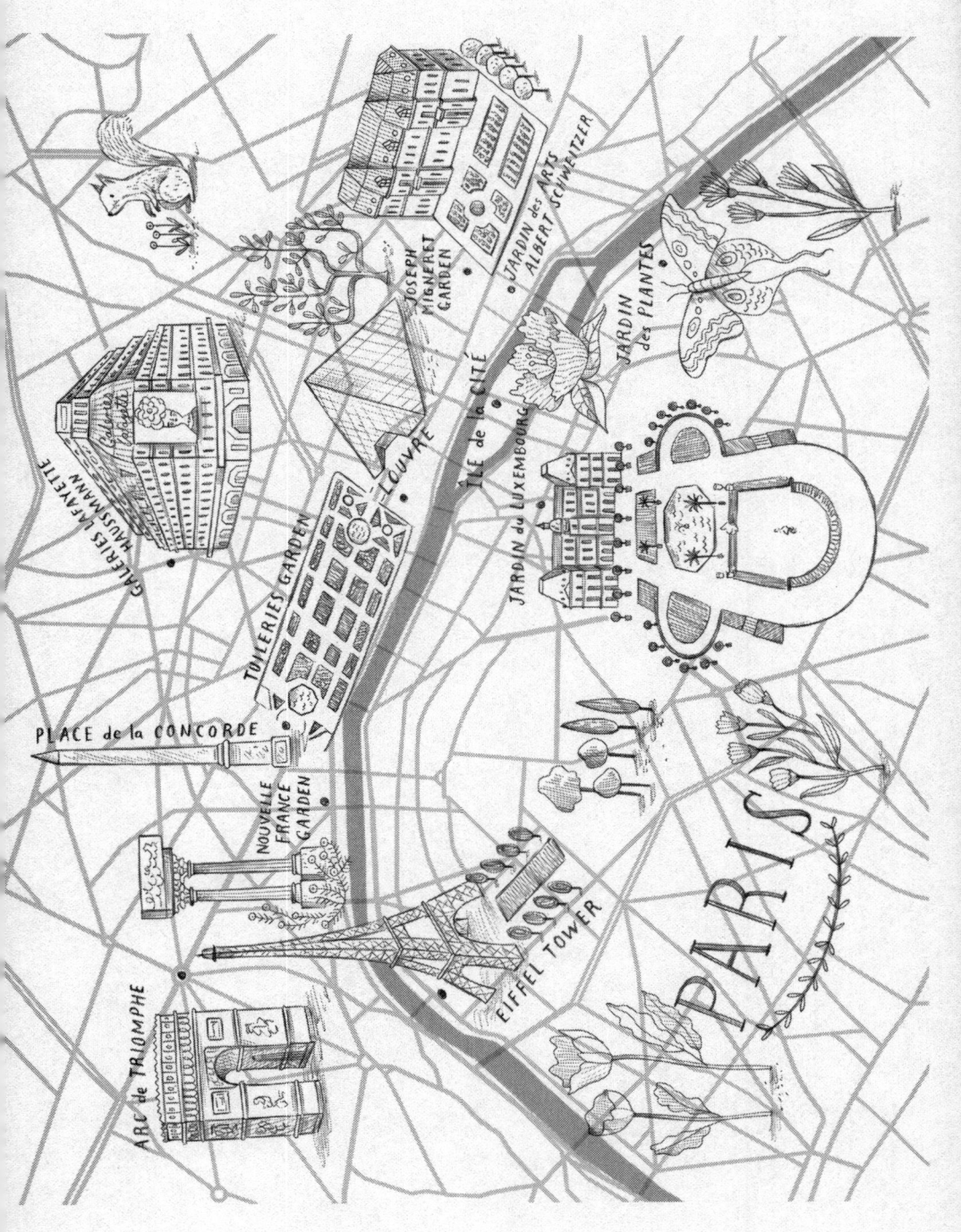

One

The dawn light was only just filtering through the curtains, but Emma Taylor was already wide awake. She had been lying sleepless for at least an hour, determinedly keeping her eyes closed, trying to ensure her mind remained empty, and failing. Now, giving up all pretence that she was going to go back to sleep, she got up, shrugged on the retro velvet dressing-gown Mattie had lent her, padded over to the window and drew back the curtains.

The bedroom looked out over the garden at the back of the house, and in the gold and pink of early morning, its overgrown vegetation assumed a fleetingly magical quality. The garden wasn't large, but it had once packed a great deal of beauty into not much more than a hundred square metres. There had been soft grass to sit on, a big wisteria against one wall—you could still see it, even now—rosebushes and hydrangeas, and carefully tended beds bright with flowers from spring to autumn, as well as a few edibles such as tomatoes and herbs. The garden had been her grandfather Alain's pride and joy, but since his death two and a half years ago, it had been slowly neglected to the point where now, overtaken by weeds and rank long grass, it would take quite a lot of work to get right again. Her grandmother Mattie simply hadn't had the heart to tackle it.

Emma opened the window, breathing in the fresh morning air. The sounds of Paris waking up came floating above the high wall of the garden. Sounds that she'd already become accustomed to, even though she'd arrived jet-lagged from the other side of the world only a week ago. It was a cocktail of mechanical noises: the hum of early-morning traffic on the boulevards, the underground rumble of trains in a nearby Metro station, the swish of street-sweeping machines, the muffled thump of van doors as shop deliveries were made, and the distant sirens of police and ambulances. But interwoven with that was a glittering thread of birdsong: blackbirds, warblers, robins, thrushes and wrens, taking part in the dawn chorus. Emma could hear them but couldn't see them, for they were hidden in the garden below and the surrounding trees.

As she stood there, an image came into her mind of her mother as a girl, standing at this very window, listening to the birds. A lump formed in her throat, and she was about to turn away when her attention was caught by a flash of red in the garden below. 'Monsieur Leroux took up residence here last autumn,' Mattie had told her on her first day, 'but he doesn't keep regular hours, so you can never be sure when he might appear.' This was the first time Emma had seen him since she'd arrived.

'Bonjour, Monsieur Leroux,' Emma whispered as the red squirrel scampered lightly across the grass before vanishing into the undergrowth. Monsieur Leroux—Mr Redhead. It was typical of her grandmother to have given the little creature a name. There was something childlike about Mattie, something sweet yet clear-eyed.

Emma didn't remember the first time she'd met her grandmother because she'd been three years old when her French grandparents had come to Australia. It was their sole visit. And Emma had only been twice to her grandparents' lovely old house tucked away in a quiet street of the 7th arrondissement of Paris. The first time, she was seven years old and her stepfather, Paddy, had persuaded her mother, Corinne, to visit. What Emma most remembered from those three dreamlike weeks were impressions: a cosy house with lots of stairs, her grandfather's slow smile and slow speech, her grandmother's sparkly manner and eccentric way of dressing, so different from her mother's understated chic. There were memories of riding ponies and sailing toy wooden yachts in the nearby Jardin du Luxembourg and listening in delight to her grandmother's story of the dancing faun statue there. She remembered eating divine cakes from the local patisserie—such as the best chocolate éclairs she'd ever eaten—and riding on the Metro, visiting the little zoo in the Jardin des Plantes and playing in the garden while her grandfather weeded around her.

Then they'd gone home to Australia, time had passed and passed. Somehow, her childhood went by and they didn't return to France. Mattie had a heart condition that made flying difficult, so her grandparents didn't come back to Australia either.

There were letters exchanged—Emma always wrote a special one at Christmas—and phone calls for birthdays, but that was it. As a child, Emma didn't wonder about her mother's attitude, and if, as a teenager, she occasionally asked herself questions about her mother's past in France, she didn't voice them. And so her grandparents remained as vague, kindly presences in her memories of that first time in Paris. There seemed to be no particular urgency for Emma to see them again, or perhaps it was just that her mother's detached attitude towards them had affected her more than she had realised.

In any case, it wasn't until two and a half years ago that Emma had finally come back to Paris. And that was for her grandfather Alain's funeral. She'd come with her mother and they'd stayed ten days. It had been hard, and not only because of the sad occasion. Paddy couldn't come because of work and Corinne hadn't wanted Emma to come, but for once Emma put her foot down. Emma wasn't sure if her mother had agreed because her daughter's unusual firmness had taken her by surprise, or because she was more vulnerable than she cared to admit. It was a big thing to lose your father, no matter how strained the relationship had been, and Corinne did seem to be genuinely affected. Emma had thought that might trigger a proper reconnection between her mother and grandmother, but unfortunately, once they were in France, the old barriers seemed to go up. Although Corinne tried to provide comfort to her mother, it was clear that it was an effort, and Mattie must have seen that, though she never reproached her.

Sometimes it felt as though her mother's life had only really started when she'd set foot in Australia thirty-two years ago as a pregnant twenty-year-old; or perhaps when she'd met Paddy, several months later. Corinne talked readily enough about her life in Australia, before and after Emma was born. But although she had spoken a bit about her childhood, the years of her adolescence and the period just before she left France were a closed book, which she passed over in silence. She'd never spoken about Emma's father, other than to say that it hadn't worked out with him.

Emma had always thought of Paddy as her real father. He'd been there from her earliest babyhood, steady, kind, funny, and full of love. For her, and for her mother. And that was all that mattered. But now . . .

She turned from the window, her gaze falling on the photograph propped up on the mantelpiece. It was a black-and-white shot of her mother as a very young woman, late teens maybe, lying in long grass, laughing, chin propped up on her elbows, a crooked chain of daisies on her head. It was a beautiful picture but it made Emma's eyes prickle with tears.

'Emma?' Her grandmother's voice, surprisingly deep for such a small woman, came suddenly through the door. 'You're awake, *ma chérie*? I thought I would make some hot chocolate to warm us, it's such a chilly morning.'

Emma blinked away the tears. 'That sounds perfect, Mattie,' she said. It was, in fact, not particularly chilly for a May morning, but she'd learned that her grandmother was *frileuse*, a succinct but untranslatable French term for someone who easily felt the cold.

Emma would have preferred coffee, but she could have that later, and she'd got used to the morning ritual of watching Mattie in the kitchen downstairs, fiddling about with the little saucepan she kept specifically for hot chocolate, and chatting about this and that, letting Emma enter the flow of talk when she felt ready. During such moments, Emma knew how much she'd missed. But also how right she had been to come at last.

Across the river, Charlotte Marigny jogged through quiet leafy streets, earbuds pouring in a stream of her special Paris running playlist. It was an eclectic mix of classic Parisian songs—Piaf and Brel and a smidgen of old-school French rock, like Johnny Hallyday and Michel Polnareff and, just for a bit of fun, '*Ça plane pour moi*', Plastic Bertrand's bizarre earworm of a punk song. She remembered hopping up and down to that as a little kid, delighted at being invited into the world of her teenage brother, Nicolas. The one-hit wonder still had cult status in France, but Nicolas had long outgrown it and the quiff of dyed blond hair that he'd affected at the time, in homage to the singer. Now he had an important job somewhere in the corridors of the European Parliament in Brussels that he could be a little pompous about explaining, so she didn't ask. She was staying at their aunt Juliette's place in the 16th while Juliette was off on some jaunt in Prague with an old friend who Charlotte suspected had once been a lover. Her aunt obviously knew something was up because she had told her to stay for as long as she needed, but she hadn't probed at why her niece felt she needed to get away so precipitously.

The sun had fully risen by now, and the city was really coming to life. Boulangeries were already busy, disgorging puffs of warm, appetising smells every time their doors opened and the breakfast customers emerged, fresh baguettes under arms and bags of croissants in hand; early-shift workers lined up at café counters to throw down thimblefuls of black coffee before hurrying on; stalls and shops were being readied to open. Turning down the next street, Charlotte found herself by the river, where dogwalkers and the occasional fellow runner passed by, as the silver-grey water lapped softly against the quays and the odd boat chugged slowly on its way to somewhere. She stopped for a moment to catch her breath and take a swig of water from the bottle at her waist. She gazed across the river and for a moment she was entranced all over again by the sheer enchantment of this city that had once been *her* city, the place where she'd been born and brought up. Her home was in London now, had been for many years. She'd married there, brought up a family, founded a very successful garden design business, and over time had grown to love London, in a different way from how she loved Paris, but almost as much. Her Paris playlist was all about nostalgia, she thought as she took a final swig and put the bottle away, but her London playlists were an embodiment of a busy life and her confidence in her work, marriage, children . . .

A face flashed into her mind, and she almost groaned as the all-too-familiar pain and confusion struck her hard. Pushing the earbuds further in and turning up the volume, she set off again, running faster than before, trying to outpace her thoughts. For the first time in a very long time, Charlotte Marigny had no idea what to do.

Several Metro stops away, Arielle Lunel rushed down the stairs to the platform just as a train drew in. It was already crowded, and she hoped she didn't smell too much of the sweat she could feel trickling down the back of her neck. *Ouf*, well at least she wouldn't be late for work, and Pauline, who worked from home as a translator, would make sure the children got to school as usual. Normally Arielle wasn't in such a rush, but for some reason the alarm hadn't sounded this morning and that had thrown everything out of kilter. It was hard enough as a single working mother trying to organise everyday life around two lively children while living in a space that wasn't really their own. Her sister never said anything about the invasion of her previously quiet and ordered apartment, but occasionally Arielle caught an expression of exasperation on Pauline's face which made her feel a pang of guilt.

She was so grateful to Pauline, who once again had put her life on hold for her. When their parents had died, Pauline had been only twenty but she had thrown herself into parenting her thirteen-year-old sister in the best way she could. Twenty-five years later, she had offered to let Arielle and the then three-year-old twins move in with her, after the trauma of Ludovic's death in a car accident was followed by the shocking revelation of a mountain of debts he'd incurred, unbeknownst to her. Arielle had been forced to sell pretty much everything of value to pay off the debts, including, most painfully, her beloved flower shop, which she'd owned from well before she'd married Ludo. And she'd also had to give up the grand apartment in the 4th that they'd previously rented.

Pauline's apartment in the 18th was a long way from where Arielle worked now, managing a stall in the flower market on the Île de la Cité, but she could at least contribute to the rent and household expenses, with some money left over for treats. And the apartment was a reasonable size, with two bedrooms plus a small study that had been converted into Arielle's bedroom. The twins had to share a room, but they preferred that even though they had very different personalities—Alice was outspoken and impulsive, Louis quieter and gentler.

Slowly, as first one year passed, then two, their lives had settled into a new pattern. Three years since Ludo's death, Arielle still missed him, but the grief was softer now, a dull ache rather than a sharp pain. The children they had made together were the light of her life. And her job managing Monsieur Renan's beautiful stall in the flower market, which had started off as a temporary position on fairly basic wages, had become not only permanent but also better paid, and satisfying in a way Arielle hadn't expected.

It wasn't the same as running her own flower shop, but it had its own distinctive pleasures—and, she had to admit, it was less stressful than owning your own business, especially as Monsieur Renan gave her free rein when it came to the day-to-day running of the stall. There was just one problem—not something to do with the stall itself, but . . .

The train doors opened and people spilled out onto the platform. But the carriages didn't move on, seemingly delayed by something. It was the stop before Arielle's and she decided to get off. She'd still be there before opening time if she walked really quickly.

Unfortunately, the crowds were thicker than she'd thought, and as she finally made her way over the bridge onto the island and hurried into the flower market, she saw that Jacques Vella was already there, fussing unnecessarily around his display. He raised his eyebrows as she approached and tapped his watch significantly. She ignored that and gave him a cursory nod before hurrying on to her stall, her pleasure at opening marred by irritation. Why couldn't that man ever let up?

Two

The day before Corinne had died, Emma had been on an out-of-town shoot for Thornton's, the fine arts and antiques company she worked for as digital media manager. She had been in the middle of photographing the glorious, and very rare, set of Clarice Cliff ceramics found in the attic of a local house, when a phone call had come from the hospital in Sydney. Her mother was asking for her, the nurse said, she was quite agitated, she had something important to tell her daughter and it would be good if Emma came today.

Emma hurriedly finished the shoot, packed everything up and headed back to Sydney. The trip should have taken her no more than three hours but, as fate would have it, an accident on the motorway delayed traffic for ages and by the time she reached the hospital five hours had passed. She was met by an ashen-faced nurse who told her that Corinne had suffered a massive stroke and was unconscious.

Her mother died a day later. Even though Corinne's cancer diagnosis had not allowed any room for hope, and Emma had been prepared for something like this for months, it had been a shockingly sudden end. Amid the grief, there was a sense of relief that her mother's suffering was over at last. But there was another thing, which gnawed at her still. Her mother had wanted to tell her something important, and she should have been there to hear it. It wasn't her fault, Paddy kept telling her, and she knew in her rational mind that was true. But in her heart, she felt a sense of guilt. If only she had got there sooner! She was sure her mother had wanted to tell her about the past, maybe even the secret Corinne had kept for so long: the identity of Emma's biological father.

Paddy had no idea what Corinne might have wanted to tell her, or who her biological father was, for Corinne had never told him either. 'And I preferred it that way,' he'd told her, with sad honesty.

The only clue Emma had was that photograph of her mother long ago in the tall grass. It had been on Corinne's bedside table at the hospital that day, as if she had been intending to use it as a prop for the story she wanted to tell.

It was a photograph Emma had never seen before and which Paddy said he'd only seen once. 'She told me it was taken in France, before she left to come here,' he said. 'Not in Paris, but on holiday somewhere in the country.' That certainly accorded with the look of the background—the meadow with a church spire or pointy tower in the far distance. There was also a scrawl in an unknown hand—not her mother's—on the back, reading, simply, '*un jour de printemps*', one spring day. Paddy didn't know who had written that either, or any other details. 'You know what Corinne was like,' he had said. 'If she didn't want to explain something, she simply didn't.'

Emma knew that all right. Even though Corinne had loved her daughter deeply, she had been a private, even secretive person. So the fact that she had finally been ready to open up was doubly affecting, and Emma couldn't get it out of her mind.

Four weeks after the funeral, she had left Australia to stay with her grandmother in Paris. It was Mattie who had urged her to come, knowing instinctively that her granddaughter needed time with her, in the place Corinne had grown up. And Paddy had encouraged that, telling Emma she wasn't to worry about him as he had his three lively sisters for support. They and their families had been towers of strength in the last few months.

From the start, being in Paris with Mattie had felt right. Unlike last time, when Emma had tried mediating a situation she didn't understand, there had been no awkwardness. Being with her grandmother felt both consoling and utterly natural. And sharing her gentle, peaceful routine made Emma feel as if she was taking up again the lost threads of that first visit to Paris, starting to weave a relationship with Mattie that was all the more precious for having taken so long.

This morning, after a simple breakfast of coffee and fresh baguette with butter and jam, Emma had accompanied Mattie to the bustling local market and shops. Mattie was clearly well known and greeted warmly at every shop and stall they visited. On the first day they'd gone together, she'd proudly introduced her granddaughter to everyone, and a week on, Emma seemed to have become part of the scene, welcomed by name and asked about her day.

It reminded Emma so much of doing the Saturday morning shopping as a child with Paddy, who often stopped to chat with people he met in their small country town. When Emma remarked on it, Mattie said, smiling, 'Paris is at heart a series of villages, and it's in our home village we feel most comfortable, just like people in the country do. It's a natural human thing.'

Not for everyone, Emma thought, remembering her mother's strictly practical style of shopping back home. Corinne didn't go with Emma and Paddy on those Saturday morning expeditions, telling her husband she couldn't stand all the chit-chat. She said she knew that, as a well-liked GP in their close-knit community, Paddy had to pretend to show interest, but she worked in system management at the local council and there was no need for her to be forced into an interest she didn't feel. Paddy smiled and said that he wasn't pretending, but Corinne had simply raised an ironic eyebrow. So how had she coped as a child being trotted around this neighbourhood by her chatty mother? Not well, presumably. But, on the other hand, she'd been happily married to someone with the same sociable temperament as the mother she'd left so far behind.

People could be so complicated.

Another of her mother's paradoxes was that though she no longer considered France her home, she had ensured that her daughter could not only speak but read and write French. And thank goodness she had, as French was a necessity with Mattie, for Emma's grandmother only spoke that language. And they talked so much in those early days! Mattie loved hearing about Emma's childhood, and she delighted in sharing stories of Corinne's childhood, as they pored over photos in the old family photo album and her own drawings from long ago. Mattie had once been a commercial illustrator, and still kept a visual art diary for when the mood took her. Her sketchbooks were full of studies of Corinne as a child, playing, or reading, or sleeping: small moments of her mother's life that touched Emma deeply.

So far, though, Mattie had only briefly mentioned Corinne's departure from France thirty-two years ago. There had been no big fight leading up to it, she'd reassured Emma. Her parents knew Corinne was itching to get away and see the world. They'd known she was going to Australia on a working holiday visa and would be away for up to two years. But they had no idea she was pregnant. In fact, neither had she, for her periods were often late, and quite irregular. It wasn't until a month after her arrival in Australia that she'd known for sure, after visiting a doctor. But she hadn't told her parents about it until Emma was three months old. Why, Emma wasn't sure. Perhaps she was afraid they would try to dissuade her from having the baby. Or perhaps she had thought they would try to make her come home. Or maybe she had simply wanted to keep it to herself, till she was ready to tell.

Time passed, Paddy successfully sponsored Corinne to stay and the move to Australia became permanent. It wasn't that she cut her parents off because she did keep in touch by fairly regular letters and an occasional phone call, but Corinne made it clear her life was in Australia. And so the pattern was set.

Today, over a simple but delicious market-sourced lunch of pan-fried fish with herbs, the conversation, which had started by Mattie asking about Emma's work with Thornton's, soon came to an intriguing turn. Emma had just told her grandmother how she'd got the job by chance because they'd come across her Instagram posts about vintage and charity shop finds, when Mattie smiled and said, 'You know, Alain once had a shop selling those kinds of things.'

As far as Emma had known, her grandfather had worked in a newspaper printing office most of his life. 'I had no idea! When?'

'A couple of years before we got married. It was where we met, in the late 1960s. I was twenty-five, working for various magazines, and that day I'd gone to the river to sketch and happened across his shop, not far from here.' Her eyes shone. 'It was a fascinating place, every square millimetre of its tiny space crammed with unusual old things he'd picked up all over France, but I was the only customer. We got talking and I soon realised that, though he was the most interesting man I'd ever met, he didn't have the slightest idea about publicity. So I offered to take it in hand.'

Mattie smiled mischievously, and Emma imagined her grandmother as she'd seen her in one of the photos: a lively young woman in a minidress and boots, dark kohl-rimmed eyes under a thick fringe, turning up to the quirky shop of the quietly handsome, kind man who would become the love of her life. Mattie's hair might be a shining silver-white now, instead of a lustrous jet black, but her eyes were just as sparkling as she happily reminisced.

'I designed a series of pop-art flyers and took them around the places where people my age gathered.' She shrugged. 'Our version of social media, I suppose.'

'And did it work?' Emma asked, delighted by this unexpected glimpse into her grandmother's youth.

'It certainly brought in a whole new clientele, mostly young people. But most of them didn't have much spare cash, so they tended to hang around and talk philosophy or lament their turbulent love affairs. Alain didn't mind.' A momentary sadness flitted over her face. 'He was always happy to listen to people.'

Emma squeezed her grandmother's hand. 'Pappy was so kind.' Pappy, the common French version of grandpa, was what she'd called him, but its female equivalent, Mamie, was too confusingly close in sound to the English 'Mummy', so instead, Mattie, short for her grandmother's given name of Mathilde, had stuck. 'It is what I remember most about him.' She glanced out of the window. 'That and seeing him work in the garden.'

Mattie followed her glance. 'Alain always loved plants, but we didn't have a garden in our first home, which was a cramped little flat. But when Corinne was three years old, my uncle unexpectedly left me this house, with its hidden-away garden. It was a dream come true for Alain.' She looked at Emma. 'You know, in France there's a saying: *Tout le monde a son jardin secret.*'

Everyone has their own secret garden, Emma thought. Aloud, she said, 'Like in the book?'

Mattie looked puzzled, and Emma belatedly realised that her grandmother wouldn't have read *The Secret Garden* by Frances Hodgson Burnett. It was an English classic, not a French one. 'Sorry,' she said. 'I thought you meant something from a book I really loved as a child. What does it mean?'

'A private space,' Mattie said. 'A peaceful place that offers escape and relieves stress. It can be in your mind, where memories and dreams and ideas gather, or it can be something you actually do, like a long-running journal, or my sketchbooks. It can also be a secret, like forbidden love or a double life . . . Occasionally it can be an actual place that has a deep meaning for you.' Her gaze turned back outside. 'For Alain, the garden was his haven *and* his way of expressing himself. But that is why . . .' She paused, and Emma saw the sudden shine of tears in her eyes. 'I couldn't keep it up, after he died, even if—if it broke my heart.'

'Oh Mattie.' Emma hugged her grandmother tightly.

After lunch, Mattie always retired to her room for a *sieste*, leaving Emma to her own devices for an hour or two. The first day, exhausted by the trip, she'd crashed out herself. The next two days it was raining solidly so she'd explored the house. She had a good sense of it now. On the ground floor were the kitchen and laundry—which opened onto the garden—the living room and dining room, and a small room which had once been a study but was now a makeshift library. On the first floor were the bathroom and three good-sized bedrooms, the smallest of which was currently unused but neatly furnished. Finally, up a steep flight of narrow stairs that Mattie never went up anymore, was the second or attic floor, with a room that had clearly once been a *chambre de bonne* or servant's room but now only contained two trunks full of mothballed old clothes and an impressive collection of spider webs, as well as a separate storage room. Full of paintings, books, faded but lovely carpets and well-worn furniture, the house was cosy in the way beloved old houses are.

The last couple of days, however, the weather had been bright and soft and Emma had left the house to go for a walk; the first day to the Boulevard St Germain and then the Jardin du Luxembourg—where, she was delighted to see, children still sailed toy yachts and the dancing faun still capered happily on his pedestal. The second day she'd gone to the Latin Quarter and its charmingly ramshackle backstreets.

This afternoon she decided to head to the stalls of the *bouquinistes* on the banks of the Seine, only a short distance away. And it was there, happily browsing among the stalls, that she happened upon *the* book.

It was a plain hardcover volume with a very plain title: *Petit guide pratique du jardinage*. A practical little guide to gardening.

It had been published in Paris in 1897 and was arranged in sections about trees, shrubs, flowers, vegetables and fruit. There were rather nice black-and-white drawings too. But it was something else that made her buy it: a bookplate, pasted on the flyleaf, which read *In memory of our beloved sister Jeanne-Marie Merlin du Bosc, born 2 October 1895, died 20 August 1918, in her twenty-third year.*

That simple yet startling dedication seemed freighted with such love and sorrow that it immediately spoke to Emma's own loss. Jeanne-Marie had clearly been a gardener, she thought. Her family had wanted to honour her memory and celebrate her short life in a book she had loved. And it was then, as Emma thought of the conversation with her grandmother, that the decision took root in her mind.

She would restore her grandfather's garden. And this book would be her guide.

Three

The fine weather had brought out the crowds in the streets and Charlotte was already regretting not taking the Metro back. She'd been across the river to record an interview for a radio program created by an old acquaintance. The program was called *Au Vert des Prés*, literally *To the Green of the Meadows*, but intended as a play both on his surname—Auvert—and the neighbourhood where he lived, Saint-Germain-des-Prés in the 6th, which had once been a village outside the walls of medieval Paris, nestled amid what were then the meadows of the Left Bank.

Before she'd left London, Charlotte had listened to previous episodes of the program, which told stories of gardens and gardeners in Paris through the ages. The introductory episode was centred around an imagined walk in the gardens of the sixth-century abbey of Saint-Germain-des-Prés, through the eyes of the patron saint of gardeners, St Fiacre, a seventh-century

Irish monk who'd moved to the Brie region, just north of Paris, establishing famous vegetable and herb gardens. It had been lively and engaging, and Charlotte had immediately listened to the next two episodes: one on the seventeenth-century writer Charles Perrault, author of such famous tales as *Cinderella* and *Sleeping Beauty*, who had been instrumental in the opening of the first public garden in Paris, the Tuileries Gardens; and another as a mosaic of overheard stories from the flower market on the Île de la Cité. It was that which had stimulated Charlotte to walk back from the recording session—which had been about how Paris gardens had inspired her work in London—because her journey would take her past the flower market, where she hadn't been for a long time.

Recently officially renamed as *Le Marché aux Fleurs Reine Elizabeth II*, in honour of the late queen, the flower market was mostly housed in a couple of late nineteenth-century iron and glass pavilions on the side of the island that overlooked the Right Bank, but outdoor flower stands also spilled out onto the quay. Stepping into one of the pavilions, Charlotte was immediately plunged into a humid, muffled world of narrow alleyways lined with shops and stands, filled from top to bottom with a vast, colourful array of flowers and plants of all sorts, as well as garden tools, accessories and decorations. At this fertile time of the year, the flowers showed off their full beauty and gawkers and customers were out in force. Weaving her way through the throng of people, Charlotte took in the scenes of market life, to the soundtrack of a babble of tongues:

an elderly French couple haggling with a sour-faced man about the price of a bunch of daffodils; an excited group of Americans exclaiming over a display of cacti to the obvious pleasure of the cheerful female stallholder; a beautifully dressed Korean family having their photo taken against a background of hydrangea blossoms; a woman with a Slavic accent hesitating over various garden ornaments, to the growing impatience of the stallholder.

It was in this way that she happened upon a flower stand at the end of the pavilion. The stand immediately caught her eye because the flowers—a mix of fragrant spring blooms such as peonies, jonquils, lilac, sweet pea and magnolia—were grouped in a pattern that had been so skilfully arranged that it created a dreamlike harmony of colour and shape. It had been a long time since Charlotte had seen anything quite so naturally beautiful. And yet so artful too.

To one side, talking to a customer, stood a petite woman in a deep green sleeveless pinafore apron over jeans and a simple white shirt. She had her back to Charlotte, so all she could see of the woman's head was a mass of auburn curls. But then she turned, and Charlotte saw that the colour of the pinafore almost matched the colour of her eyes, set in a pleasantly round face. And, despite the fact she wasn't blonde, wearing a puffy white dress or carrying a wand, she somehow reminded Charlotte irresistibly of the fairy doll which had once perched on top of her family Christmas tree back in London in happier times.

'*Madame? Je peux vous aider?*'

Charlotte started. The woman's voice was clear, level, with a distinct trace of a Midi accent, probably Provence. 'Er—I wondered if you might suggest flowers to give to a favourite aunt.'

Why had she said such a stupid thing? Any flowers she bought today would be dead by the time Juliette returned. But the woman smiled at her and said, 'It is wonderful to have a favourite aunt. Did she look after you when you were young?'

Charlotte shook her head. 'She was often away, travelling the world. But it was always good to see her. And she'd unfailingly bring something back for me and my brother, something that smelled of faraway places.' She hadn't meant to say all that. And she noticed with some discomfort that the man the stallholder had been speaking to earlier was still there, hovering.

The flower-seller's face lit up with genuine pleasure. 'How happy that must have made you!'

At that moment, Charlotte's phone pinged in her pocket. A text. Normally, she'd have ignored it, but right now it felt like an excuse to cut the pointless conversation short. 'I'm sorry. I have to take this call,' she lied, and hurried outside.

It was Aidan, her assistant back in the office. *Sorry to disturb, Charlotte. It's re Mrs Browning.*

She exhaled. *Mrs* Browning, as she insisted on being called—no first names for her!—was a wealthy Mayfair widow who was obsessed with her garden but whose understanding of landscaping could have fit on half a Post-it note. She was always wanting to remodel her garden based on what she'd seen in magazines, even when it was completely unsuited to the actual conditions. She also imagined that she had a natural flair for design which only needed a final tick of approval from a professional. From long experience, Charlotte knew how to handle her. But Aidan had never had to deal with Mrs Browning's whims on his own before.

She texted rapidly back. *Hey, Aidan, what's up?*

She wants to change things again ☹ *Like this.* It was a photo of a luxuriant tropical garden. *And I'm afraid I don't think I handled it well.*

Concerned, Charlotte abandoned texting and called him. 'What happened?'

'I remembered how you said to make her think a small tweak is more effective than a big change.' A pause. 'But—er—then I made the mistake of saying that she should pick something that inspired her, and we could definitely do it for her . . .'

Charlotte winced. 'Okay. So what did she say?' She had visions of palm trees and waterfalls and miniature jungles complete with tigers. She wouldn't put it past Mrs Browning to suggest tigers.

'Well—' Aidan sounded reluctant. 'I'm afraid she said what she really wanted was that awful bird bath thing in the picture. The one shaped like a flamingo.'

Charlotte couldn't help laughing, relief mixing with amusement. 'Oh dear.'

'Sorry, Charlotte,' Aidan said, 'I know it's going to really spoil the look of what you created for her but—'

'Don't worry, Aidan. Given what she could have demanded, this is very small beer. Just go ahead with the flamingo monstrosity. She'll get sick of it soon enough. You did well.'

'You really think so?' She could hear the relief in his voice.

'Absolutely.'

'Thank you,' he said, cheerfully. 'It's a real weight off my mind. Oh, I meant to ask. How's your aunt?'

Charlotte briefly closed her eyes. The lie she'd told her staff, to cover the reason for her sudden departure. 'Better. Thanks for asking.'

After the call ended, Charlotte stayed put, feeling rattled. Had it been unfair to expect Aidan to step up in her absence? Was she letting her clients and her staff down by not being there to deal with the day to day? What if being away hurt her business more than she'd imagined it would? *Stop it*, she told herself. *You told him he did well, and that's the truth. He wanted reassurance, sure, but he had* done the right thing. So don't micromanage. Don't imagine problems where there aren't any, when the truth is you can hardly bring yourself to think about the very real problem that . . .

'Madame? Are you all right?'

She turned to see the redhaired flower-seller from the market looking at her with concern. Embarrassment made her draw herself up. 'I have to go,' she said stiffly, and hurried off to the nearby Metro without a backward glance.

Four

Daniel was still there when Arielle went back to her stand. 'Mobile phones can be such a curse,' he said, shaking his head. 'They make people forget their manners.'

In the past year, since he'd been coming regularly to the market to buy flowers, Arielle had come to know and like Daniel Auban. He was a kind man, courteous, reserved, and somewhat old-fashioned though he didn't look much older than her. He was also a good listener, and never pushed himself forward. In fact, he seldom expressed himself directly.

'She didn't mean to be rude,' she said. 'She was just unhappy.'

He looked at her. *How do you know that?* was written in his eyes, but he didn't voice it, as she knew he wouldn't. Instead, he said tentatively, 'I wonder what you would have suggested, for her aunt.'

Arielle smiled, and turning to her display, she picked out first one flower, then another, and another, until she held seven stems.

'Her aunt travelled the world, so I would pick seven types of flowers to represent the seven seas and seven continents,' she said. 'But each of them should mean something too, something relevant to the receiver and the giver.' She pointed to each flower in turn. 'Pink carnation, to symbolise family love. Lily of the valley, for joy. Blue cornflower, for courage. White peony, for thankfulness. Red poppy, to remind us to savour each moment in the fragility of life. White tulip, for new departures. And cosmos, because its name means world.'

He shook his head. 'That is extraordinary. Truly. I . . .' He hesitated, just as a large group of chattering tourists appeared, claiming Arielle's attention. Daniel lifted a hand in farewell and was gone. She was sorry he had decided to leave but didn't take offence because that was his way. He was uncomfortable around crowds—except, she had heard, at the Cluny Museum, where he worked as a botanical historian specialising in the Middle Ages.

After she'd dealt with the gaggle of tourists, Arielle put the flowers she'd shown Daniel in the vase full of water that she always kept nearby. It was a very busy day in the flower market, and thankfully that meant Jacques Vella wouldn't come and cast a critical eye over her display. He never did it when customers were about. And certainly not when Monsieur Renan was there. In fact, Vella was charm itself with Arielle's boss. This was despite the fact it was Monsieur Renan who had rejected his offer last year to buy the stall, not Arielle. Maybe he thought he would win Arielle's boss over. There was no chance of that, but unfortunately, there was one other thing the man was, other than unpleasant. And that was persistent.

Glancing at the vase of flowers, Arielle's thoughts turned again to the woman she'd seen that morning. With her well-cut short dark hair, subtly made-up face and elegant clothes, she'd looked the epitome of the chic, confident Parisian, but Arielle had seen the shadow in her eyes and known something was wrong. She wished that the woman had stayed long enough to at least see the flowers. Their simple beauty would have given her heart a moment's lift, and those moments counted. *Well! Now the flowers will come home with me*, she thought, *and I'll give them to Pauline.* Because, aside from the world travel, everything else about the blooms' meanings could be applied to her sister too.

A few hours later, she'd just left work with the flowers but thankfully without a parting shot from Vella, when a text from Pauline pinged on her mobile. *Can you pick up something nice from the traiteur on the way home? Also a good Bordeaux.*

Arielle smiled. *Sure. What are we celebrating?*

If only! We have unexpected visitors and the stew I've made for us won't make the grade ☹

Arielle frowned down at her phone. *Who's there?*

The Grandiers.

Arielle felt her stomach clench. Ludo's parents! They hadn't visited in months. The last time had been a quick visit two days before Christmas, when they'd dropped off presents for the children. Arielle never felt comfortable around her in-laws. They didn't understand why their son had chosen her as his wife.

She was an orphan, from a much more modest background than the Grandiers, and she didn't have a university degree or even an ambition to acquire one. She didn't have *une bonne situation*—meaning a well-paying, prestigious job. Being a florist certainly didn't cut it with Thierry and Virginie Grandier. Plus her accent was too southern for their liking. And how scandalous that she hadn't even taken on her husband's name after marriage!

None of this was said overtly. It was communicated through patronising attitudes and snide remarks that stung Arielle, but she hated confrontation and so didn't challenge them. Besides, she wanted to get on with her beloved Ludo's parents. Ludo had said airily she should ignore their jibes as they treated everyone like that, even him. It was part of the reason why he'd taken so many risks to create a showy façade about their life that would mute his parents' criticisms and chime with their vision of achievement. But now Ludo was gone, Arielle was of even less consequence to her in-laws, although the children, being blood, did merit some attention. Not much, mind you.

So why were they here today? They lived two hours away, in a superb old house in the Champagne countryside, and rarely ventured to Paris, a city Virginie especially decried as 'not being what it used to be'. Whatever that meant.

Arielle decided to call her sister. 'What's happening, Pauline?'

'Hang on,' Pauline whispered, then Arielle heard her say, 'Sorry, I have to take this, be back soon.' Then Pauline came back on, saying, 'I'm in the kitchen now, it's okay to talk.'

'Did they say why they were here?' Arielle asked, as she hurriedly made her way towards a *traiteur* that she knew would still be open.

'They said they'd come to see you and the children, and seemed put out that you weren't here. They're talking to the children while they wait for you.'

Arielle tried and failed to see the Grandiers making conversation with two six-year-olds.

Pauline clearly had the same thought. '*Pauvres gamins*,' she said with feeling. Poor kids. Dropping her voice a little, she went on, 'I *had* to invite them for dinner, expecting they'd refuse as usual, but to my horror they said yes.'

'It's okay.' Arielle looked at the appetising window display in front of her. *Traiteurs* offer a range of high-quality pre-cooked dishes, ready to reheat at home. They had existed since the nineteenth century, and although frozen meals and takeaway places had made inroads into their trade, classic *traiteurs* still operated. 'We'll cope. I'll bring some nice things home.'

'And I'll feed the kids now, then they can escape to their room,' Pauline said.

'Good idea. I'll see you soon.'

A few minutes later, Arielle left the shop with a delectable cargo in a carrier bag: tiny asparagus tarts and a salmon tartare with capers for entrees, quail fillets with red-currant confit and seasonal vegetables for a main, and a pistachio and white chocolate mousse, accompanied by delicate lacy biscuits, for dessert. *Plus we have cheese and bread at home and I can whip up a salad too*, Arielle thought cheerfully. She'd gone a little overboard with the food, but never mind. Thierry and Virginie were just an excuse, this would be a treat for Pauline and herself. And the children would love the dessert!

But when she arrived at the apartment, hands full with the meal, a bottle of good Bordeaux and the flowers, Arielle's cheerful mood began to evaporate. Pauline's expression was strained. And the children hadn't come out to greet her, which was unusual.

'They're in their room still,' Pauline said, guessing Arielle's thoughts and taking the parcels from her.

The children's room was just down the hall, away from the living room where the Grandiers were installed. Louis and Alice were lying on Alice's bed, fair heads bent over a large picture book. It was one of the *Babar* books that they'd loved when they were younger. But last year, when they started school, the twins had declared that the *Babar* books were too babyish and they had been banished to an upper shelf. Yet here they were now, poring over one. Was it for comfort?

As soon as they saw her, their faces lit up. 'Maman!' they cried, scrambling off the bed to throw themselves at her.

'Hello, my darlings,' she said, hugging them. 'I am so glad to see you.'

'We are too,' said Louis, his eyes shining. 'We missed you,' said Alice, nestling deeper.

'How was school today?'

'Good,' they chorused. It was sincere. They really liked their school. That was one thing Arielle didn't have to worry about.

'You know what?' she said. 'I've brought us some really tasty dessert, we can have it soon together and—'

'We don't want to go with Grand-maman and Grand-papa,' Alice interrupted, with a catch in her voice, while Louis nodded. The rather old-fashioned terms of Grand-maman and Grand-papa were what the Grandiers insisted on being called by the twins.

'Go where?' Arielle said uneasily. But the twins didn't answer, so she kissed each of them on the forehead, told them she'd be back soon, and headed to the living room, where Thierry and Virginie were sipping on glasses of Cinzano and picking at a bowl of nuts.

'Ah, Arielle, *bonsoir*,' Thierry said, rising and pecking her on the cheek.

'*Bonsoir*. Are you in Paris long?' she asked, as Virginie offered her own cheek.

'Just overnight. We have booked a *very* nice hotel in the third,' Virginie said with a smug little smile. 'Now, Arielle, there's a long weekend coming up and we thought the children might like to come and stay with us for it. Oh, and you too,' she added as an afterthought, 'if you can spare the time off work.' She made the words sound like disapproval, but that was hardly unusual.

What *was* unusual was her invitation. Arielle had rarely been invited to the Grandiers' when Ludo was alive, and since his death, never. And there was a look in Virginie's eyes that troubled her. Skin prickling with unease, she said politely, 'That's very kind, but we already have plans to—'

At that moment, Pauline came into the room. 'Dinner is ready,' she said. 'Please come to the table.' But neither Arielle nor the

Grandiers responded. Instead, Virginie said with a tight smile, 'Then please consider changing your plans. It would give us pleasure.'

Could it be true that they wanted to spend time with her and the children? 'Thank you,' Arielle said, feeling shaken. 'I will let you know.'

'That's fine,' said Thierry quickly.

But Virginie ignored him and said, with a set expression, 'It would also be a good occasion for the children to get used to . . .' Thierry shot her a warning look, but too late.

Arielle's unease was full-blown now. 'Get used to what?' she asked sharply.

Virginie drew herself up. 'The children are nearly seven. And we think it's time to think about their future. Their schooling.'

It was Pauline who interjected this time. 'What *about* their schooling? They are doing perfectly well.'

Virginie shot her a quelling look. 'We know paying for a good school would be difficult for you, in the circumstances,' she said to Arielle, 'so we are prepared to help. We can pay in full, if necessary, isn't that right, Thierry?'

Thierry nodded weakly. 'That is so.'

Arielle frowned. 'That's a very generous offer, but there's no need to—'

'We also think the children would benefit with more space than what they have here,' Virginie interrupted. 'And there's a really good school close to us. So this is what we propose: the children are enrolled there, and they live with us during the school year. We'll pay for everything.'

Pauline gasped, but Arielle was speechless.

'Or you could also come and live with us,' Thierry said, glancing at his wife, with a trace of anxiety in his voice. 'You see, we are in a position to offer much, and we truly want the best for our grandchildren. And you too, Arielle,' he added, hurriedly.

Everyone looked at Arielle.

She was trying to control the rage rising in her throat, but managed to say, 'No.'

'But why not?' Virginie replied sharply. 'You surely can't be satisfied with . . .' she waved contemptuously around the room. 'This limited life, with limited prospects for the children.'

'Please stop,' Arielle ground out.

'Think about it,' Thierry said. 'No need to make a decision now, is there?'

Arielle wanted to scream, to throw everything in their smug faces—not only this outrageous proposal, but all the put-downs she'd endured, their past indifference towards the children, the way their expectations had twisted Ludo, all of it. But she controlled herself enough to say, in a voice that was unnaturally calm, 'I'm sorry, but I think it's best you leave now.'

Virginie's eyes flashed. Her hands shook. 'Remember, Arielle,' she hissed, 'they are our son's children as well as yours, and we have a perfect right to—'

She was interrupted by her husband, who gently took her by the arm, saying, 'Come on, my dear. We can talk another time when everyone's calmer.' He looked at Arielle and Pauline. 'Goodbye, then.'

Pauline nodded stiffly and escorted them to the door, but Arielle stayed where she was, her ears still ringing with what the Grandiers had said. Even given their relentless self-absorption, how *could* they have imagined she might agree to such a proposal? If Ludo had been alive, would they have dared to try? But maybe, she thought bleakly, they would have, and maybe he'd have given in to them. She clenched her fists. She certainly wouldn't let it happen. Never!

Pauline returned and hugged her. 'Are you okay?'

'Not really,' whispered Arielle. Then a thought struck her and she stared at her sister. 'But I've just realised, the children—oh my God, the children thought they were going to be sent away!'

She hurried to the twins' room, flinging open the door. 'Grand-maman and Grand-papa are gone,' she said, and the immediate rush of relief she saw in their beloved faces pierced her heart. Hugging them tightly, she asked, trying to sound cheerful, 'Are you still hungry?' When they nodded, she went on, 'That's good, because Tati Pauline and I have so much to eat that we really need a couple of hungry children to help us—especially with a very delicious dessert!'

Five

It was midday on a Sunday, the church bells were ringing all over the city and Emma and Mattie had been to Mass at the Abbey of Saint-Germain-des-Prés. Within the sacred space of the magnificent ancient church, with its glorious deep blue, red and gold vaulted ceiling, the words of the priest seemed to float in a timeless serenity that enveloped Emma. Afterwards, she and Mattie had lingered to light candles for her mother and grandfather, and it felt consoling, rather than sad, unlike when she'd spoken with Paddy last night.

He'd video-called from Sydney airport where he and his sisters were about to catch a flight to Colombo before embarking on an eight-day Sri Lanka cruise. It was a trip that Corinne had really wanted to go on, and Emma knew that was the reason he was going, to honour her wishes. They'd talked for a while and she'd told him about her garden project, which, as an enthusiastic gardener, he warmly approved.

It had been good to talk to him, but after the call, Emma had found herself in tears, thinking of the catch in Paddy's voice as he'd spoken of her mother looking through travel brochures . . .

Today, though, she felt more at peace, and once she and Mattie had settled at an outdoor table in the neighbourhood restaurant where they'd decided to have lunch, she said, 'Guess what I'm going to do this afternoon, Mattie.'

Mattie smiled. 'Something young and energetic, I suppose.'

'Remember that gardening book I bought the other day at the *bouquiniste*?'

Mattie nodded. Like Emma, she'd been touched by the dedication, and said it was exactly the kind of book Alain would have loved.

'Well, I've been reading it,' Emma went on, 'and I thought I could begin putting it into practice.' She took a deep breath. 'I'd like to make a start on clearing Pappy's garden and . . .' She stopped, seeing the change in Mattie's expression. 'If that's all right with you.'

'Oh, Emma, it certainly is. And I confess I did wonder if that's why you wanted that book. But . . .' Her grandmother hesitated. 'I know I should have done more to preserve the garden, but it was all I could do to maintain the house . . . I didn't have the heart to tackle the garden, or the funds to employ someone to do it for me.'

'You don't have to explain, darling Mattie,' Emma said, clasping her hand. 'I understand completely. Think of me as your personal gardener. You can tell me exactly what needs doing and when.'

'I left all that up to Alain,' Mattie said. 'I would not have a clue how to proceed.' Her expression lightened. 'So I give you my blessing to do whatever you like.'

Emma kissed her on the cheek. 'I will keep it simple, not that I have the skill to do anything else, anyway. And I won't do anything expensive, I promise! Though I might buy some extra plants. Do you know the best place to go for those?'

'The flower market on the Île de la Cité,' said Mattie promptly. 'Alain used to patronise a stall held by a man called Renan, whose father had run it before him.' She was quite animated now, her eyes sparkling. 'I don't know if it'll still be there, but there are lots of stalls, and the prices are quite reasonable.'

'It sounds perfect,' said Emma. 'Will you come with me? I'll need some advice.'

'It will be like both of us groping in darkness,' said Mattie, laughing, 'but I will gladly go with you, whenever you like.'

After a delicious lunch of asparagus vinaigrette, rare roast beef with Madeira sauce and chocolate mousse, they went back to the house, and Mattie retired as usual while Emma made herself a cup of coffee, intending to start planning her garden project. But the trouble with a full midday meal in the sunshine is that it makes the idea of a *sieste* terribly alluring, even after coffee. Just a few minutes, Emma told herself, finally giving in to the languor and heading for the sofa. She lay down and closed her eyes, the peace of the house like a low, comforting hum, and before she knew it, she was fast asleep.

A sudden noise jerked her awake, and she sat bolt upright. The back of her neck was sweating, and her eyes felt gritty. She picked up her phone from where it lay on the floor. It was 3 pm!

She'd been asleep for well over an hour. She heard a door opening, and voices, and realised what the noise had been: the entry buzzer.

Scrambling to her feet and picking up her shoes, she planned to sneak up the stairs to the bathroom unseen. But Mattie was already ushering the visitor into the hall.

Tall and broad-shouldered, with hazel-brown eyes under a sweep of very dark brown, almost black hair, stood a man. He looked to be in his mid-thirties and was undeniably good-looking, with a casual elegance that reminded Emma of a younger version of Grégory Fitoussi, one of her favourite French actors. Their eyes met and she was the first to look away, embarrassed and confused.

Mattie said, 'Oh, Emma, darling, there you are. This is Marc-Antoine. He's recently come back to Paris and has called in to see how I'm doing.' She held up a little cardboard box. 'And to bring me some of my favourite macarons.'

Emma had not a clue who this Marc-Antoine was, yet her grandmother had spoken as though she expected her to know.

'Mattie,' Marc-Antoine said, 'I think your granddaughter is falling from the moon . . .' In French, *tomber de la lune* means you have not the faintest idea what is going on. Well, that was true. But *he* clearly knew who *she* was, given what he'd said.

Mattie clapped a hand over her mouth. 'Oh! Marc-Antoine is Alain's grandson, from his first marriage to Vivienne Frey, you know?'

Emma knew about her grandfather's first marriage, and had vaguely heard the ex-wife's name, but she'd never heard anything about Alain having children and grandchildren with Vivienne.

Before she could gather her scattered wits, Marc-Antoine cut in smoothly, saying, 'I'm not his *actual* grandson, you understand. I'm not even a step-grandson, more of an honorary one. My grandmother was a widow with a nine-year-old child when she married Alain. That child was my mother, Claire. The marriage didn't last long, but the split was amicable and Alain kept in touch with them, especially with my mother.'

'Oh,' Emma said blankly. Maybe, she thought, reeling from this unexpected development, her mother had never told her about this unusual relationship because she'd never met Claire or her son. But Mattie saw her expression and said, 'Claire visited us from time to time over the years. I liked her very much. She was a lovely girl,' she added fondly to Marc-Antoine.

He touched Mattie's shoulder. 'And she liked you very much too. You and Alain made a big difference to our lives.' He turned to Emma. 'I was so very sorry to hear about your mother,' he said.

Emma swallowed. 'Thank you.'

'Marc-Antoine never met Corinne,' Mattie said, 'but he has heard me talking about her, and you, and your stepfather. Likely more than he ever wanted to.'

Marc-Antoine made a noise of polite protest, but Emma caught the ghost of a knowing smile in his eyes and thought, with a sudden flash of annoyance, that he probably thought it was funny that he knew a good deal about her, when she knew practically nothing about him. Aside from the fact he seemed *much* too sure of himself.

'Now then,' Mattie went on, 'let's not stand around in the hall any longer. Tea, I think, with macarons. Yes?'

Emma muttered something about needing to freshen up and fled to the bathroom while she tried to process what she'd heard. Even if Marc-Antoine had not met Corinne, it was clear his mother had. But Corinne had never so much as mentioned Claire in passing. Perhaps she had resented her father's continuing relationship with his first wife's child, and her mother's gentle acceptance of it, or perhaps she simply hadn't got on with Claire. Another thought struck her. Why hadn't they been at Alain's funeral? Emma would have *definitely* remembered him if he had been there.

Back downstairs, desperate for something practical to do so that she could hide her agitation, she volunteered to make the tea while Mattie and Marc-Antoine sat at the table, chatting. They might not be related by blood, but they *sounded* close, and she felt a sharp stab of pain. It was pure jealousy, she knew that, just as she knew it was unreasonable to dislike him simply because he'd had years of knowing Mattie and she had only started to get to know her grandmother. But she couldn't help it. Here she was, thinking she was building a unique relationship with her grandmother, when this stranger had already claimed a place in Mattie's heart. He and Mattie even resembled each other, with their striking dark looks. Like her own mother, but quite unlike herself, with her blue-grey eyes and the mid-brown hair that she once dyed all the colours of the rainbow, and the freckles on her nose that she used to try to conceal but now didn't bother. When she was a kid, people who didn't know Paddy was her stepfather would say she looked like him, but that was only because they both had blue eyes and brown hair of vaguely similar shades. She didn't really look like him, any more than she looked like her mother or grandparents. She had wondered if maybe she'd got her features from her biological father but knew better than to ask her mother.

She was shaken from her uneasy thoughts by Mattie saying, 'Emma, I was just telling Marc-Antoine how you're going to restore the garden, and he thinks it's a great thing to do.'

As if I need his seal of approval, Emma thought, bristling. Trying to keep her voice steady, she said, 'I am going to *try* to restore it, anyway. I don't know much about gardening, but I do remember Pappy's garden and it was lovely.'

'Perhaps it could be lovely but in a different way,' he said, meeting her defiant gaze with an unreadable expression in his eyes. 'More . . . modern. Easier for you to maintain,' he turned to Mattie, 'even when you have no one here to help you.'

'That would be good,' Mattie agreed, with a quick glance from one to the other, 'but we don't have to decide now.'

We, meaning Marc-Antoine too? *No*, Emma thought, heat rising in her again. *He won't take my project as well.* 'It has to be tidied up first and that will take some time,' she said, briskly, as she started pouring the tea into the cups.

'Of course, but—' he began, before Mattie hastily interrupted him, saying, 'Are you back in Paris for good? With your new position, I mean.'

He smiled. 'There will still be a fair bit of travel, but I'll be mostly based in Paris. So I should be able to see you much more often.'

'Marc-Antoine has been working for a New York bank for quite some years,' explained Mattie, as if Emma had asked.

Trying to cover up her grimace—she might have guessed he was a banker!—Emma picked up a macaron and bit into it. Huh! It was delicious.

'And what about you, Emma?' he asked, seemingly oblivious to, or deliberately ignoring, her expression. 'Mattie told me you left your job to come here. That was brave.'

Emma shrugged. 'Not really. I've saved up quite a bit, and I'm still doing freelance work for my old employer. Even before my mother . . .' She paused, then went on, 'I'd been in the job for a while, and it felt like it was time to move on. I needed a new challenge.'

'And do you think you'll find that here?'

His cool gaze was itself an irritating challenge but she refused to be fazed. 'Maybe. But right now, what's most important to me is being with Mattie.'

Mattie beamed and reached for her hand. 'And that's what's most important to me too, darling. I am so very happy that you are here and that we can finally get to know each other. Even if . . .' Her eyes filled with tears.

Emma touched her hand. 'I know,' she said, feeling a little guilty. She shouldn't waste time sparring with this guy when there were more important things to think about. He glanced at her then and she caught an expression in his eyes that she couldn't quite read. It was only the merest flicker before he got up, scraping his chair back. 'Would you mind if I went into the garden for a moment, Mattie?' he said. 'Just to refresh my memory.'

'Of course I don't mind, dear boy,' she said. 'Maybe Emma can go with you, she can probably tell you more than I can.'

'If she likes,' Marc-Antoine said, just as Emma said, 'I don't mind.'

Both of us are lying, Emma thought ruefully, as she led the way.

It wasn't exactly a comfortable experience, surveying the garden with Marc-Antoine. They spoke in a stilted way about pruning trees gone wild and clearing undergrowth and cutting back rampant ivy, and Marc-Antoine peered into the shed at the cobwebbed tools. He gazed in a speculative way around the garden, as if he were measuring it up, and it made her bristle once more. But to her relief he made no more remarks about modernising. She didn't want to clash with this man, because she could tell that he was important to her grandmother. But she wasn't going to let him interfere or boss her around, either.

Finally, to her relief, he looked at his watch, an elegant vintage Piaget. *Of course!* Expensive retro chic was *exactly* what someone like him would go for, she thought, blithely ignoring the fact that she rather fancied those old-style watches herself.

'I regret to say, but I've got a meeting,' he said, not sounding regretful at all. 'It was good to meet you.' He held out a hand, which Emma shook, murmuring a similar insincere pleasantry, glad that he hadn't done the normal French thing of *la bise*, the kiss on each cheek.

Six

Charlotte had explained her sudden Paris trip with two different stories. To her staff, she'd said she was going to spend time with her elderly aunt, who, she intimated, hadn't been well recently. But she couldn't use the same story with her children, who were fond of Juliette and would be worried if they thought she was sick. So she'd told them that she wanted to revisit the gardens of Paris as inspiration for new designs. And that wasn't altogether a lie.

Right now, she was on her way to the Carnavalet Museum in the Marais. Housed in two superb ancient mansions, the Carnavalet was Paris's oldest museum, fittingly dedicated to the history of the city. Charlotte knew that it had undergone a major renovation recently, including the rejuvenation of its gardens, which were of the formal French sort. Apparently, she had read, it now boasted a more contemporary interpretation of that classic style. Charlotte was rather curious to see exactly what that meant.

She had lived long enough in England to find the formal French garden style, with its gravel paths, geometric patterns and regimented plants, a little unwelcoming, though undoubtedly elegant. And she had immediately taken to the traditional English approach, with its homely profusion of vegetation, green nooks, rustic benches and cheerfully mixed flowers. It amused her, too, that the French caricature of English people portrayed them as cold and uptight, and the English caricature of French people imagined them to be frivolous and exuberant, yet their garden traditions were rather the opposite. But you could generalise too much, she thought, as she got off at the Saint-Paul Metro station. Plenty of English people had regimented gardens and plenty of French people had cosy ones. Her aunt's garden was one of the latter, while her parents-in-law's stiff patch, with not even a blade of grass allowed to misbehave, was one of the former. It didn't reflect their characters, though. Tom's parents had always been kind to her, even warm. But they didn't seem to have noticed what was going on with their son, and she couldn't bring herself to tell them.

To be fair, she herself couldn't pin down exactly when she realised that something was wrong between her and Tom. In a long marriage such as theirs, and with such different personalities, there had been ups and downs but deep love for each other and their three children had helped them weather the occasional blow-up. In the past they'd always been able to talk about things, even if it could take a bit of time and patience to winkle things out of Tom. So when he'd gone quiet, Charlotte wasn't concerned at first. She was in the middle of a hectic period at work and was pretty distracted herself. When she did eventually ask him what was up, he answered readily enough, saying he was stressed about his workload at the high-end recruitment agency where he was a senior manager. And, he'd added with a faint smile, he was having a bit of trouble adjusting to the fact he and Charlotte were now empty-nesters, since their youngest son, Jamie, had left for university. Tom had always been an involved father and a conscientious worker so Charlotte accepted his explanations. But as time went by, his mood didn't improve and he wouldn't talk about it, so she became more and more worried. Finally she suggested that even if he wouldn't talk to her, maybe he could consider speaking to a professional. But Tom rejected the idea with such force that she immediately backed off.

Since then, he had pretty much withdrawn. He went to work every day, he didn't get drunk, or stay out, or rage at Charlotte. She knew he wasn't seeing anyone else because, somewhat to her shame, she had checked up on him. He was going from home to work to home to work to home, day after day after day. But despite his physical presence he wasn't *there*. Not in any of the ways that counted. He made an effort if his parents or the children were visiting, but when they left, it was back to square one. Her beloved husband had become a stranger who communicated only when he absolutely had to. And sex was a distant memory.

She began to dread going home and spent more and more time at work, but the old satisfaction seemed to have waned, infecting her daily routine, making her more distracted, less disciplined, and . . .

Enough! Being here was meant to be an escape, she thought, halting in front of the window display of a small clothes shop. Concentrate on the here and now, she told herself—like that beautiful embroidered green top in the window that is calling to you, though it's not the kind of thing you usually wear, not these days anyway. *Well, these days can go and screw themselves*, she thought defiantly, pushing open the door of the shop. *I want to be back in a simpler time, a time when it was just me, in Paris, young and carefree.* She felt a spurt of guilt at that—was she really wishing her life away, her darling children, the work she'd taken such pleasure in, the long years of love with Tom? No. She needed a break. *And* that top. Right now.

She tried it on and smiled at herself in the mirror. She'd leave it on, she told the saleswoman, along with something else she'd scooped up: a retro brooch she would have loved at nineteen. The jewellery she wore these days was made of real gems and of a discreet design. This one was exuberantly shaped like a seahorse and studded with sparkling clear and green rhinestones. The saleswoman smiled as she rang the items up on the till. 'A new look for spring, madame?' she said.

'Why not?' said Charlotte, lightly.

The saleswoman's smile broadened. 'We all need it sometimes, don't we?'

'We do,' Charlotte said, feeling strangely, deliciously untethered, as if her responsibilities had left her. If she *had* been nineteen, she'd have been on her way to meet friends in a café, not heading off to a museum alone. She felt a sudden lump in her throat, wishing she could visit one of those friends and reminisce about old times. But they'd all scattered.

Just after leaving the shop, her phone pinged, bringing her back to the present. It was a text from her daughter Elise. *Hey Marm, thinking of going to Paris next weekend, you still going to be there? xx*

Charlotte hesitated. Could she really be away from London that long? But then she thought of what awaited her back home and found herself typing, *Sure. Still have quite a lot of people and places to see.* Then she added, *Aunt Juliette is away for a while. It'll just be me.*

I know, Elise wrote back. *She WhatsApped me the other day. She's going on to Krakow after Prague, and maybe Budapest too. Revisiting old haunts, she said.*

Well, Charlotte thought, amused, her aunt told Elise more than she told her. But those two had always shared a *complicité*, an instinctive understanding of each other. She was about to answer when another message from Elise appeared. *She also said you might need company.*

Charlotte's chest tightened. *I'm okay. But I'll be very happy to see you.*

Me too. I'll see you then. Love you, Marm.

There were tears pricking at Charlotte's eyes now. *Love you too, darling.*

Charlotte stood there for a moment longer, scrolling through the exchange of messages. How was she going to hide her turmoil from her daughter? Well, she had six days to cut her way through the thicket of painful thoughts and messy feelings to arrive at a decision. She couldn't continue living with the situation as it was. Was her relationship with Tom still salvageable, or was it better to think about separating, painful though the thought was? She was good with deadlines, they made her work more efficiently, and also think more clearly. In six days she'd come to a decision whether her marriage was over or not. And then she'd know what needed to be done.

Firmly ignoring the cynical little voice in her mind that said, *Fat chance*, she walked on and soon reached the museum. Never mind mooning about the joys of hanging around in cafés when she was a carefree girl, she had to be who she was *now*. And that was a mature, self-assured professional woman going to look at something that might give her new ideas. At the very least, it would give her a few moments of pleasure. And that would do, right now.

Seven

It had been Pauline's idea to go to the Carnavalet. The twins had been given a homework task: finding out about when Paris was called Lutetia, back in Gallo-Roman times. They could have looked it up on the internet but when Pauline had suggested going to the museum, Arielle had readily agreed. She knew that her sister was distracting her from worrying about that awful clash with the Grandiers. Arielle was indeed anxious that they might come back to the charge, the thought of it keeping her awake at night. But several days had passed and there hadn't been another peep out of them, so she tried to put it to the back of her mind. A day out would definitely help with that.

Besides, it was a lovely Sunday, her only full day off. They'd had a picnic lunch in the Place des Vosges and then went on to the Carnavalet, which was nearby. Arielle had been to the museum before and remembered it as a lovely, hushed old place, with long corridors and lots of historical displays in a multitude of rooms. Now, spaces had been opened up and it seemed both to highlight the beauty of the building as well as make it easier to take in the intriguing weaving of Parisian history. The courtyard garden had changed, too. Before, it had been formal, elegant but perhaps a little stiff, with gravel paths, long border beds filled with regimented flowers and bonsaied bushes in soldierly lines, and central beds of dwarf box plants trimmed sharply to look like paisley-printed carpets. She'd loved that curve of living green paisley.

Today, it was still there, and bursting with depth of colour, the glossy leaves of the box shining in the sunlight. What had changed had been a softening of the stiffness: the gravel less dominant, the living paisley carpets trimmed less sharply and bordered by flowering plants with blooms in tones of pink, violet and white. These had been allowed to bush out more than before, and there were climbing green vines on one inner courtyard wall. There were café tables scattered around and there was an air of relaxation. The garden was still elegant but it no longer felt like it was demanding to be admired. Rather, it was inviting you to pause a moment, draw a breath and look closely.

Just as the woman in the green top was doing. She was so absorbed that she started when she heard the twins' running footsteps on the gravel behind her. *Oh, it's her*, Arielle thought, *the woman who wanted flowers for her aunt*. She looked different today, in that embroidered top with a bright brooch pinned to it, but it was definitely her. 'Sorry,' she said, while Pauline went after the fleeing twins. 'We didn't mean to disturb you. The children can be a little lively and—'

'It's all right,' broke in the woman, with a polite smile, 'I know how children can be.' Then she stopped, and looked at Arielle, plainly recognising her, and faintly colouring. 'Oh. Hello.'

'Hello,' echoed Arielle. She waved around at the garden. 'It's the first time I've seen it since they redid it.'

The woman blinked. 'Me too. I—' She hesitated, then plunged on, 'I thought I might get some ideas.'

Arielle smiled. 'For your own garden?'

A shrug. 'Maybe.' Then she looked directly at Arielle and said, 'What do you think?'

'I think they have done a beautiful job of—'

'No, I mean, what strikes you first here? What one element would you take away to recreate?'

Taken by surprise, Arielle looked around at the graceful tumble of greenery down the wall, the paisley beds, the flowering plants almost encroaching on the gravel paths, and said, 'What first struck me was that the garden had found a balance with itself. I mean,' she said, seeing the woman's expression change, and thinking she'd not explained properly, 'it used to be almost stiff in its formality. Now, it's not that it's turned informal, because it can never do that, and you wouldn't want it to, you wouldn't want to get rid of that,' and she gestured towards the exquisite living carpets, 'but it's found a place between the two. Or at least,' she added, smiling, 'whoever designed it has found it.'

The woman nodded, slowly. 'I think you are quite right.'

'And the one element I'd take away with me,' Arielle went on, 'if it was for my own garden . . . well, it wouldn't be about a particular plant, or a specific feature. I think I would take away a sense of time suspended, as if . . .' she groped for an image, 'as if this was Sleeping Beauty's garden, in the first year of her enchantment. The castle is asleep, but the garden has just awoken.'

The woman stared at her. 'What an extraordinary way to look at it.'

'I'm sorry,' Arielle said, embarrassed, 'you probably wanted me to pick something practical, and instead—'

'And instead you gave me something inspired,' said the woman. She put out a hand. 'Charlotte Marigny. I'm a designer of gardens. In London.'

'Arielle Lunel,' said Arielle, shaking the other woman's hand. To cover her embarrassment—she'd been giving advice to a professional designer!—she added lightly, 'And as you know, I sell flowers. In Paris.'

Charlotte laughed. 'You clearly do much more than that.' Then she said, in a rush, 'And I'm sorry about the other day. Walking off like that. It was—a problem. At work.'

'Please don't worry. I understand.' Arielle was sure there was more to it than that, but that wasn't her business. 'What are London gardens like?' she asked.

'There are many beautiful public gardens like this one,' Charlotte said. 'But I think there are more private gardens there than in Paris, even if some are very small.' She gave a sudden smile. 'But that's not very helpful. Have you ever been to London?'

Arielle shook her head. 'I'd love to one day but . . .' She gestured towards where Pauline was coming towards them, shepherding the twins firmly in front of her. 'I doubt it will be soon.'

'They are your children?'

Arielle made the introductions and was glad to see Charlotte Marigny knew how to be with children. They were fascinated by her seahorse brooch, so she took it off and let them handle it, and she didn't talk down to them at all. Pauline shot her sister a questioning look, but didn't actually ask any questions until Charlotte had excused herself and headed off, after giving Arielle her card. Then Pauline turned to Arielle. 'Okay. Who is she, and what was that all about?'

Arielle explained, adding, 'It was the day that Thierry and Virginie came . . .' She glanced at the oblivious twins, who were intently watching the progress of a ladybird on the leaf of a bush. 'I'm glad I talked with her today. She seemed happier.'

Pauline shook her head, affectionately. 'You and your befriending of sad strangers!'

Eight

On Sunday evening, after a light supper, and before the viewing of an old episode of Mattie's beloved *Inspecteur Barnaby*—known to the English-speaking world as *Midsomer Murders*—Emma had brought out the family photograph album again. This time she was looking for any pictures that showed the garden. She found a handful of them, most with the garden as a backdrop to people, but a couple with it as the focus. Mattie had also shown her some lovely watercolours she'd done of it over the years.

Now, on this cool but bright Monday morning, Emma—dressed in her shabbiest T-shirt, gumboots and an old pair of Alain's overalls (fortunately he'd been short and wiry so they didn't totally float on her)—was in the garden, surveying the array of tools she'd collected from the shed and cleaned. There was a rusty but sturdy wheelbarrow; a fork and a spade; a pair of secateurs, which had been a bit stiff to open at first but a drop of oil had worked wonders on them; a battered watering can; and a pair of ancient gardening gloves. They'd all belonged to her grandfather, and it felt right to use them.

After a close reading of parts of the *Petit guide pratique du jardinage*, the consultation of some online sites as well as gardening snippets she vaguely remembered from Paddy, Emma had drawn up a plan of attack, deciding that the best way to handle this project was to divide the garden into sections. She'd get each one cleared completely before she started on the next.

Time to get to work. She squared her shoulders, picked up the handles of the wheelbarrow, and trundled it to a spot near the big old wisteria vine that spread against one wall, and which she'd decided would be her starting point. Though weeds had grown around the vine, its age and toughness meant it had survived. It had even put out a few of the fragrant violet-coloured flowers that hung in grape-like clusters here and there among its spreading branches.

As she cleared the weeds, she'd dump them in the wheelbarrow and trundle it to the spot she'd earmarked for green waste. She would take it all in logical stages, starting with what looked like the easiest section, near the wisteria, and proceed in order of difficulty as she got more experienced. In between she'd also write down what she had found growing, and what might be missing. She had a small notebook and pencil for that very purpose, jammed into the top pocket of her overalls. And then, at the end, she'd have a good idea of what had to be done next.

If she worked to the plan, then she should get it done quickly. The last thing she wanted was to give Marc-Antoine an excuse to pop in and start throwing his weight around.

Alas, nature had other ideas. Emma had imagined that most of the weeds would be relatively easy to get rid of with the aid of secateurs, fork and spade, as well as her gloved hands; however, the thick undergrowth put up a stronger battle than she had expected. There were no overgrown rosebushes with vicious thorns in this first section at least, like there were in other bits. But she knew that there should be a couple of hydrangea bushes. She remembered her grandfather telling her hydrangeas were magical plants because their flowers could change colour. She would take great pleasure in freeing them from the invading weeds.

She worked steadily through the first section and found one hydrangea—sadly the other appeared to have died. Clearing around it, giving the straggly bush room to breathe, felt like a triumph. Another victory was uncovering three or four smaller plants that had also survived. They didn't look like weeds to her untrained eye, although she didn't know what they were, exactly. She'd try to find out later.

But after those first small successes it soon became apparent that it wasn't simply a matter of pulling up something here, chopping something there, digging out something else so the plants that had survived could breathe again. Sure, some weeds did come up easily, but others were more challenging, like the annoying sticky blades that she vaguely remembered Paddy calling goosegrass but which she didn't know the French name of yet (she'd have to learn a whole new vocabulary, she thought grimly), or the sharp sting of nettles, which caught her more than once.

But worst of all was the damn ivy, which had crept all over the garden from its original picturesque placing against the back wall of the house. It was hard to get rid of because no sooner had she discovered a strand of it creeping along like a green sneak thief and pulled it out than she saw that it had a tributary strand, and another, and yet another. Whenever she attempted to get to the source of it, she was led off in different directions. The bloody thing was even trying to strangle the wisteria! But she kept working, pulling and chopping and sweating, cursing the ivy, cursing herself for not having paid more attention to Paddy's gardening talk back home, telling herself she was delusional thinking she could do this, wishing she hadn't started, then cursing herself again for being so negative. And she had thought she was ready for it! Ha, she hadn't known a bloody thing!

Mattie came out a couple of hours after Emma had started, with a glass of water and a small jug of grenadine with ice. 'You need to stop and have something sweet, for the energy,' she said firmly, when Emma said she just needed the water. So she did as she was told, drinking the water first, then a glass of grenadine, both without stopping. And she did feel better. 'You've done very well, it already looks clearer,' Mattie said, loyally, glancing at the patch Emma had been working on. *More like it's been butchered,*

Emma thought, but she said, 'At least I managed to rescue a few things. But it's going to take longer than I thought.'

'That's gardening, Alain used to say.' Mattie smiled. 'It makes you move to its own time. Emma, I'm thinking of bringing out a chair and my sketchbook and pencils—do you mind?'

'Of course not,' said Emma, 'but I must look like a dirty old scarecrow right now. You don't really want to draw me, do you?'

Mattie gave a mischievous grin. 'Dirty old scarecrows make great subjects,' she said, and went back inside, returning moments later with a kitchen chair and her sketchbook.

At first, Emma felt a little self-conscious working under her grandmother's eye, but she soon relaxed as Mattie shared her memories of the garden, including a story about how five-year-old Corinne had decided that an elf lived under the wisteria vine. She had put out bits of food for him, including a couple of her favourite biscuits. 'A real sacrifice on her part,' Mattie observed, 'but she was so delighted to find out that they had gone! Of course, we never told her that the real culprit was a young rat which had made its home under the wisteria.' Usually that anecdote might have made Emma feel close to tears, but today, working in the sunshine in the very same garden where it happened, it felt different. She could *see* her mother here, as a child, coming out with biscuits for the elf and the image warmed her heart and made her feel even more certain that restoring the garden was the right thing to do.

Presently, Mattie went back inside to prepare lunch while Emma finished clearing a patch and threw the green matter into the wheelbarrow. She was about to wheel it over to the pile she'd made when her eye caught a flash of movement in a litter of dead leaves a short distance away.

'Monsieur Leroux!' she whispered in delight, standing as still as she could while the squirrel darted about, seemingly unconcerned by her presence. It was such a beautiful creature, red fur shining, feathery tail waving, quicksilver movements almost dizzying.

Suddenly, the squirrel stilled. Its dark eyes looked directly at her. Then, with a trilling sound, it turned and dashed into the undergrowth almost quicker than her eyes could follow.

Emma sighed deeply from sheer pleasure. Normally, she might have wished she had her phone to take a photo or video, but she was glad she'd left it in the kitchen. How could you capture that joyful liveliness, anyway? It would just have looked like a blur of movement.

She stayed there a moment longer, hoping the squirrel might reappear, but when it didn't, she finished dumping the weeds onto the pile, then slowly went around the section she'd cleared, making notes in her little book. In one bare patch of earth in a resurrected bed, she saw a bulb had come to the surface. She pushed it back into the soil, then saw several more. She had no idea what sort of bulbs they were—daffodils, irises, tulips?—but they definitely needed to stay there. She made a note of it.

And then she saw another brown bulb. When she touched it, however, intending to push it into the soil like the others, she realised that it wasn't a bulb but something harder. Scratching gently on one side of the object, she saw another colour appear—a dull silver. So it was made of metal. It was too chunky for a coin. She'd have to clean it up to see what it was.

Putting it in her pocket, she trundled the wheelbarrow and tools back to the shed, ready for tomorrow. She'd have a break this afternoon.

Going back inside, she found Mattie setting out plates and cutlery in readiness for lunch, which smelled delicious. She knew it was grilled Toulouse sausages with mustard, a big salad and fresh bread—a perfect combination. 'Ready in five minutes,' Mattie said, smiling.

Emma washed her hands and face, then took out the object she'd found and scrubbed it as clean as she could. It was revealed to be a small silver pendant, carved into the shape of a rose, and the bail that would have once attached it to a chain was broken.

'Look what I found, Mattie,' she said, holding it out. 'A silver rose.'

Mattie made a soft sound in her throat as she saw the object in her palm. 'It's Corinne's. From when she was sixteen or seventeen.' She looked up at Emma, her eyes bright. 'I remember she bought it when she was on holiday with her best friend, who also got one. When she lost it, she hunted for it everywhere. It caused quite a commotion. She was so angry! With herself, with us when we tried to suggest where it might be. And it's been in the garden all this time! It's actually a peony. Corinne's favourite flower back then.'

'I didn't know that.' Corinne had never mentioned those frilled fragrant beauties to her daughter. As far as Emma knew, her mother had preferred native Australian flowers to European ones.

She felt a surge of excitement. 'Do you think Maman might have bought the pendant on the same holiday when that photo was taken?'

'It's possible,' Mattie said. 'But I'm not sure. She's not wearing it in the photo, is she? And she wore it every day when she got back, until she lost it.'

'Perhaps the photo was taken before she bought the pendant,' Emma said. 'You said her friend had the same one. Do you remember who that was?'

'Let me think.' Mattie frowned, then her face cleared. 'Yes. I've got it. It was Charlotte. Charlotte Marigny. I remember her because she came to our house when the Chernobyl disaster happened, and she was worried about her aunt who was in Sweden at the time, because of the radioactive cloud, you see. Corinne was very good friends with her for a while. They bought the matching peony pendants when they were on holiday with Charlotte's family.'

'Do you know if they stayed in touch, at least until Maman left France?' Emma asked.

'I don't think so,' Mattie said, as she handed back the pendant to Emma. 'But I'm not sure.'

They sat down for lunch then but all the time, Emma kept turning it all over in her mind. Her mother had never mentioned Charlotte Marigny, but then she had hardly talked about any aspect of those last years in France. Perhaps she and Charlotte had fallen out or drifted apart long before Corinne had left, and there was no connection to whatever it was her mother had been wanting to tell her. But if something had happened between them that had triggered her mother's departure, then that might be the first proper clue to the mystery.

She had to try and track down her mother's old friend.

Nine

A deadline had seemed like a good idea the other day, but it turns out that when you try to apply it to life, rather than work, it makes your mind rebel. Every time Charlotte tried to think about what she was going to do, her mind skittered away into thoughts about the weather, or things she'd seen on social media, or overheard in the shops. She decided to write her thoughts down, objectively, as if preparing a report, presenting pros and cons, but she only got as far as dividing the sheet of paper into two columns when she heard a voice in her head saying, *What a pleasure, tidying away emotion in neat little columns!* It sounded just like her father's amused tone, and it made her feel both silly and sad, so she tore the paper up and went out for a run.

That was early Monday morning. After that, she'd showered, changed and spent the rest of the day in the shops, distracting herself by embarking on a marathon of browsing in the old department stores of the Boulevard Haussmann. She didn't mind shopping but only if it had a specific purpose. Buying new shoes. A new shirt. Jewellery. Make-up. Books. Her friends always joked that you'd better not arrange a day out shopping with Charlotte, unless you wanted to have it all done and dusted in under two hours. Yet there she was in Galeries Lafayette and Printemps, doing just what other people seemed to love: browsing, sauntering, idly examining racks of clothes. Except, after a while, looking wasn't enough; her credit card started to get a proper workout, and none of it from the bargain racks: a pair of round Miu Miu sunglasses with tortoiseshell frames; a smart beige and cream Lancel slim leather belt; a set of Clarins beauty products; a Max Mara silk shirt in a superb shade of burnt orange. She'd been impulsive, and it felt good. As she sat having lunch in the Printemps Brasserie, resting her aching feet, she had the exhilarating feeling that this wasn't just an out-of-character shopping spree; it was a sign that she was throwing caution to the wind, so she would see her way forward.

But that feeling only lasted till she looked at her phone in the Metro and saw an email from Aidan. With a hollow feeling in the pit of her stomach, she opened it up. But there were no issues. Mrs Browning had settled down and the team had installed the flamingo monstrosity; the woman who was replacing Shirin, their accounts manager, while she was on maternity leave, had come in and confirmed dates. *And*, he finished, *I bumped into Elise in the café this morning. She said you were staying longer in Paris, maybe even into next week. Is that right?*

If they had compared notes on the reason for her sudden departure, then they'd know she had been lying to them both. Exiting the inbox and going to Aidan's mobile number, she texted, *Got your email. Sounds like you have everything sorted. Yes, I am staying longer. Is that okay with you?*

His reply came almost immediately. *Of course. We'll cope. But are you okay?*

I'm fine. Thanks for asking, though.

No problem, he texted back. *Take care.*

He definitely seemed less stressed than last time, which was a good thing. Or was it? Was he covering up issues he didn't dare tell her about? Were things falling apart behind the scenes? *Oh, for God's sake, Charlotte*, she told herself angrily, *stop it right now!*

By Tuesday morning, after a restless night brought about mainly by too many glasses of red wine, she'd decided that she'd approached the deadline in the wrong way. Trying to force her mind to come up with a solution wouldn't lead to success.

Once at a dinner party she and Tom had attended, one of the other guests, who was a successful novelist, said that he'd learned that his subconscious mind—which he had dubbed 'Harry'—did all the heavy lifting when it came to working out what his characters would be doing next. 'Harry's not to be rushed, though,' he said, grinning. 'Any attempt by upstairs at hurrying him along leads to radio silence.' *Upstairs* was what he called his waking mind. At the time it had sounded twee and unconvincing to Charlotte, but the man must have been doing something right because his novels were bestsellers. 'Hey, Harry,' she said aloud, now, 'I'm desperate so I'm calling on you, okay? I won't force or hurry you, but for God's sake, please remember we're on borrowed time.' Shaking her head at her own absurdity, glad no one was around to hear, she finished her coffee and got ready to go out, heading to the Metro station to catch the train, bound for Versailles.

She hadn't been to the extensive gardens at the Palace of Versailles for ages, but she occasionally caught the popular radio show of Alain Baraton, who'd worked in those gardens since 1981. It was on one of the show's recent episodes that she'd heard a mention about the latest addition to the Palace gardens: *le Jardin du Parfumeur*, the Perfumer's Garden, which she'd immediately earmarked as somewhere she wanted to go.

Visiting the gardens was free, unlike the palace, so she didn't stop at the ticket office but continued around the back, past the spectacular terraces and grand fountains, down the long gravelled paths lined with neat trees, then past a garden of quiet nooks and soft green grass. Once, on a school visit, she and another student had managed to slip away from the class to find refuge here. Today, it was equally devoid of people, with birdsong in the trees and the blue sky above. Charlotte could almost imagine she was on a countryside estate as she kept on towards the grounds of the Trianon, which with its smaller buildings and gardens had once been a tranquil bolthole for the royal family, away from the intrigues of the court. It was here that the Perfumer's Garden had been planted.

Created as a collaboration between a contemporary perfume house and the Versailles gardeners, it celebrated the importance of floral fragrances. It was said the profession of perfumer had started in Versailles, a profession that over the centuries had come to be one of the jewels in the nation's crown. The garden had been carefully thought out, with three main sections: a 'garden of curiosities', filled with the unusual and the aromatic; 'under the trees', a walkway lined with Japanese cherry trees, and plots where fragrant bushes such as lilac and jasmine flourished; and a 'secret garden', a shady walled retreat where orchids, roses, laurel and giant lilies grew together.

Charlotte was particularly taken with an area featuring a selection of flowers whose scent was known as 'mute', because even though the living plant had a richly distinctive fragrance, it was impossible to distil an essence from it, and the perfume had to be recreated synthetically. Among others, these included violets, carnations, lilac and peonies. All those flowers were very popular, and she had placed many in people's gardens, as well as her own. But until now she had not known their secret: a scent spreading in the air but held tightly to the living plant, a refusal to give up its essence that had driven perfumers mad over the centuries. There was something rather wonderful about that, as well as strange, almost disconcerting. A lesson for life, maybe?

Many hours later, exhausted after a long if very pleasant day walking kilometres around Versailles and then a crowded train ride where she'd had to stand a lot of the way, Charlotte finally got back to Juliette's house.

As she let herself in, she saw that the answering machine's light was flashing by the landline phone that Juliette insisted on keeping 'just in case'. Thinking it might be Juliette herself, she pressed the button to listen to the recording and heard a young stranger's pleasant voice speaking in good but slightly accented French.

Bonjour, Madame Marigny. Forgive me for calling unannounced but I am hoping you might be able to help me. My name is Emma Taylor. I am Australian and living at the moment in Paris with my grandmother, Madame Mathilde Lenoir. I was hoping you might put me in contact with your niece Charlotte, who I believe was a childhood friend of my mother, Corinne Lenoir. It would mean a great deal to me. I can be reached on—but here, Charlotte pressed the pause button, and stared at the machine, her scalp prickling. For that other escaped student on that school trip to Versailles had been Corinne Lenoir.

Rewinding the message, she listened to it again, as her mind filled with pictures of the past.

Ten

Every second Wednesday morning, Monsieur Renan visited the stand to chat with Arielle about how things had gone in the previous fortnight, look at the new flowers that had come in, glance over the records book and exchange cheerful greetings with clients. He would always turn up impeccably barbered and dressed, a box of delicious cakes in hand, far too many for them to eat over their morning tea or coffee—the extras were for Arielle to take home to Pauline and the twins. Sometimes, he came alone, sometimes with his daughter Romaine Vinier, who worked at the Mairie de Paris, the central council which oversaw the general running of the city. Arielle wasn't entirely sure what she did there, but Romaine gave the impression it was something important. Romaine could be quite tiring at times but her heart was in the right place when it came to her father, whom she clearly adored. And she was always friendly to Arielle, even if she liked to make suggestions that revealed a rather naïve idea of how the business ran. At such moments, Monsieur Renan would wink surreptitiously at Arielle, reminding her not to take offence.

Today was a Romaine morning, which meant bringing out the sachets of green tea that she preferred and boiling the kettle for her cup. Meanwhile, Arielle and Monsieur Renan would drink coffee delivered piping hot from a nearby café, and discussions would begin, fortified by the selection of exquisite cakes. Then, when the first customers started arriving, Monsieur Renan and Arielle would return to the front of the stand and chat with them, while Romaine stayed in the back of the shop uploading photos to the Instagram page she'd created for the stand.

Arielle was relieved that Monsieur Renan had rebuffed Romaine's suggestion that social media should be part of Arielle's job; she had quite enough to do without wasting her time on Instagram. Romaine found this inexplicable: *Here you are, years younger than me*, she'd declared, *and yet you don't see this is the modern way for business success!* Arielle would smile politely and murmur that people might have shiny new tools but still craved personal connection. And what can be more personal than the choosing of flowers, for birthdays, and funerals, and weddings, or just for the joy of flowers? Romaine would raise her eyebrows but she could hardly deny that Arielle's approach brought in the customers.

As per usual when Monsieur Renan spent time at the stand, Vella just happened to come by shortly after opening to smarmily greet him and shower Romaine with overblown compliments—something he must think would help him worm his way into their good graces, but which Arielle could have told him wouldn't work. Not only did Monsieur Renan regard Vella's effusions with ironic distaste, but Romaine, scarred by her marriage to a lying philanderer whom she'd finally divorced, was suspicious of all men, especially those who tried to flatter her. So try as he might, he never got anywhere with either of them, and today was no exception.

The morning's customers included a man buying flowers for his wife's first day in a new job; a woman wanting to know their prices for a wedding; a red-eyed woman ordering a funeral wreath; a couple of Japanese tourists exclaiming over the peonies and buying a bunch for their hotel room; and Daniel Auban. He turned up just before nine thirty, a bit out of breath, his light-brown hair windblown. But although he gave the impression of being in a hurry, he said they should go ahead and serve other customers first. As he hovered, making a show of looking at the flowers, Arielle thought he seemed on edge, and she wondered what was wrong. But she could do nothing about it till the last customer had gone, and then it was Monsieur Renan who turned to him and said, 'And what about you, Monsieur Auban? Have you found the perfect flower to grace your day?'

There was a teasing tone to his words that made Daniel colour and say, in a rush, 'Well, yes, I think, I mean, I *have* decided. Those, please,' and he pointed to a bunch of flowers that the French called *marguerites* and the English called daisies.

Monsieur Renan raised an eyebrow. 'Humble but eloquent flowers,' he said, with a little smile, 'wouldn't you say, Arielle?'

She smiled back. 'Innocence, hope, a new beginning . . . the perfect flower to offer a new mother, or perhaps someone about to embark on a fresh chapter of their life. Is that who it's for, Monsieur Auban?' She always called him by that formal moniker when her boss was around.

Daniel flushed again. 'No, no,' he stammered, 'it's for—well, actually I'm giving a talk at lunchtime today at the museum, and the flowers are a kind of prop. And what you say—about their meaning—ties in very well with my subject.'

'What is the talk about?' said Arielle, wrapping the flowers.

'The signification of the garden in an illuminated manuscript from the fifteenth century,' Daniel recited. 'I'm comparing the symbolism of the garden in the manuscript to the one in *The Lady and the Unicorn* tapestries at Cluny, and how it might be relevant to contemporary life. I've been thinking about it for a while as a subject for an academic paper, but then I thought a general audience might be interested, too.' A smile lit up his usually serious face. 'And this morning, I decided I had to have a prop.' He gestured towards the daisies.

'Then I am glad you found the right one,' Arielle said warmly. 'It sounds so interesting. I would love to hear more about it when you have the time.'

Daniel shot her a glance, then said, in a rush, 'Would you like to come and hear the talk today?' Quickly adding, as he saw her expression, 'But I understand it's not possible, sorry, you must be terribly busy.'

'I wish I could . . .' Arielle began uncertainly, but she was interrupted by Monsieur Renan saying *no* in such a firm tone that he startled them both into silence.

'No,' Monsieur Renan repeated. 'She *won't* be too busy. *I* will take over the stand today, from eleven thirty till three o'clock. And I want no argument, Madame Arielle Lunel,' he added, forestalling her protest. 'I know it's been a while, but this old fellow hasn't forgotten what to do.' His face cracked wide open into a mischievous smile. 'Besides, if I want extra help, I'll put Romaine to work. It will be great material for her next phone story.'

'What's great material?' asked Romaine, emerging from the back.

'You and I, my darling,' said her father, 'are going to be keeping shop from lunchtime onwards, while these two here chat about the hidden meaning of flowers in the Middle Ages, or whatever else they feel like. All right with you?'

'Well, Papa,' Romaine said, glancing in some surprise from Arielle to Daniel and then to her father, 'I *was* planning on taking you to a fine restaurant that's supposed to be the latest thing.'

'I say *bof* to the fine restaurant,' snorted Monsieur Renan. 'I think it will be more fun if you fetch us both a *jambon beurre* from the café and we have it together, here at the stand, just like when you were a little girl, remember?'

Romaine's eyes were suddenly bright. 'I remember,' she said, 'and you're right, Papa. It will be much more fun.'

Her father touched her arm affectionately. 'Excellent! So we're all agreed.'

'Really, Monsieur Renan,' Arielle said, shaking her head in amusement, 'you are very bossy, but you are also very kind.'

Daniel's face was wreathed in smiles. 'Thank you. I hope my talk won't be disappointing.'

'Stop it right there with the *ifs* and *buts*, young man,' said Monsieur Renan firmly. 'And I have one other piece of advice.'

'Yes?' said Daniel uncertainly.

'The way you are clutching those *marguerites*, my friend, they are going to be seriously in need of a drink before they play a starring role in your talk.' The old man's cheeky grin was infectious.

───※───

Two hours later, Arielle hurried over the bridge to the Cluny Museum, just ten minutes' walk from the stall. Once inside, she went straight to the room dedicated to *The Lady and the Unicorn*—the jewels of the museum's collection of medieval art—for a moment. Arielle had seen the six large tapestries before, but today she let the feeling of the beautiful artworks' gentle mystery flow over her.

She read a notice on the wall explaining that the tapestries dated from around 1500, were designed in Paris and woven by skilled Flemish artists in wool and silk. Depicting the five senses, plus a sixth sense whose exact meaning remained enigmatic, all the tapestries featured a golden-haired lady and a pure white unicorn, as well as an attendant lion—kept mostly at arm's length—and a collection of other smaller beasts and birds. All set against the idyllic background of a neat grassy garden replete with flowers and fruit trees standing guard on either side.

Just standing there gazing at them made her feel as though she was entering a different dimension, where worries had no place, where she could put aside the nagging anxiety that if the Grandiers hadn't made any further contact that wasn't because they'd changed their minds, but because they were plotting their next move. She breathed the peace in a little longer, then slipped quietly through the crowd to find the room where Daniel had told her he would be.

He was alone, nervously fiddling with a computer projector as she came in, the daisies in a vase to one side. When he saw her, he smiled. 'Thank you so much for coming. I'm not sure how many other people are going to arrive, it was announced a bit last minute, so you might be my only audience. I hope you don't mind.'

'Not at all,' she said, 'I would count myself lucky.' She was about to say something else when the first of the attendees started trickling in. Whispering 'good luck', Arielle found a seat as more people came in and the room started to fill up. She had never heard him give a talk before, and had no idea how he would perform, but only hoped that her presence wouldn't hamper his presentation.

She need not have worried. It soon became very clear that he was in his element, talking about things he loved and understood intimately. Starting by holding up the daisies, he said, 'People have always seen meaning in plants, in gardens. These flowers, for instance, I learned today, might send a message of hope and of good wishes for a new chapter in life.' His gaze sought Arielle's then, in gentle complicity, and she felt a rush of warmth. 'In the Middle Ages,' he continued, 'people were no different. They sought signs in what surrounded them, just as we do. And gardens were prime symbols of hope and new life.' Returning the daisies to their vase, he clicked on the first slide, which showed the decorated title of a manuscript. 'I'm going to start not with *The Lady and the Unicorn*, which I presume most of you here have seen, but with a book you probably don't know. It's in the National Library of France's collection. The text is by a known medieval writer, Pierre d'Ailly, but the artist is anonymous. It's called *Le jardin de vertueuse consolation*—the garden of virtuous consolation. And here we see a wonderful example of the fantastical, playful nature of medieval art,' he said, pointing to how the first letter of the book's title had been made to look like a piece of garden trellis, with dragons and stern bearded faces hanging off it. Zooming in on the image, he said, 'Look at that dragon at the top. Is it devouring a carrot, or a bird? Or maybe,' he grinned, 'a pair of garden secateurs?' And to a ripple of laughter, he clicked onto the next slide.

Arielle wasn't the only one in the audience to gasp: the screen was filled with an exquisite illuminated page showing a lady with four attendants greeting an old woman at the gateway of a garden, the whole of the image enclosed within a decorative border filled with illustrations of fruit, flowers and birds. 'As you can see'—Daniel pointed at calligraphed words directly under the scene—'this tells you that you are entering the garden of virtuous consolation. And now, listen to words that come later in the book, and which express something of the nature of that garden.'

Leaving the picture up on the screen, he picked up a notebook and read: '*In this soil are born the herbs of humble meditation, the trees of high contemplation, the flowers of honest conversation, the fruits of blessed perfection.*' Looking up, he went on, quietly, 'You see, this book was intended as a religious text, but I think that those particular words resonate with our secular age, too. For to me the writer was not only a religious man, he was also a lover of gardens, maybe even a gardener himself. And I also feel instinctively, though without hard evidence, that he was passing on an understanding of the garden as a place of reflection and consolation, to help those in sadness or with a troubled soul.'

There was silence as he finished speaking, and Arielle, a lump in her throat, knew she wasn't the only one deeply affected. But so, she realised, was Daniel himself. Maybe he'd stopped because he couldn't trust himself to continue. After a moment, he resumed speaking. 'And here are some other words from the book, which are rather different, less contemplative but full of a joy I think many of us might recognise.' Smiling, he picked up the notebook again, and read, '*Grass is a-greening, flowers blooming, trees shading, fruits quenching, fountains playing, birds singing, friends enjoying.* Isn't that beautiful? The words feel like they are there just for the pleasure of it, like a song. As if the writer couldn't help himself . . . maybe because when he wrote it, he was looking out of the window at that sheer abundance, or maybe he was remembering it from last spring. We'll never know for sure. But across the centuries he's reached out to us, and we understand. There's a deep joy in that, which we can take into our own lives. I know someone,' he continued, 'a beekeeper who was inspired by manuscripts like this one to create a garden like you might have found in that time, when the humble bee was seen as a symbol of inspiration, because of the way it wanders around the flowers, gathering nectar that is then magically transformed into honey, like a poet or artist might transform a simple idea into something that distils the sweetness of life. And that's what we see too, when we step into the garden of *The Lady and the Unicorn*.'

He went on, the slides changing to images of the six tapestries as he spoke entertainingly about what each of the elements of the garden depicted in them might mean, but Arielle's mind lingered on what he'd said, and the expression on his face as he read out the words from that book, a book she'd never heard of before, but which she knew she would never forget.

Eleven

'Come and see, Emma, quick,' Mattie called from the living room, where she was watching the morning news. Leaving the washing-up, Emma did as she was told. 'What's the . . .' she began, but trailed off as she saw who was being interviewed on screen.

'So, Monsieur Hugo,' the reporter asked brightly, 'what does it feel like to be appointed as the youngest director ever of Aurora International's Paris office, the nerve centre of the company in Europe?'

'It feels like an honour,' said Marc-Antoine smoothly. 'I am very grateful for the trust the board has put in me.'

'Some people might say the board has taken a risk appointing someone so young to this important position. What do you say to that?'

'I am hardly a teenager,' said Marc-Antoine, with a humorous lift of an eyebrow. 'Unless thirty-four is the new sixteen.'

Mattie chuckled. 'He handled that silly question well,' she said.

Emma nodded without comment, thinking that he probably had had more than enough practice at dodging questions.

'Long before it was fashionable, Aurora International built an impressive reputation in the field of ethical investment,' the reporter went on. 'But now most financial institutions want to get in on the act. How will you ensure that Aurora International remains competitive?'

Marc-Antoine gave a faint smile. 'You surely don't expect me to give away our secrets. But let me assure you that we will remain ahead of the rest.'

'This new appointment means you will now be based in Paris; will you regret leaving behind your life in the *Big Apple*?' The reporter said the last two words in English.

Marc-Antoine smiled. 'I was born and lived for quite a lot of my childhood in Paris, I still have family here, and I love this city. I can hardly regret coming back here to live.'

'Just one last question then, Monsieur Hugo. Most directors have an eye to their legacy. What do you hope yours to be?'

Marc-Antoine gave a little laugh. 'It's a bit soon to ask me that, don't you think? I'm focused on getting the job done, with my team.'

The reporter thanked him, Marc-Antoine inclined his head somewhat regally, and then he and the journalist disappeared as another story came up.

'Well,' Mattie said, muting the TV, 'I'm so glad for him. He's worked so hard. Much too hard, sometimes,' she added, 'it seemed to take over his life in New York. I hope that now he's back home in Paris, he can start to relax.'

'I don't think you can relax in his sort of position,' Emma said. *And he doesn't look like the type anyway*, she thought. Ambition was written all over him. Even his name conveyed it. A given name linking you back to an ancient Roman general, and the surname of one of the greatest French writers ever, Victor Hugo: clearly something to live up to. But she highly doubted his New York life was completely about work. He'd probably had a string of glamorous girlfriends, as polished as himself.

'I suppose you're right,' Mattie said. She glanced at Emma. 'Anyway, I'm going to call him to congratulate him and maybe, if you don't mind, he could come to lunch or dinner today or tomorrow. I'll cook.'

Emma saw the slightly anxious expression on her grandmother's face and immediately felt a twinge of guilt. 'Of course I don't mind, Mattie,' she said, squeezing her grandmother's hand. 'And I'm happy to cook, if you like.' She winked. 'I'm told I'm not too bad at it.'

'That is absolutely true, darling,' Mattie said. Emma had cooked dinner two or three times since she'd arrived: dishes from her repertoire that she knew would come out right, and which Mattie had enjoyed immensely. 'But you're working hard in the garden and you need to relax too. I'll make something simple but sumptuous, the kind of thing I know Marc-Antoine loves.' She beamed at Emma. 'I'll call him now.'

'And I'll go and finish washing up the breakfast things,' said Emma.

Relaxing is the last thing I'll be doing, she thought as she washed up, *if I have to make small talk with that guy over a meal.* Or worse still listen to him blathering on about his highly important job in an investment bank. Correction, *ethical* investment bank. Her lip curled. Was there really such a thing? Pulling out her phone, she googled Aurora International. After reading several news articles, she had to conclude that Aurora International did indeed appear to be that rare beast. She couldn't find anything that even hinted at scandal. But it's still a bank, making big fat profits presumably . . .

'So Marc-Antoine is coming on Saturday for lunch,' Mattie said from the doorway, without preamble, 'because he's about to leave for Berlin and won't be back till Friday evening.'

So he's going to take over our Saturday instead, Emma thought, with a twinge of spite. 'Do you want me to start doing some shopping for you?'

'No, no, it's fine,' Mattie said a little distractedly. 'I've got to decide on a menu first. The shopping can be done tomorrow.'

'All right. Well, I'm going to get dressed then head back into the garden.'

Mattie shook her head. 'You are overworking yourself, my darling Emma. You've been at it every day since Monday'—it was now Thursday—'and you must need a break. Why don't you go and see a bit more of Paris this morning, instead? You can potter in the garden this afternoon, if you must.'

I don't mind the work, I enjoy it, Emma wanted to say, but instead she found herself saying, 'Maybe I *do* need a break. I might visit the flower market and see if that stand you told me about still exists.'

'Excellent idea,' said Mattie. 'And say hello to Monsieur Renan for me, if you see him.'

'Would you like to come with me and tell him yourself?' Emma offered, but Mattie shook her head. 'Not today, darling. I'm going to sit down with my recipe books and decide on the menu for our Saturday lunch.'

~

An hour later, Emma emerged from the station just a few steps from the flower market. Glancing at the lovely old cast-iron fountains and displays of ready-to-plant small trees and bushes outside the charming pavilions, she was immediately enchanted. It felt as though she'd arrived in a bucolic old-world haven far away from the busy modern city. Entering the first pavilion, she wandered happily down the aisle, stopping here and there to take photos and noting everything with great delight: colourful rows of flowers in pots and bunches, some of which she knew, such as tulips, hyacinth, lilac, lily of the valley, and yes, hydrangea and peonies, but also many others whose names she had no idea of. There were also decorative baskets hanging from hooks, displays of elegant or kitschy garden ornaments, and lots of packets of seeds to rummage through. Some of the stalls really pushed the boat out when it came to decoration, with chandeliers and glass baubles and colourful paper lanterns hanging from the ceiling.

But she'd had no idea that there would be so many stands, and this was only the first of the pavilions! How was she going to find Monsieur Renan's place? She'd forgotten to ask her grandmother exactly which pavilion it was in, if it even still existed, that is. She couldn't phone Mattie because her grandmother would be having her *sieste* right now. Asking a stallholder would be the easiest. And if she bought something, they'd be more likely to answer questions.

Stopping at the closest stand, she selected a new pair of gardening gloves—the old ones were threadbare and would soon have holes. Taking them to the counter, she paid for them and said, 'I wonder if you might know if Monsieur Auguste Renan still works here?'

The stallholder, a surly middle-aged man who had barely glanced up from his phone, now looked up and said, 'Not so you'd notice.'

Emma was taken aback. 'Oh. I see.' She *didn't* see but wasn't sure how else to respond.

He shrugged. 'The old man's semi-retired and he's got that Lunel woman doing all the work for him now. At least she's supposed to do all the work, but I wonder if . . .' He broke off, seeing Emma's expression and added, grudgingly, 'Renan's stand is the last before the exit.'

'Thank you.' Emma gave him a weak smile and left, glad to escape from the man's inexplicably spiteful manner. But she forgot all about him as she got to the Renan stand. There were many lovely displays in the market but this one had to be her favourite, resplendent with layered patterns of gloriously exuberant flowers, among which she recognised some truly magnificent pink peonies, whose sweet scent filled the air.

Standing watering the flowers with a long-necked plastic can was a woman with curly red hair. She saw Emma and smiled. 'Bonjour.'

'Bonjour,' Emma echoed, liking the woman's bright face and the quick intelligence in her eyes. 'You really have the most beautiful stand in the market, Madame.'

The woman looked pleased. 'Thank you.' Setting down the watering can, she asked, 'Is there something I can help you with?'

Emma explained about Alain visiting the stall and the woman, introducing herself as Arielle Lunel, Monsieur Renan's manager, said she would ask him about it. 'He has an excellent memory, and I'm sure he'd remember your grandfather, if he was a regular customer.'

'Thank you,' Emma said. 'In fact, I'm trying to restore Pappy's garden, and so far all I've done is clearing and weeding, but I do want to grow things too. Maybe you could advise me?'

A smile lit up Arielle's face. 'I'm no expert but I'd be very happy to make suggestions. What a lovely thing to do, restoring your beloved grandfather's garden!'

It was Emma's turn to beam. 'Thank you. I thought maybe I could buy some seeds today. What would you suggest?'

'Cosmos, nigella and rose campion,' said Arielle, at once. 'They are very pretty and easy to grow from seed. You'll have a lovely display in a few weeks.'

'That sounds perfect.' Emma took out her phone and showed Arielle photos she'd taken of the plants she'd uncovered in the garden but hadn't been able to identify. 'None of them are flowering, and I can't tell what they might be.'

Arielle looked at each in turn. 'These are dahlia. That one's heliotrope. And this one'—she pointed to a picture showing a couple of small-leaved clumped plants—'they're peonies.'

Emma was delighted. She'd known her grandfather had grown them but hadn't thought they had survived. 'Really?'

'Absolutely. They may flower soon but it depends if they've been set back by being in the midst of weeds. They look healthy enough, so even if they don't flower this year, they probably will next year. You know,' she went on, 'peonies are extraordinary plants. They can live for up to a hundred years.'

'Wow! How old do you think these ones are?'

Arielle glanced at the photo. 'I can't be sure—how long ago did your grandfather start his garden?'

'About fifty years ago, I think,' Emma said. 'If he planted peonies then—do you think these might be them?' *They might have been blooming when Maman was just a little girl*, she thought, awed.

'It's certainly possible.'

'And if I wanted to plant more, could I do that now?' Emma asked.

'No. You have to wait till autumn. And they take a few years to flower. Four or five, sometimes.' Arielle smiled. 'So you have to be patient.'

'I'm getting the idea that gardening is not something you expect results from in a hurry!'

Arielle laughed. 'Very true.'

Emma could see a group of people approaching the stand. 'I won't hold you up much longer,' she said, 'but as well as the seeds, could I buy some flowers too? A mixed bunch of the flowers you identified for me, at least those you have here—and hydrangea too, because that's another one I rescued.'

That beautiful smile lit up Arielle's face again. 'I don't have heliotrope at the moment, but yes.'

As Emma left the market, clutching the gorgeous bunch Arielle had put together—pastel-blue hydrangea, creamy-white dahlia, and a few of those gorgeous pink peonies—she felt buoyed by the encounter. It was great to know she had someone she could go to for advice, especially someone as *sympa* as Arielle.

At that moment, she felt her phone vibrating in her pocket. The call was from a number she didn't recognise, and she let it ring out. If it wasn't a scammer, then whoever it was would leave a voicemail. Sure enough, instants later came the buzz announcing a voicemail, and Emma clicked through to listen.

Hello, a woman's voice said, in French. *My name is Charlotte Marigny. I believe you telephoned my aunt. Can you call me back on this number?*

The voice sounded brisk, assured and Emma's pulse quickened. It had been two days since she'd tracked down Juliette Marigny's number. Juliette had become a travel writer after leaving the diplomatic service and there were several reviews of her books, and a couple of magazine interviews but no mention of a niece called Charlotte—until Emma had hit on something buried in the social pages of a magazine. It wasn't an article but rather a photo that showed a cheerful group of people raising glasses against a background of greenery. The caption read: *Well-known writer Madame Juliette Marigny's superb garden in the 16th arrondissement was the setting for an unusual launch this week, as the prestigious Paris Cooking School announced its latest venture, a bespoke catering service. Pictured from left to right are Sylvie Morel, owner of the Paris Cooking School; Damien Arty and Kate Evans, assistants to Madame Morel; and on the far right, Juliette Marigny and her niece Charlotte, who designed the garden.* And that had given her the final clue she needed to work out which of the listed numbers in the directory for 'Marigny, J' was the right one.

She took a deep breath, hit the number that had called her, and waited. After the first couple of rings, the brisk voice answered. 'Yes?'

'I'm Emma Taylor, daughter of—'

'I know who you are,' Charlotte Marigny said, not rudely, but clearly wanting to cut to the chase. 'You're Corinne's daughter.'

'Yes. My mother—Corinne—died six weeks ago. Cancer.' Emma swallowed, the words still hard to say out loud. 'She had cancer and had been very ill for months.'

'I am so very sorry,' Charlotte Marigny said, her tone quite changed. The French adjective she'd used, *désolée*, seemed so much stronger to Emma than its equivalent in English, 'sorry', even though she knew that like sorry it could be used on a sliding scale of emotion, from mere politeness to heartfelt sympathy. 'What a very sad time for you,' Charlotte went on, softly. 'Cancer is so cruel.'

Tears sprang into Emma's eyes, and she couldn't speak. Then Charlotte said gently, 'Are you still there, Emma?'

'Yes. I—excuse me,' she said. 'Thank you so much for your kind words, Madame Marigny. And also for getting back to me.'

'Charlotte, please. Excuse me for not calling before now, but things have been rather busy. I'm in Paris on business and have had a lot of appointments.'

'I understand,' Emma said. Taking a deep breath, she went on, 'This might sound strange, but I know practically nothing of my mother's life before she went to Australia. She never talked about it. My grandmother has filled me in on a few things but she told me that you and my mother had been good friends, and I thought, maybe you might know more and could tell me about it.' She trailed off, a little spooked by the silence at the other end, then added, hurriedly, 'But I completely understand if you don't want to.'

'It's quite okay, Emma,' Charlotte said. 'I'm happy to talk. But perhaps it would be better if we met in person.'

Relief flooded over Emma. 'That would be great.'

'How about tomorrow, three o'clock at the Jardin du Luxembourg, near the Grand Bassin, where children sail toy yachts—do you know it?'

'I certainly do,' said Emma. 'That's perfect.'

'Then it's settled. I'll be wearing a red jacket.'

'Great. I'll . . . well, I'm not sure what I'll be wearing, but I will look out for you. And I look forward very much to meeting you.'

At last, Emma thought, with a surge of relief and excitement. At last she was going to speak to someone who might be able to shed some light on her mother's secrets. She thought of the silver peony and the actual peonies still there in her grandfather's garden. Her mother's favourite flower back then . . . A tingle went up her spine. It felt like the jigsaw pieces were starting to fall into place.

Twelve

Charlotte had not been sure at first that she would respond to Emma's message. She was meant to be thinking about her future, not taking an irrelevant detour into the past. Sure, it had been weird, getting that message on the very day when she'd thought of Corinne for the first time in many years. But it was only a coincidence, life was full of them. In the end, however, she'd decided that a distraction might be just what she needed in her present situation, her subconscious mind having stubbornly refused so far to give her any help whatsoever.

She was genuinely sorry to learn that Corinne Lenoir was dead, and now the memories came flooding back.

After that first chat in the Versailles garden when they'd escaped from the boring guide, the girls had begun hanging out, talking a lot, listening to music and going to parties. They even holidayed together once, when Charlotte's parents had invited Corinne to the place they'd rented in the remote Morvan hills in Burgundy. The girls were very different—Charlotte was outgoing and sociable and Corinne was reserved and sometimes intense—but they enjoyed each other's company. Corinne was a one-off in many ways—aloof but not shy, with a sharp, even unforgiving intelligence that saw her hold her own at school. Even the troublemakers and macho sexists never dared to bother her. She was also strikingly beautiful, yet neither flaunted nor denied it. Charlotte's brother, Nicolas, when he was still trying to persuade himself that he was straight, had said that she had an '*air de Joconde*'—a Mona Lisa aura—which fascinated boys, and quite likely a few girls too. But Corinne didn't seem to be fascinated back.

Not until she met Pascal on that holiday. And though Charlotte could have told her it would end in tears, Corinne wouldn't have listened. She was an all or nothing kind of girl, and once she decided on something, she stuck to it, no matter what. Not only about Pascal, but other things too. Such as the idea that her parents were uniquely, embarrassingly annoying and inadequate, when to Charlotte, they seemed rather cool, unlike hers. Most teenagers thought their parents were awful or boring, or both, but Corinne took it to another level.

Charlotte winced, remembering the last time they'd talked. Although *talked* was not the right word, a *blazing row* was much more like it. It was the year after they left school and, though it had started from a silly insensitive remark, it had escalated quickly because, away from the bubble of school, the difference in the girls' personalities had become more pronounced. Charlotte had become fed up with Corinne's trenchant, take-no-prisoners nature and Corinne couldn't cope anymore with Charlotte's easy-come-easy-go attitude. But it wasn't Corinne who'd blown up; it had been Charlotte.

Charlotte had chosen to meet Emma at the Luxembourg Garden because, even though she hadn't been there for some years, she'd always liked it as a child, and her own children had too, when the family was on holiday in Paris. It was a real pleasure garden of the classic sort, with something for everyone, from gorgeous flowers to pony rides, lovely water features to tennis courts and a host of statues. It always made Charlotte feel relaxed.

She had just reached the central square when a voice called her name. Turning, she saw a young woman of around thirty, dressed in a loose flowery top, blue jeans and sneakers. She had an appealing face, fresh and naturally smiley, though there was more nervousness than pleasure in the smile. Corinne's daughter was definitely pretty, but she did not look much like her mother or have her startling beauty: that rippling mass of wavy dark hair, those long-lashed brown eyes and full pink lips, and most of all, that indefinable air which hung about her.

'My red jacket did its work then,' Charlotte said, in English, holding out a hand. 'Emma, I presume?'

'Yes, it's me,' Emma replied, sounding nervous, as they shook hands.

This young woman was definitely not like Corinne, Charlotte thought. At least, not the Corinne she remembered, who never got flustered.

As they began a slow circuit around the square, Charlotte said, 'So, why did your grandmother tell you about me?' It wasn't exactly what she'd planned to open with, but it would do.

'Two things.' Emma stopped, fumbled in her jeans pocket and brought out something which flashed in the sun. 'I was working in Mattie's garden—that's my grandmother—and I found this.' She handed it to Charlotte. 'When I showed it to Mattie, she said you had one too, that you had bought it at a market when you were on holiday with Mum, and that you were best friends as teenagers. But before that I had never heard . . .' She hesitated, but Charlotte filled in the blanks for her. 'You had never heard of me, because Corinne didn't tell you,' she said flatly, turning the silver peony around in her palm.

'Mum wasn't really a talker,' Emma said, sounding defensive. 'Not about the past, anyway.'

'Not even to your father?' Charlotte asked. God, she had completely forgotten about the peony pendants. Where had hers gone? Lost somewhere in her many moves.

'No. At least, I don't know. Well, he's my stepfather actually. So, was Mattie right? Did you have one of these too?'

Charlotte nodded. 'Corinne and I bought them from a market stand when we were on holiday with my family in the Morvan, in Burgundy. It was when we were both seventeen, the summer before we took the *bac*.' The bac, or *baccalauréat*, is the French school leaving exam. 'I wasn't all that keen on the pendants, but Corinne persuaded me to get one. I think she wanted to please Pascal.' She caught Emma's expression. 'Your grandmother wouldn't have told you about him because she wouldn't have known. A boy called Pascal Lamartine was looking after the stand where we bought the pendants. He was a few months older than us and a local, or rather, he'd been living there since his parents had uprooted the whole family and moved to the area a couple of years before. The Morvan is very rural but also quite wild, with massive native forests and remote hills. It has a few smallholdings run by people fleeing the city to try to live a simple country life.'

'We call them tree-changers in Australia,' Emma said, nodding.

Charlotte smiled. 'That's a great term. I must remember it. The Lamartines were like that. They lived on a smallholding just outside a village called St Jean de la Forêt. They raised goats and chickens and had a market stand to sell eggs and cheese and the jewellery Pascal's dad made. Pascal was expected to help out, with the animals and the market stand.' She gave a little laugh. 'He wasn't too keen on that! He was a real city boy, itching to get back to the bright lights.'

'And Mum fell for him?'

'Big time. But he fell for her too. They were pretty much inseparable. That summer, the three of us hung out together, sometimes joined by one of Pascal's mates from the village, a local lad called Eric. He was nothing like Pascal, kind of weedy and quiet, but it turned out we had a shared interest in nature, so we talked about that. And though he and I didn't click romantically, we got on okay. It went on like that for a while, and then the holiday ended. We went back to Paris. Corinne couldn't call Pascal because the Lamartines didn't have a house phone. And it was in the days before everyone had mobile phones. So she sent him a letter. She waited ages, but there was no answer. She thought it had maybe gone astray so she wrote again. Still he didn't answer. And that was that.'

'Are you sure?'

There was an intent expression on Emma's face that suddenly reminded Charlotte of Corinne. 'Absolutely sure,' she said. 'She stopped talking about him, and when I told her that she was much better off without him, that there were plenty more interesting guys out there—*ouf*, did I get the blackest look! I had vaguely thought of getting in touch with Eric, to ask him if he knew what was going on, but I knew to leave well enough alone after that.' She handed the peony back to Emma. 'She lost this not long after we got back to Paris, before the whole thing fizzled out. She was very upset about mislaying it.'

'That's what Mattie said,' Emma said. 'But she didn't know about Pascal.'

'I was the only one who knew, apart from Eric. I don't think Pascal's parents knew or cared—they weren't really focused on their kids—and my parents didn't know, either. My brother, Nic, was already at university and had gone away with his own friends that holiday. Corinne and I did pretty much what we wanted, as long as we were back by evening. And, as you know, all teenagers keep things from their parents. I didn't find it strange that she didn't tell them.'

'You said you told her she was better off without him. So you didn't like him?'

'He was okay. And very good-looking.' She shrugged. 'But a bit of a show-off. Immature, I guess. I no doubt thought I was so mature back then, when I wasn't really either. But for someone as intense and single-minded as Corinne, I felt instinctively that he was a bad match.'

'And you're sure they never saw each other again?'

'Not that I know of. She never mentioned him again, anyway.' She looked at Emma, suddenly remembering what the other woman had said at the beginning of their conversation. 'Two things, you said. The peony's one. What's the other?'

Emma blinked. 'What? Oh, yes. This.' She brought out her phone, fiddled with it then handed it to Charlotte. 'I have the original at home. It was taken somewhere in France, when she was on holiday. She left it for me but I'd never seen it before. Have you? Was it taken by you or someone else during that holiday when she met Pascal?'

Charlotte stared at the lovely black-and-white image of a young Corinne, and a sharp pang of real sorrow struck her. 'What a beautiful portrait! I did have a camera back then, but I didn't take this, and I've never seen it before. I suppose it *could* have been taken in the Morvan, though it's hard to tell. I'm certain it wasn't taken that summer though. Corinne's hair was down to her waist back then, but her hair is shoulder-length in this picture, like yours. Didn't she say anything about it?'

A spasm of pain crossed Emma's face. 'She never got the chance. She died before she could explain it.'

Gently, Charlotte said, 'Is there anything written on the back of the photo by any chance?'

'Just this,' Emma said, swiping to the next photo, and Charlotte saw the scrawled words. *Un jour de printemps.*

'Do you recognise the handwriting?' Emma asked, a hopeful look on her face. 'It isn't Mum's, I'm sure of that.'

Charlotte looked closely at it, then shook her head. 'Sorry, no.'

'Could it be Pascal's?'

'I never saw his handwriting. I'm sorry.'

'It's okay.' She looked at Charlotte. 'Did you stay in touch with my mother after school?'

It was the question Charlotte had been dreading, but she knew she had to answer as honestly as she could. 'We did, for a while. But then one day we had a big blow-up—my fault, I'm afraid—and the friendship ended.' She saw the question in Emma's eyes and explained, 'It started stupidly over a cutting remark Corinne made to me about a guy I was seeing. I was used to her harsh judgements of people, but this time I was really furious. After all, I had kept my thoughts about Pascal to myself when she was seeing him. The whole thing escalated pretty quickly.' She sighed. 'Afterwards, I regretted it and tried to make amends—she heard me out, but then said it was better we didn't see each other anymore. And that was it.'

There was a pause, then Emma said, 'That must have been hard.'

A lump came into Charlotte's throat. 'It was. But also—and this sounds awful—I was kind of relieved. Our friendship had run its course.' She looked at Emma. 'I do remember your mother fondly, and I regret that our friendship ended the way it did. But we had different dreams, different ways of looking at life. For a time, that didn't seem to matter. And then, it did.'

'I understand,' said Emma. She gave a faint smile. 'Mum clearly just accelerated the process; she wouldn't have tolerated anything half-hearted.'

Charlotte smiled back, ruefully. 'You're right.' On an impulse, she added, 'Look, Emma, if there's anything more you'd like to know, I'd be happy to talk again. How long are you here for?'

'I'll be here for a few months. It's really nice, staying with Mattie and getting to know her properly at last . . .' Charlotte saw a shadow pass over Emma's face as she spoke. She could see there was a world of regret there, but all she said was, 'I only met your grandmother a couple of times but I thought she was lovely. And your grandfather—he had such a beautiful garden! I'm a garden designer now you know, and I still remember how well he'd used the space.'

Emma's eyes lit up. 'Actually, I'm working a lot in his garden. Pappy passed away two and a half years ago, and Mattie has found it hard to keep it up. It's rather overgrown and I'm trying to clean it up and maybe get it back to what it was.' She hesitated. 'I know you're very busy, but would you like to come and see it some time? I'm sure Mattie would like to see you as she remembered hearing about your dashing aunt.'

Charlotte laughed. 'We were all so proud of Aunt Juliette. She led such a glamorous and exciting life, although she told me later that it was nowhere near as fun as I'd imagined. Anyway, I'd love to pop in and say hello. Would this weekend work?'

Yes, it would indeed, Mattie said, when Emma called her, and so they arranged for Charlotte to come for lunch the next day, with Elise, who would be with her by then. Emma said there would also be a family friend present, but she didn't elaborate, other than to say his name was Marc-Antoine.

As they parted company, Emma said, 'I am very glad to have met you, and to know a little more about my mother. It means so much to me.'

Charlotte was touched. 'Then I am glad as well,' she said simply. As Emma walked away, Charlotte watched her go, thinking of when she and Corinne had been friends. It was such a long time ago but regret about the manner of their parting filled her again. She and Corinne would never have the chance to reconnect, however remote an outcome that might have been. But she'd been handed the possibility of helping Emma, and that might provide some kind of closure. For herself, as well as for Emma. *And*, a cynical voice deep inside her whispered, *it will handily distract you from thinking about your own problems.*

Thirteen

On most Saturday mornings, Arielle took the children with her to work. She only had to work a half-day on Saturdays because in the afternoon and the whole of Sunday the weekend assistant, Coralie Ferreira, took over. But having the children at the market meant that they didn't miss out on being with her, and it also gave Pauline a break. Since they'd moved in with her, Pauline had pretty much had to co-parent the twins, and Arielle sometimes worried that it placed too much of a burden on her sister *and* put a crimp in her love life. Pauline scoffed at the latter, saying that she had pressed pause on dating. And, she'd added, since Arielle and the twins had moved in, she was happier than she had been in years. Even if she was rather more tired too.

But despite that, Arielle knew her sister was pleased to sometimes have Saturday mornings to herself, pottering around the shops or simply taking her book to read in the sun in the park without interruptions. Plus the children loved coming to the stand, commenting on the flowers, competing as to who knew the most plants, and just being with their mother. And despite the inevitability of Vella's raised eyebrows, the children's bright-eyed presence at the stand on Saturday mornings certainly didn't put customers off, quite the contrary. Monsieur Renan had even joked that he should put the twins on the payroll. Instead, he'd arranged something they appreciated much more: a standing order for tall glasses of grenadine or Orangina at the local café, delivered soon after the stand opened. They came with coffee for Arielle, and croissants for them all, and the second breakfast—because they only had time for a quick round of toast and jam before they left—made the early start something to look forward to.

Today, however, Louis and Alice were in a grumpy mood. They had woken up late and complained when Arielle told them to hurry up and get dressed, and then squabbled in the Metro. By the time they arrived, it was right on opening time, and Arielle—who had not slept all that well—was flustered and not in the mood to listen to any more nonsense, so she told them to go and sit quietly in the back till their second breakfast arrived. Scrambling to get everything in order before customers arrived, she could hear the twins grumbling to each other in the background but chose to take no notice. Sometimes parenting required you to turn a deaf ear or a blind eye and this was definitely one of those occasions.

The weekends were usually very busy, with large tourist contingents: everything from busloads of weekend trippers from the UK, Germany or Belgium to the individual travellers from further afield.

Most of the tourists browsed but a few did buy, and more than a few liked to ask questions and take photos. There were some local customers, Parisians buying flowers for special occasions, but most of the regular weekday customers didn't come on Saturdays, though occasionally Daniel Auban came by.

The other day, after his talk, they had gone for lunch in the museum's café and chatted about flowers and manuscripts. He'd told her more about the beekeeper he'd mentioned in his talk, a man called Franck who had a smallholding in the Chevreuse Valley south-east of Paris, and had come to one of Daniel's previous presentations, becoming inspired to change how he did things. 'But I think he always had it in him,' Daniel had said, 'and hearing my talk and seeing the manuscripts simply unlocked it.'

The conversation had turned then to other topics. The only personal information she'd gleaned from their chats before was that he came from Lorient in Brittany, had travelled a lot in his twenties and had only embarked on a career as a botanical historian thirteen years ago when he was thirty, comparatively late for an academic. Apart from that, she knew very little about his background and nothing about his private life. But at lunch that day, she'd learned something that had surprised her: for the last five years he'd been a member of a community group, one of several around Paris, that created *jardins partagés*, shared gardens in empty or degraded spaces. Unlike allotment gardens, which were only found at the edge of the city, these shared gardens were within central Paris.

It had touched her, the thought of his long frame in gardening overalls, soft scholar's hands deep in soil, trying to coax a recalcitrant seedling into standing up straight. As always, he was humble about his role in the shared garden but he clearly took pleasure and pride in it. No wonder he'd been able to talk about the joy of gardens in that warm way in his talk. She put those thoughts aside as the first of the human tide flowed into the market.

Arielle had just dealt with a lively tour group from the US when she saw Charlotte approaching, accompanied by a young woman whose looks marked her immediately as a close relative. 'Arielle,' Charlotte said, 'this is my daughter, Elise, she's over from London for a few days.'

The children, who had ducked down below the counter to play some sort of game, popped their heads up, and Elise said, 'Hello!'

The twins looked at her uncertainly, then a shy smile broke over their faces. 'Hello,' they said, in unison. Louis said, 'We are helping with the flowers,' and Alice added, 'Do you want to buy flowers?'

Elise laughed. 'I think we do,' she said, 'don't we, Marm?' She spoke fluent French, with only a slight trace of an English accent.

Charlotte was smiling at the children. 'Thank you for reminding us.' They beamed, and she turned to Arielle. 'We'd like a bouquet of flowers in memory of a dear friend of mine from long ago. Peonies were her favourite flower, but the people we are giving it to are her mother and her daughter. Her daughter lives in Australia but is visiting her grandmother in Paris—'

Arielle broke in. 'Is your friend's daughter called Emma, by any chance?'

Both Charlotte and Elise stared at her. Charlotte murmured, 'How did you . . .'

'She came by my stand a couple of days ago,' Arielle said, 'looking for advice about the restoration of her grandfather's garden. He'd visited our stand when Monsieur Renan—my boss—ran it. She didn't mention her mother's death, but I saw the shadows in her eyes and knew there was sorrow there.'

'Corinne, her mother, died recently, much too young,' Charlotte said softly.

Arielle drew in a breath. This would be a very special creation indeed. 'Memory, love, consolation, shared bonds—those must be the elements in this bouquet. Red and white peonies in the centre to express the love you all had for Corinne, surrounded by blue forget-me-nots and white roses for consolation, and memory. The bouquet would then also be in the colours of the French flag, and of Australia's too, if I'm not mistaken. And Britain's,' she added, 'as you, the givers, live in London.'

Charlotte's eyes were bright with emotion. 'That will be beautiful. Thank you, Arielle.'

'How do you know what all those flowers symbolise?' Elise asked, more matter of fact.

'I've been working with them a long time,' said Arielle. 'And Monsieur Renan, my boss, taught me a lot too. But it's also about listening to the flowers and feeling what they might say to people . . .' She broke off, her throat tightening as she spotted two familiar figures heading her way. Familiar but not welcome. They had been hovering near Vella's stand but were now heading purposefully towards her, just ahead of a cluster of tourists. 'I'm really sorry,' she said hurriedly, 'but I'm going to have to put these together for you later. Would that be okay? I can have them ready for you by eleven o'clock.'

'We'll come back then,' said Charlotte, looking a bit surprised by the abrupt change in Arielle's manner.

Arielle was dismayed by her unintended rudeness as the pair of lovely customers walked away, but all her anxiety returned in full force at the sight of the couple rapidly approaching.

'Virginie, Thierry,' she said, pasting a smile on her face as they drew near. 'What a surprise to see you.'

'Pauline told us you were here,' said Virginie, an accusatory tone to her voice, 'and your colleague over there—' she pointed vaguely in the direction of Vella's stand—'told us you let the children have the run of the market.'

I bet he did, Arielle thought, grimly, but aloud she said, 'They like it here.'

'Um—yes—well, we thought we could spend today with the children, and you,' Thierry said, with a tentative smile.

Arielle stared at him. How could he possibly think she'd be happy for them to spend the day together after what they'd proposed?

At the sound of their grandparents' voices, the children had scuttled away into the back, but eagle-eyed Virginie had seen and looked ready to storm the counter in search of them. The tourists who had been heading to the stand now reached it and were soon exclaiming and asking questions. The Grandiers had to retreat, but as soon as the coast was clear, back they came—and away the children vanished, into the recesses of the storage room.

Arielle began putting together the beautiful bouquet for Charlotte and Elise, and that helped her to keep calm when Virginie opened her mouth and said, 'Did you think any more about what we discussed the other day?'

Arielle tried to keep her voice steady. 'I wasn't aware that it *was* a discussion.'

There were spots on Virginie's cheeks now and her eyes were hard. Visibly controlling herself, she said, 'As a good mother, surely you know you can't provide adequately for the children? Your wage is low so you are forced to live with your sister—'

'I *choose* to live with my sister,' said Arielle tightly, as she arranged the flowers for the bouquet, trying to focus on their beauty, and not on what Virginie was saying.

'And you don't have parents who could help out,' Virginie ploughed on, 'or any chance of promotion, so you should—'

'We'd just like to make it easier for you, Arielle,' Thierry interrupted.

Arielle's stomach was churning. Why weren't any customers approaching? Where had the crowds gone? She didn't want to be alone with these two horrors.

Virginie snapped, 'You cannot possibly afford to give them what they should have, what *we* could give them, what Ludo himself had.'

Arielle lifted her head then and stared directly into her mother-in-law's eyes. '*What Ludo had,*' she repeated, bitterly. Now the words she had never spoken before gushed out of her. 'You mean, wanting for nothing—except for the most important thing of all?'

She saw Thierry go pale, looking so stricken that for an instant Arielle regretted her words. Then Virginie spat out, furiously, 'How dare you! What would you know about anything, least of all about our son? *Our* son, who you tried to turn against us. Only you didn't succeed, did you?'

'Virginie . . .' Thierry began, pleadingly, but his wife ignored him.

'And look at you, Arielle,' she hissed, 'so guilty about not spending enough time with Louis and Alice that you drag them to your place of work, in the midst of dirt and goodness knows what nasty bugs that might be crawling around. What kind of mother does that to her own children?'

'The kind of mother I wish I'd had,' said a voice, so suddenly that they all started. In the heat of the confrontation, no one had noticed Daniel approaching. 'The kind of mother those lovely children are very lucky to have,' he went on, moving closer to Arielle and fixing the Grandiers with an expression she had never seen before on his face. It stopped Virginie in her tracks—but not for long. Giving him a hot glare, she snarled, 'And who do you think you are, Monsieur, interfering in a private conversation?'

'Hardly a conversation,' he said. 'More of a bullying session. You should know the difference, Madame.' His tone was soft but his eyes were steely.

'Now then,' Thierry began to stammer, 'there is no need for unpleasantness, no need at all, we just . . .'

But no one took any notice of him. Virginie looked from Daniel to Arielle, then back again. 'Ah, I see. He is your *friend*,' she said.

Arielle deliberately ignored the implication, her head held high. 'Daniel *is* my friend. But you are not. You never have been, although once upon a time I longed for it.' Unexpectedly, she choked then.

'You don't understand,' Thierry said. 'We never wanted to—'

That made her snap, 'Oh, I know you never wanted me in your precious family!'

'That's not what I meant,' Thierry began, but Arielle had had quite enough.

'You're worse than her, you never even say what you really think. Go. Please go, both of you.'

Virginie looked ready to spit more insults, but Thierry put a hand on her arm and drew her away, throwing an unreadable glance over his shoulder at Daniel and Arielle. In a moment, they were gone.

'Are you all right, Arielle?' Daniel's tone was so gentle that she almost burst into tears. She shook her head. 'Not really, but thank you, Daniel.'

He nodded, faintly colouring, shy again. 'It's okay.'

'I'm sorry you had to witness that,' she said.

He waved a hand. 'Don't be. I'm only glad I could at least help a bit.'

'You helped *a lot*,' she said. 'And I should explain what that was about, but right now I have to talk to the children—I don't know what they heard, but . . .'

'You must go to them,' he said. 'And you don't have to explain, not unless you want to.'

She felt a catch in her throat, knowing he understood. She started to go but turned back. 'Would it be all right if the children and I came to visit you tomorrow in your shared garden?'

His face lit up. 'It would give me the greatest pleasure.'

Fourteen

Emma had gone to bed late the previous night, after spending hours on Google searches. 'Pascal Lamartine Saint Jean de la Forêt Morvan' first—nothing had come up—then 'Lamartine' and 'Morvan'—still nothing. 'Pascal Lamartine' had yielded the social media profiles of only four men, none of whom matched the approximate age the Pascal she was looking for must be, and none of whom had any connection with the Morvan.

She tried 'St Jean de la Forêt, Morvan' and came up with a brief Wikipedia page, offering bare details about how this tiny Morvan hamlet dated from the early Middle Ages, its population dwindling over the centuries till it was almost uninhabited. Aside from the usual location map, there was a blurry photo of a scatter of stone houses and a village well. And that was it for St Jean de la Forêt.

The search around Morvan yielded pages about the region: history (including a theory that it was connected with the 'real

King Arthur'); ecology (there was a massive national park there); towns; customs; demography; tourism; local news, etc. No mention of Lamartines, though.

It frustrated Emma, who was used to finding information on almost any subject on the internet. Finally, in desperation, she'd even applied the Google Lens app to the photo of her mother in the long grass, trying to focus it on the spire or tower in the distance, hoping against hope that it would come up with a location. Of course, it was in vain, with the app coming up with ridiculous options, such as Cleopatra's Needle in Paris.

Looking at those useless search results, a wave of grief ambushed her and tears filled her eyes. She'd been so excited after seeing Charlotte, thinking she was closer to finding out what her poor mother had wanted to tell her that day. But now the answer felt more elusive than ever. Finally, exhausted from crying and staring at the screen for too long, she had shut down the laptop and gone to bed.

When she woke, her eyes felt gritty and her head ached. Feeling better after a shower and a couple of paracetamols, she found her grandmother at the kitchen table, busily making mayonnaise, a list of the final things she had to buy at her elbow. There'd be shopping first—the markets to buy fresh vegetables and cheese, roast potatoes from the local rotisserie, fresh bread from the *boulangerie* and from the local butcher, the *poulet fermier*, they'd ordered a traditional free-range, corn-fed farmhouse chicken. The main course would be that chicken, roasted to golden perfection and served with a sauce made of its own cooking juices, with lemon, garlic, salt, pepper and tarragon, accompanied by the rotisserie potatoes and a selection of seasonal vegetables—Mattie was to decide exactly which on the spot in the markets. There would also be two starters: smoked salmon with a cucumber salad and boiled eggs with home-made mayonnaise. There would be a green salad and cheese, after the main course, and then Charlotte had promised to bring some cakes. It was a veritable feast! Simple and sumptuous, just like Mattie had said.

'Bonjour, Mattie.' Emma dropped a kiss on her grandmother's head. 'Can I do anything?'

'Pass me the salt and pepper,' said Mattie, doing a final turn with the whisk and looking in satisfaction at the bright yellow emulsion of egg yolk and oil. She took the salt and pepper from Emma and ground some in. 'Now all it needs is to go in the fridge and set nicely. I've already boiled the eggs, they're cooling.'

Emma covered the mayonnaise bowl with some cling wrap and put it in the fridge. 'Mattie, you are amazing! I feel useless.'

Mattie patted her hand. 'You can make that delicious vinaigrette of yours. And you can carry all the things home from the market. Then you can slice tomatoes, wash lettuce, set out the salmon and the eggs, arrange everything on platters. And set the table. But right now, you can make me some more tea and yourself a cup of coffee. Is that enough work for you?'

Emma laughed. 'Sure.'

'I am so very glad you made contact with Charlotte,' Mattie said, suddenly changing the subject.

Emma kissed her. 'Me too.' Taking a deep breath, she said, 'Can I ask you something, Mattie?'

Mattie smiled. 'Whatever you want, my darling.'

'Why was Maman so distant with you and Pappy?' She swallowed. 'I'm sorry. It's probably not something you want to talk about, it's just that I don't understand.'

Mattie reached over and touched her hand. 'I do want to talk about it, sweetheart. But I'm not sure I can really explain it, except to say that Corinne saw the world differently from how Alain and I did. We loved her dearly, but it wasn't always easy to understand her. She could be very black and white, even as a child—shades of grey troubled her. But in adolescence, things became really difficult for her. I think she suffered from a feeling she didn't fit in, and to defend herself she became quite intolerant and haughty—to us, and others. We tried to be as accommodating as we could, but maybe that was a mistake. Fighting with her would have made it so much worse though.' She sighed. 'By the time she left, she wasn't overtly angry or resentful, as she had been as a teenager, but she was no more communicative. And in a way, when she went, it was a relief. We thought that the trip to Australia would do her good, that she'd come back with a new perspective . . .'

Emma knew what had happened next. Corinne hadn't come back to Paris with distance and time having softened her views. Instead, after months of little contact beyond a brief call to announce her safe arrival in Australia, and a few postcards, she'd informed them of three dramatic things: that she had borne a child, that she'd met Paddy, and that she wasn't coming back.

'How did you feel when she told you that I was born?' Emma asked.

'It was a shock, as you can imagine. We'd had no idea she was even pregnant in the first place, we'd never met a boyfriend and she'd not even mentioned anyone before Paddy—and we knew *he* couldn't be your father because of the timing. So learning about you was both thrilling and worrying, because we didn't know how she would manage, we wanted to help. But she told us not to be concerned, she was fine, you were fine, and she sent us that photo. I can't tell you how much that delighted us.'

Emma knew the photo she meant. It was of her as a bald, bright-eyed baby in a bouncer and was in a silver frame on the mantelpiece in the living room.

Mattie continued, 'Corinne made it clear she wanted no questions, and we respected that. We were glad she kept us regularly informed of your progress and it was such a delight when we came out to Australia when you were nearly three. It was clear that Corinne was so much happier in Australia than she'd been in France, so even though our visit was short, we returned with much lighter hearts. And then that visit when you all came, and you, my darling, were such a delightful, inquisitive, joyful child—I can't tell you how happy it made us both.'

In a shaky voice, Emma said, 'I loved it too, and I'm very sorry I didn't try harder to persuade Maman to come again. And after I left home, I *should* have come to see you and Pappy well before he . . .' She couldn't say any more, her voice was suddenly choked with tears.

'My darling,' said Mattie, taking her hand, 'you were a child, it wasn't your responsibility. We knew our daughter, and accepted her as she was, even if at times we wished the situation were different.' She looked straight into Emma's eyes. 'And later—well, here you are now, and that is an immense joy to me, even more than you can imagine. I know Alain is smiling down at us right now. So don't be sorry, my dearest child, and don't think you have to fix the past. Your mother and I made our own kind of peace with each other, and you and I can't let regrets and what ifs taint the present.'

Feeling you didn't fit in, and wanting to make a new start in a new country was understandable, Emma thought. But why did that have to mean freezing out the people who loved you? And why couldn't you love both places, the one where you were born and the one you chose to live in as an adult? Even in such a short time here, Emma felt as though she could. *But I am not my mother,* she thought. *She was very different from me. If I am to try to come to terms with it all, then I have to accept that, and not grudgingly, but generously, lovingly, as Mattie clearly does.* She squeezed her grandmother's hand.

'And now,' Mattie said, her tone changing, 'we still have a lot of work to do. Shall we finish breakfast and go to the market?'

Everything was done. The table was set, the starters and salad rested on platters and in bowls, the green vegetables were in the pan ready to quickly steam, the rotisserie potatoes were keeping warm, the white wine was in the fridge and the chicken was roasting very nicely in the oven. In the living room, a tray with glasses, various bottles of aperitifs, and bowls of nibbles waited for pre-lunch drinks. Emma could not keep still, checking and rechecking everything, much to Mattie's amusement. 'No need to be so nervous,' she said, 'it's only lunch.'

You could have fooled me, Emma wanted to say, *all those elaborate preparations we've been making*, but actually she was annoyed with herself for being so jumpy at the idea that Marc-Antoine was coming, because what did it matter, really? Except that mixing her mother's old friend and Mr Big Shot probably wasn't the best way to learn more about her mother. He would want to go on about his shiny new job and they'd all have to sit there and listen.

A short time later, Charlotte and Elise arrived, the latter carrying a big cake box, the former a magnificent bouquet. After a flurry of greetings and introductions, Charlotte handed the flowers to Mattie, who exclaimed, 'How absolutely glorious!' Her eyes were full of tears as she put her nose to the beautiful, fragrant flowers, breathing them in. 'Peonies. You remembered.'

'They are in honour of Corinne,' Charlotte said. 'And the other flowers mean consolation and memory, always in our hearts.'

'What a wonderful choice,' Emma said.

'Oh, we didn't make it—the bouquet was made for us by one of the most extraordinary florists I have ever come across,' Charlotte said, smiling. 'I think you've met her before. Arielle Lunel.'

'I certainly have,' said Emma happily.

They had just deposited everything in the kitchen—the cakes in the fridge, the bouquet in a vase which would go into the living room, when the entry buzzer in the hall sounded again. 'Emma, can you go and get that?' Mattie asked. Emma went, reluctantly, but not wanting to show it.

'Hello,' she said into the intercom. 'I'm buzzing you in now.'

'Aren't you going to ask who it is?' came the amused voice of Marc-Antoine.

'I hardly think that's necessary,' she said stiffly, 'you're the only one missing.'

Now he sounded perplexed. 'The only one missing?'

Of course, he didn't know about Charlotte and Elise. 'We have two other guests. So, do you want me to let you in or not?'

Too late, she realised the rudeness of her words, but she couldn't take them back. Flustered, she immediately pressed the button. 'Everyone's in the living room,' she stammered, when he came in, 'we're going to have a drink first.'

'Okay,' he said, 'then I better give you this.' He handed her a bottle of chilled champagne. His voice was equable, but he was unsmiling.

'I believe congratulations are in order,' she said, feeling like a fool. She should simply usher him through and not make things worse by gabbling.

'Thank you.' He paused. 'And I look forward to meeting the other guests.' This time there was the ghost of a smile on his face. Amusement that he'd embarrassed her? Relief that he wouldn't be stuck talking to her all afternoon?

'Hello, my dear Marc-Antoine.' Mattie came into the hall, wreathed in smiles. He bent down to kiss her on both cheeks.

'Come through and meet Charlotte and Elise. Has Emma told you about them?'

'In a way,' he said, shooting Emma a look that she tried to ignore.

'Emma, my darling, can you take that bottle into the kitchen, open it and bring it with some champagne glasses to the living room?'

Emma was relieved to have a few moments alone to regain her poise. She had to calm down, and not react to Marc-Antoine in that absurd way. She shouldn't be so bothered by his presence, but his easy, affectionate familiarity with Mattie emphasised all too clearly the fact that, until now, she had not been a part of Mattie's life in the way he had, and that hurt. But it wasn't only that. It was something about *him*, something that put her on edge, that made her act all wrong.

It was going to be a long lunch.

Fifteen

'What an idea your father's parents had to give him that name!' Elise shook her head. 'No wonder he changed it.'

'He almost changed his last name too,' said Marc-Antoine, 'until he realised that while being called Victor Hugo made you the butt of jokes, just having the surname Hugo made you sound distinguished. So Roland Hugo he became.'

The conversation at the table had ranged widely over the last hour and a half; they'd talked at first about the last time Charlotte had been in this house, thirty-six years ago, imagine! That led on to a discussion about Corinne, but innocuous stuff—school memories from Charlotte, then Emma's memories about growing up with her mother and Paddy in small-town Australia. Then Mattie had switched the topic to London, how Charlotte had first gone to live there. From there, it had meandered on to several other things, ending up now, after a question put by Elise, with a discussion of

Marc-Antoine's estranged father, who headed a prestigious Belgian finance company.

'And the name swept all before him?' Charlotte asked, mopping up the last of the delicious chicken juices with a piece of bread.

Marc-Antoine shrugged. 'The way he would tell it, yes.'

'How would *you* tell it?' Elise asked.

If it had been anyone else, Charlotte would have thought Elise was flirting. And Marc-Antoine was definitely flirt-worthy material. But Elise didn't flirt. She was too direct for that. If she found a man sexually attractive, she made it very clear. There was no coyness about her. Her daughter had ambition. And ideals. A holiday internship with Aurora International would advance both those things. But she knew instinctively to avoid a hard sell. She was simply herself, interested in people, focused, and people responded naturally to that. Including Marc-Antoine.

'Well, I would tell it like this,' he was saying now. 'Roland Hugo is not one to let anything stand in his way. Whatever the cost.'

'Some might say that is the mark of a good businessman,' Elise said.

'Not me.' A pause. 'Roland and I don't see eye to eye. He has never been a part of my life. I only kept his surname because my mother used it too.' His tone was quiet, but firm, indicating that further discussion on the subject was closed. Elise took the hint, moving on to talk about something else.

Just then, Charlotte caught Emma looking at Marc-Antoine with what seemed like frank dislike. She was pretty sure it wasn't due to what he'd said, though. Before he'd come in, Mattie had quietly explained who he was, and Charlotte thought it couldn't have been easy for Emma, learning yet another thing her mother had kept from her. But it was hardly Marc-Antoine's fault, was it?

Presently, Emma got up to clear the table, and Charlotte helped her, seeing that Marc-Antoine, Elise and Mattie were still deep in conversation.

In the kitchen, she said quietly, in English, 'Do you want to talk about it, Emma?'

Emma had started stacking the dirty plates and dishes in the sink, but now seemed to think again. She pulled the dishes out, put in the plug, ran in water and squeezed in some detergent. 'Mattie really should have a dishwasher,' she said. 'I think I'll buy her one.'

'Come on, Emma,' said Charlotte, picking up a tea towel. 'I can see something's up. It can help to talk.'

Emma slid the plates into the soapy water, not looking at Charlotte. She cleared her throat. 'It's just—I didn't sleep at all well last night. It still hits me so hard that Maman . . .' She was such a big presence, she had such an amazing life force, and it seems impossible that she is no longer there and . . .' She stopped abruptly and began vigorously scrubbing the plates so that they clattered against each other.

'I'm so sorry, Emma,' Charlotte said, touching her arm. 'I didn't mean to be insensitive.'

'It's okay,' Emma said, still not looking at her. 'It's not only that. I—' she hesitated, then went on, 'I stayed up too late on the internet, trying to find Pascal. I didn't find anything remotely useful. Which was pretty disappointing.'

'Pascal knew your mother when she was seventeen, Emma, but there's no evidence he did later and I don't think he could tell you much about her. So why do you want so much to track him down?'

Emma stopped washing. She turned to face Charlotte and said in a low voice, 'When my mother arrived in Australia, she was two months pregnant. With me.'

Charlotte stared at her. She remembered Emma had said she had a stepfather but she had assumed that her biological father was Australian, too. 'Are you sure?'

'About me being conceived here, in France?' Emma's smile was forced. 'One hundred per cent. I turned thirty-one in February. And my mother arrived in Australia seven months before I was born. She didn't know she was pregnant,' she added.

Charlotte remembered Corinne complaining about her irregular periods when they were at school. Charlotte had told her that she should count herself lucky because it meant she didn't have as many periods as other girls. Corinne had just given her *that* look.

'That must have been quite the shock.'

'I imagine so,' Emma said dryly. 'Anyway, she decided to have me. She didn't come home, though. She only told Mattie when I was three months old. And even then she never told them or anyone else, not even Paddy—my stepfather—who the father was.'

'Oh my goodness.' Charlotte exhaled.

Emma gave an unamused laugh. 'I had the best father in Paddy, and that's all I need in the dad stakes, but I still—'

'Emma,' Charlotte interrupted her. 'Forgive me, but if your mother never told you who your biological father was, it was most likely because she didn't *want* you to know.'

Emma's eyes flashed. 'Maybe before. But not at the end. I think that was what she wanted to tell me before she died. That's why she had that photo ready to show me, because it's connected to him, whoever he is. It kills me that I wasn't in time to hear it from her own lips. But it's also why I *must* find out.' She looked at Charlotte, her gaze direct and unflinching, uncannily like Corinne's, for a moment. 'And, yes, I know she met Pascal three years before she left France, but he is my only real lead at the moment.'

Before Charlotte had a chance to respond, Marc-Antoine appeared in the doorway. 'I'm sorry to interrupt,' he said, 'but Mattie sent me out to ask if everything was okay. Is there anything I can do to help?'

'We don't need anything,' Emma began, in a rather snitty tone, but catching Charlotte's glance she added, grudgingly, 'but maybe you could get the cakes out of the fridge?'

'Sure,' he said, giving Emma an unreadable look.

There were definitely sparks flying, Charlotte thought, and not the good sort. She said, 'Emma, if you tell me where the dessert plates and cake forks are, I'll take those out too.'

'They're in—' Emma began, just as Marc-Antoine said, 'I think you'll find them in—' They both stopped abruptly, then Marc-Antoine made a gesture of what might have been either apology or exasperation and, taking the cakes out of the fridge, he left the kitchen.

Charlotte glanced at Emma, who was busying herself pulling out some lovely gold-rimmed dessert plates from a cupboard. She almost said something about what she'd witnessed, then thought better of it. Instead, taking up their conversation from before, she said, 'I completely understand. You must find out. Look, I'm heading off to Normandy tomorrow with Elise for a couple of days, but I'll be back Monday night. If I can help in any way, please let me know.'

Emma's expression lightened at once.

After the cakes had been demolished, they all went out into the garden. Mattie and Emma walked with Charlotte around what Emma had cleared—about a third of the garden now. The cleared part looked raw, with exposed earth and dead weeds, and there was still a lot to do in the other sections, but Charlotte could easily see how it might look once the heavy work was completed and planting began. The bones of this garden were strong, she told the two women, the soil friable and well drained, and you could even tell its fertility by the way the weeds had flourished. You can build on such good bones, she said, work with its potential; maybe not recreate Alain Lenoir's vision but pay homage to it. She was hopeful about the hydrangea's prospects, confirmed Arielle's judgement on the health of the dahlia, heliotrope and peony plants Emma had uncovered, and approved of the seeds she had bought. And she was touched to see how much Emma lapped it all up.

Meanwhile, Marc-Antoine and Elise stood chatting by the back door and Charlotte was not surprised to hear later from her daughter that he'd advised her to apply for an internship at Aurora International's London office. After a while, Mattie called him over, and Charlotte saw Emma stiffen momentarily, but she stayed civil, and when he offered to help with the work if she needed, Emma thanked him and said she would keep that in mind. Not exactly the most enthusiastic of responses, but Marc-Antoine didn't seem to take offence. Clearly, he had understood it was Emma's baby, and if he was smart, he'd keep well out of it. And there was no doubt that he *was* smart.

Sixteen

Yesterday afternoon, after work finished, Arielle had taken the children straight home. To her relief, they seemed okay—ensconced in the storage room, they had not heard the confrontation with the Grandiers. But she was far from okay. She kept replaying the moment in her mind, and it made her shudder. Only Daniel's intervention had stopped things from escalating further, and she was immensely grateful to him for it.

Back home, Pauline had been furious when she'd heard what had happened. She was keen to file a harassment complaint against the Grandiers, because, as she said, 'they came to your place of work, they insulted you in front of the children and in front of an adult witness, they made not-so-veiled threats, and that's definitely grounds for a complaint, the law provides for that.'

Arielle had shaken her head. 'I don't want the law involved, I don't want the children or Daniel dragged into it.'

'But they are already!' Pauline snapped. 'And next time, Daniel might not be there to send Virginie and Thierry packing.'

Arielle knew that her sister was right on one level, but wrong on another. 'This is something *I* have to work out, okay?'

Pauline shrugged. 'If they turn up here again, I won't be responsible for my actions.' She looked so very fierce that Arielle could not help smiling. She gave her sister a hug. 'I'm sure they will not dare to face you again,' she said. 'Not if you pull that fearsome face!'

Pauline held her sister at arm's length and looked seriously at her. 'Even if you don't want to involve the law, you will need to do *something* to stop them. They have a lot more money than us and they are better connected—I wouldn't put it past them to fabricate some story that puts you in a bad light.'

'Please, Pauline, don't let's talk any more about it. I don't want to worry the children. And I have to think.'

The rest of the afternoon and evening had passed quietly enough, but Arielle lay awake for ages that night, thoughts of what on earth she could do whirling round and round in her head, without any real solution. Fighting the Grandiers directly would only bring more turmoil for the children and herself.

All her life, she'd hated confrontation, and perhaps that had been a mistake when it came to people like the Grandiers. If she'd fought them earlier, when Ludo was still alive, then maybe they wouldn't be trying to strongarm her now.

As she tossed and turned, the despondent thought came to her that maybe she was also hesitating because she felt they had a point. She *couldn't* give the children everything she wished she could.

Like the things she and Pauline had experienced in their childhood—space to run around in, and nature close by, fields, and woods, and the sea. Had she been selfish keeping them here in Paris just because that's where she loved to be, where she'd met Ludo, where they'd had the twins and made their home? She was not about to capitulate to the Grandiers' wish that the family move to Champagne, and she certainly couldn't afford a place with a garden in central Paris, but if they moved further out, into the sprawling suburbs around Paris, or the countryside close by, she might be able to find a suitable place. And that would take the wind right out of the Grandiers' sails.

But that was panic speaking. Her children were happy here. She saw that every day. They loved their school. They loved the flat. They loved the neighbourhood, where they had lots of friends, and where there were many little parks they could play in. They didn't miss what they didn't have. And she wouldn't be driven from her home. Their home. Besides, she knew that moving wouldn't stop the Grandiers. They would find something else to harass her about. She would have to stand up to them, permanently.

She managed to fall asleep then, but at breakfast Pauline had seen the shadows under her eyes and offered to take the children out so Arielle could stay home and rest. But that was the last thing she wanted. 'I told Daniel we'd go and visit his garden,' she said, 'and I don't want to let him down, especially not after what he did for me yesterday. And I've always wanted to see a shared garden.'

'I see,' Pauline had said, raising an eyebrow, but she'd made no more comment.

Now, Arielle sat on a bench in the sun, one eye on the bees working in the flowers of a nearby thyme bush, the other on the twins who were happily digging with the miniature trowels that Daniel had found for them. He was over in the corner in animated conversation with the diminutive, bright-eyed older woman whom he'd introduced earlier as Maeva and who seemed to be in charge.

The shared garden was lovely—a sheltered, sunny green refuge, walled off from the nondescript grey buildings around it by simple wicker structures. It had two sections: one which contained long rectangular plots with herbs, vegetables and strawberries, while raspberry canes and blackberry bushes separated the other part of the garden, devoted to flowers and other non-edible plants. And down one end, straddling the two parts of the garden, were tall wooden compost bins. There was a shed for tools and a small greenhouse, a metal water tank covered in climbing plants, and shady spots where you could sit and contemplate. Such as the spot where Arielle sat, grateful to be resting quietly in the sun after her disturbed night. She hadn't protested when Daniel declined her offer of help this morning and waved her over to the bench. 'You look exhausted,' he said. 'Relax and let me take care of the children. I'll come and sit with you soon, but I just need to talk to Maeva about planting schedules.' He'd pointed the children in the direction of a patch of dirt which he said they could help prepare for tomato seedlings. 'Will we be allowed to eat some tomatoes?' Alice asked, and Daniel smiled and said, 'When they're ready.' And then

Louis said, 'That won't be till the summer,' and Daniel nodded. 'You're quite right. Bravo,' he said, making Louis beam with pride.

Daniel looked different today. The faded blue floppy hat he wore should have looked ridiculous but instead softened the angular planes of his face and brightened the deep blue of his eyes. He was dressed in a loose black T-shirt over olive-green cargo pants and lace-up boots, when she had only ever seen him before in a tailored shirt and pants, sometimes with a jacket or coat, sometimes without. Now she could see the strength in his tanned arms and the confident flex of his long fingers as he demonstrated something to the children. A smile crept over her face.

Arielle had been aware for some time that he was attracted to her, but she had not thought of Daniel like that, no matter what Virginie had implied. But over the last few days, things had changed, and now she looked at him and knew there *was* something more than friendship there. Something had been growing, slowly, out of sight, like a deep-buried seed getting ready for spring. And she was glad to be here now because *he* was here. And that meant . . .

'Maman! Maman, come and see!' The children's shouts scattered her thoughts. Going over to where they were standing proudly beside their patch of earth, she saw they had smoothed it out beautifully, and made holes where the seedlings might go. 'Do you think they'll be happy here?' Louis asked. 'Do you think they'll give us the best tomatoes ever?' said Alice.

Arielle took a grubby little hand in each of hers. 'They will be bursting with happiness and juicy fruit, I am sure.'

'You two must come and plant the seedlings with us,' said Maeva, approaching with Daniel.

'Can we, Maman, please?' shouted the twins, and Arielle nodded, smiling. Over their heads, she caught Daniel's eye and her heart gave a lurch as his cheery expression changed to one of such wonder that his whole face seemed lit up from within. And she knew that he had understood.

'Well,' Maeva said, her shrewd glance noting their expressions, 'I think it's time for Louis and Alice and I to inspect the seedlings and see if they're ready to be planted soon.'

The children eagerly followed Maeva to the greenhouse.

Arielle and Daniel looked at each other before he said quietly, 'Shall we sit down?'

'Yes,' whispered Arielle, 'let's.'

Back on the bench, they fussed around unnecessarily for an instant, Daniel taking off his hat and Arielle smoothing her skirt. Neither of them spoke until Arielle said, 'Daniel, I . . .'

He looked at her, and her breath caught. *He is so beautiful, and I never saw it till now. But now I've seen it, I can't look away.* She took his hand, brought it to her lips, and softly kissed it.

'Oh, Arielle,' he said, and his voice was full of delight, as well as a kind of steadiness. 'Beautiful Arielle.' And he took one of her hands, turned it palm upwards, and kissed it too. He put an arm around her, and she nestled into him. They stayed like that for a moment, before Arielle looked up at him and said, 'Daniel, I don't know how we are going to do this—we lead such different lives—but I want to try, anyway.'

'I am so very glad,' he said, 'because that is the thing I most want in all the world.' Bending down to her, he kissed her again, on the lips this time, deliberately, and she kissed him back, giving herself up to the delight of it, the taste of him on her lips, the warmth of him against her, and that expression in his eyes. It felt like the kiss went on for a long time, but it was less than a second before they drew apart, looking at each other and laughing in shared surprise, as if they couldn't believe what had just happened.

Arielle heard the children coming back, and sat up straight, pushing back her curls. 'Will you be working here all day?'

He shook his head, smiling at her. 'I am free whenever you want.'

'Then come back with us to the apartment for lunch. It would only be simple, a few cold things and salad, but we are close by, and—'

'You don't need to persuade me,' he said, his smile teasing now. 'It will be an honour.' And he sketched a little bow.

Laughter bubbled in her throat. 'Just wait till you see the chaos in our house, you'll soon change your mind about honour!'

Seventeen

*E*nthused by Charlotte's words the day before, Emma spent most of Sunday working in the garden, stopping only for an hour over lunch. She'd started by digging over a bed in the cleared section and sowing the seeds she'd bought from Arielle. It felt surprisingly good, getting her hands into the damp soil as she carefully sprinkled in the fine seed. Then, following Charlotte's advice about how to revive the rescued hydrangea, she'd carefully watered the plant and gave it a touch of liquid fertiliser from a bottle she'd found in the shed. She'd buy some compost, as well, to make sure the moisture stayed in the soil. After that, she set to work clearing more weeds, in the process uncovering two rosebushes, one of which, amazingly, had the tightly furled beginnings of three or four yellow buds.

Emma worked so hard that by four o'clock, when Mattie came out with a tray of tea and homemade *madeleines* and a firm order that work was to cease, Emma was exhausted but also happy with what she'd achieved. Almost the whole garden was cleared now, aside from one section near a stunted, gnarled old tree in a corner of the garden. As she sat on the grass with Mattie, Emma explained how she planned to leave that bit, weeds and all, because she was sure that was where Monsieur Leroux lived: there was a hollow some way up the tree trunk that was perfect for a small animal. She hadn't seen the squirrel all day but felt that those bright dark eyes were watching her, discreetly, yet without fear.

Mattie thoroughly approved of everything. 'I can hardly believe it, Emma. What you've done is wonderful—it's like our garden's come out of hiding and is beginning to show itself to us again!'

Shyly, Emma said, 'Well, it was there all along, just a bit overgrown . . .'

'Just *a bit*,' Mattie echoed, with heavy irony and a wave of her hand towards the tall piles of green waste. Some of it would be turned to compost but a lot of it would have to be taken away. 'What's next, my darling modest gardener?'

'Planting,' said Emma, and she and Mattie walked around the garden arm in arm, looking at what had survived, now the weed blanket had been ripped off. This included the wisteria, hydrangea and rosebushes, and the peonies, heliotrope and dahlia, but also a straggling honeysuckle against a section of wall, and a holly bush near another. There were the bulbs, too, which Charlotte had said might produce something even now, depending on what they were. But soon, hopefully, Emma told Mattie, there'd be much more—the seeds she'd planted and the plants she intended to put in, including more peonies. 'And I'll speak to Charlotte and to Arielle about other things they would recommend,' she said.

Mattie smiled. 'You sound as if you are getting rather hooked on this gardening thing.'

'Maybe I am. And that's as much a surprise to me as anyone!'

It was true—the work had been hard and, at times, had made her hot, sweaty and aching. When her skin had tingled from nettle stings, she'd cursed herself for even attempting it. But now the clearing was done, she felt a real sense of achievement and an absolute determination that those plants that had survived against the odds would now flourish, as well as a feeling of anticipation about what was to come.

Tired out by her long day, she only lasted halfway through another old episode of *Inspecteur Barnaby*, before admitting to Mattie that she really had to go to bed. It wasn't quite 9 pm but she was sound asleep pretty much as soon as her head hit the pillow.

She woke early the following morning, Monday. After trying and failing to get back to sleep, she spent the next two hours at her laptop, finishing up a freelance job for Thornton's. She'd been putting off completing it but this morning she felt infused with new energy, so it was easy to put the final touches to a series of teaser reels she'd created for a special auction event focused around items of French provenance. Her photos of Paris provided a useful background to the treasure hunt narrative she'd created, with mini episodes that could be posted over two or three weeks that would intrigue potential buyers into registering for the event. She sent it off to the man who'd been her immediate boss at Thornton's, and who had wangled it so that she'd get the occasional bit of freelance work. 'Just to keep your hand in,' he'd said, though she knew he hoped she would come back to her old job. She was pretty sure she wouldn't, but it was best to keep the door open. Plus the extra money would come in useful.

When she went into the kitchen, having showered and dressed, she found it empty, but she could hear Mattie talking to someone on the hall phone. She must have already gone to the *boulangerie*, judging by the fresh baguette and brioche sitting on the table. Emma fetched the rest—butter, jam, plates, cups—and started making coffee and tea, waiting for her grandmother to finish her conversation.

The drinks were almost ready when Mattie came into the kitchen. She smiled at Emma, but in a rather distracted fashion. 'Good morning. Did you sleep well?'

'Very well,' said Emma, kissing her on the cheek. 'I woke up a bit early. Still, I used that to good effect, I—'

'Emma,' broke in her grandmother, who rarely interrupted, 'I've just been speaking to Marc-Antoine.'

Emma stilled. 'Oh,' was all she said.

'And I wondered—well, it was my suggestion he speak with you.' She looked at Emma.

Emma remembered his offer the other day to help her clear up the garden. That must be why he was calling. She hadn't wanted his help then, and she didn't want it now. 'What is this about?' she said, realising too late her voice sounded more peremptory than she'd meant it to be.

'Well, it's a little complicated,' Mattie said. 'But will you please speak to him? He will explain it better than I can.'

Emma saw the anxiety in her grandmother's face and quickly agreed.

In the hall, she waited a beat of time, took a deep breath then picked up the receiver. 'Bonjour, Marc-Antoine.'

'Bonjour, Emma,' he said, a hint of surprise in his voice. Maybe he hadn't expected her to actually come to the phone. Exactly how rude and immature did he think she was? Probably very, she thought, wincing.

'Mattie said you wanted to speak to me,' she said.

There was amusement in his voice now as he answered, 'Well, actually, *she* wanted me to speak with *you*.'

'Okay, I'm listening.'

'I know a rather lovely Australian lady called Elizabeth Flynn,' he began in English. He had a slight American accent when he spoke, not surprising given he'd lived for some years in the States. 'Liz, as she prefers to be called, has recently retired from a stellar career as a project manager for a big healthcare company in London. She's Australian like I said, but she lives in Ireland—her husband, Martin, is an Irish philanthropist and a potential collaborator in one of our community projects.'

'By *our projects*, you mean something for the company you work for, I assume. But why should that concern me?' Emma said, somewhat tartly.

'Let me finish,' he said. 'Please.'

'Go ahead then.'

'Martin is in meetings all day with us,' he said, 'and Liz is at a bit of a loose end. She has been to Paris years ago and seen the obvious sights. She doesn't want to do that again. She's not interested in shopping either.' His tone was wry, and Emma's hackles rose.

'Not all women adore shopping,' she snapped.

'I know,' he said, unruffled, 'but I do believe Paris shopping is pretty special, and not just for women either.'

Emma had to admit he was right, but she wasn't going to say so.

'At dinner last night Liz talked about her garden back home, and I said she should visit the gardens of Paris, and the flower market, but she said she would feel intimidated on her own.'

Emma snorted. 'Hasn't she heard of Google Maps?' She could see where this was going, but to her surprise, found it rather intriguing.

Marc-Antoine laughed. It was a nice laugh, she thought, surprised. 'She says they send you in the wrong direction or disappear right when you need them. Look, Emma, I didn't mention this to her, but I wondered if . . .' He hesitated, and she realised it was the first time she'd heard him sound unsure.

'You wondered if someone could hold her hand and take her around, which would make her happy and make her husband happy too. Which would also make for a good business atmosphere. Am I right?'

'Yes,' he said, 'but Liz is also a genuinely nice woman, and it would be a pity if she spent her time in Paris sitting in a hotel room watching gardening shows on TV.'

It was Emma's turn to laugh. 'That sounds like an exaggeration. But surely you must have access to someone more qualified than me in your vast network of contacts?'

'I've been living abroad a long time,' he said. 'My network, as you call it, is not vast at all. Certainly not in this field.'

'But I don't know much about gardens!' she protested.

'What matters is interest, and you have plenty of that,' Marc-Antoine said. His tone changed as he went on, 'Mattie told me just now what wonders you've worked in Alain's garden already, and I've seen for myself how passionate you are about restoring it. That's what Liz will respond to.' A pause before he continued again, 'Plus you speak perfect French, but you're Australian. She would feel comfortable with you in a way she wouldn't with a French guide, no matter how knowledgeable they were. Look, Emma, to be honest it was Mattie who suggested asking you. But the more I think about it, the more I agree with her.'

Emma's thoughts were in a whirl. She should be annoyed with Mattie for dropping her in it, but she wasn't. She was unexpectedly touched by his obvious consideration for this Liz lady. She had not thought him capable of such thoughtfulness. But now she was struck by the unreasonableness of that. He had known Mattie a long time, he cared about her, that went without saying. But he'd also not put a foot wrong with Charlotte and Elise. He'd listened, not just talked, and he'd never tried to dominate the conversation as she'd imagined he would. Uncomfortably, she thought, *I may have been unfair to him.* And he had obviously sensed her hostility—how could he not?—but hadn't responded in kind.

Recovering her composure, she said, 'What about Charlotte? She's away in Normandy with her daughter till tonight, but she speaks good English, she knows heaps about gardens, and loves them too. She would be better than me.'

'Martin and Liz are leaving Paris first thing tomorrow morning,' he said quietly. 'So, you see, we can't wait for Charlotte.'

Emma's voice rose. 'Hang on. Do you mean to say you want me to do this *today*?'

'I don't want—that is—' he sounded flustered, 'I am *asking* you. Humbly requesting. If it's possible. I know it's very short notice, but if you would do it, I would greatly appreciate it. And we'll pay you.' He named a figure that had Emma's eyes widening. A day jaunting around gardens with Liz would bring in three times more than she'd be paid for the freelance job she'd just finished. And it would be considerably more fun than the Thornton's stuff. Unless . . .

Warily, she said, 'Is that danger money you're offering me?'

Sounding startled, he said, 'What do you . . . Oh, you mean, is Liz a tartar?'

Such an old-fashioned word, she couldn't help smiling. 'A pain in the bum, yes.'

'Not at all! I told you, she's a really nice woman. You'll like her.'

Emma took a deep breath. 'Okay.'

'Really? You'll do it?' There was relief in his voice.

'It might even be fun.'

'I think it might be too,' he said, and again she could hear the smile in his voice. 'Shame I have to be in meetings all day.'

Emma felt an unexpected catch in her throat. 'That's kind of the point, though, isn't it?'

'I suppose it is,' he said.

She gave him her mobile number so they could set up the details, and when Emma put down the receiver, she realised something very surprising: she'd actually *enjoyed* the give-and-take of their conversation. Shaking her head ruefully, she headed back to the kitchen where Mattie was waiting, her expression carefully non-committal.

'You don't need to worry, I said yes to him,' Emma said, without thinking, then blushed. 'I mean . . .'

Mattie laughed. 'I know what you mean, sweetheart. Now sit down, let me reheat that cold coffee, and you have some breakfast and tell me all about it. Sorry I couldn't wait, I got too hungry.'

'I'm glad you didn't,' said Emma, pulling apart the remaining brioche and buttering each half. 'So I'm going to take this lady on a Paris garden tour. Will you help me decide on the best gardens to see? And will you come with us?'

'Yes to the first, no to the second,' Mattie said, as she heated up the coffee. 'One garden is enough for me, a whole day tour of them, a bit too much. Now, if you'll wait a moment, I'm just going to fetch something.'

As Mattie left the room, Emma's phone pinged with a text from Marc-Antoine. *Liz is absolutely delighted*, he'd written, in English. *Meet her at 10 am in the lobby of the Cours des Vosges hotel, in the 4th. She'll be wearing a white hat. Thank you again, Emma.*

All good, Emma texted back. *I'll look for the white hat.* Then she added, *Have a good meeting with Martin.*

Thanks 😊 *You have a good day too, à bientôt.*

Emma found she was smiling as she looked up the hotel location. Maybe it was that unexpected emoji.

Mattie came back into the room, carrying an A4 sketchbook, pencils, a sharpener, and a battered little red book that Emma already knew was full of maps of Paris—it had been the Google Maps of its day.

'I've been thinking of the more unusual gardens you could go to,' Mattie said, 'but a list is confusing, so instead I thought I might draw you a special map that you could take with you, with all the gardens marked on it. And we'll start with one close to this lady's hotel.'

Eighteen

The last time Charlotte had been in Étretat, she'd been a mother with three lively children under the age of eleven, a business that had taken off after years of hard slog, a gorgeous husband, and parents who were always delighted to see them.

It had been a lovely family holiday—even if not strictly speaking a beachy one, though the children and Tom, who never seemed to feel the cold, had a dip in the chilly waters of the Manche, the Sleeve, otherwise known in English as the Channel. Meanwhile Charlotte and her parents had sat chatting on the pebbly beach in the shadow of the spectacular cliffs and rock formations made famous by great painters like Monet and Matisse. They'd browsed in the picturesque town, the children buying funny souvenirs; eaten delicious meals; read the motley collection of books in the shelves of the holiday house—including mysteries by the town's other claim to fame, author Maurice Leblanc, who'd created the gentleman burglar Arsène Lupin—and played dominos and Monopoly.

The house had beautiful views across the cliffs and the sea, but no TV, no internet and mobile reception was so patchy that Tom and Charlotte had simply turned off their Nokias. So for the whole of those ten days, the family had lived in a timeless bubble. Some days were punctuated with small events: going to the market, watching the fishing boats coming in, visiting the Arsène Lupin museum, trying their own hand at sketching the cliffs. But mostly, the family slid into a gentle pattern of doing nothing much at all, except being together.

No wonder Elise had such fond memories of it, Charlotte thought, glancing sideways at her daughter as they walked together on that same pebbly beach, in the shadow of those much-painted cliffs. She had fond memories of it too, but they were bittersweet now, for her parents were far away, having retired to Tahiti where her mother originally came from, and Tom—well, the laughing man who'd swung his daughter and her younger brother, Jamie, round and round on the beach, who'd gone on bug-hunting expeditions with his eldest son, Theo, and indulged his parents-in-law's reminiscences, that slow-burning yet passionate man who made love so exquisitely that even now the memory of it sent tingles down Charlotte's spine—that man seemed to have vanished, leaving a stranger in his place. And the pain of that struck her again, so sharply that she had to quickly turn her head away and stare at the sea, trying to stop the tears from falling.

'Marm,' Elise's voice was soft. 'Are you all right?'

'I'm fine,' Charlotte said in a not-quite-steady voice. 'Just a bit nostalgic.'

'Oh, *Marm*.' The name she'd adopted long ago for her mother, halfway between English and French, made Charlotte feel even more unsteady. Elise looped her arm in Charlotte's, and said quietly, 'Are you and Dad splitting up?' To her horror, Charlotte burst into tears.

She hadn't cried in such a long time. Not even in all the long bruising weeks watching helplessly as Tom turned into an unreachable stranger and her understanding of her own life began to disintegrate. Now she sobbed in Elise's arms as if *she* was the child in need of comfort. Elise simply held her, her warmth conveying more than words. It was one of the things she'd loved about Tom, his warm kindness when you were hurting, his instinctive knowledge of when to speak and when to shut up. She had to learn that skill, but it came naturally to him. Except for now . . . and that thought made her weep all the more.

Presently, though, the storm passed. Charlotte took a deep breath. 'Forgive me, darling,' she said shakily. 'You really didn't need that.'

'There is nothing to forgive,' Elise said, relinquishing her hold and looking directly at her mother. 'You don't have to be so brave all the time, you know. I need to be let in. I've felt for some time that you were unhappy and that things between you and Dad weren't what they once had been. And Theo and Jamie feel the same.'

'You've been speaking about this with the boys?' Charlotte asked, dismayed.

Elise shrugged. 'You know we talk a lot. They were just nervous about broaching the subject.'

'So they sent you as emissary,' Charlotte said, with a faint smile. Wasn't that always the way! Elise the middle child, the mediator, the one who was sent to plead their case to parents, grandparents, teachers.

'I wasn't *sent*,' Elise said, with great dignity. 'I decided it was time, especially now that you're away from home. Besides Dad has gone into full tortoise mode, so we can't get through to him.'

Charlotte stared.

'Dad's doing that thing tortoises do,' Elise explained, 'they go into their shell if you look at them, and they pretend they're really a rock. You can rap on their shell all you like but they're much more patient than you are, so you give up and go away, which is what they want.'

Her tone was light but her eyes were sad, and Charlotte felt a lump in her throat. Taking her daughter's hand in hers, she said, 'Exactly.'

'What's up with him, Marm?' Elise said now.

Charlotte shook her head. 'I wish I knew, darling. But he's in full tortoise mode with me too. And it's been very hard to live with. It's affected everything. I can't seem to concentrate like I used to.'

Elise squeezed her hand. 'That's why you're here, in France.'

Charlotte nodded. 'I hoped it might give me space.' She had been worried about the children finding out, but now, as she looked at her daughter's loving, concerned face, she felt relieved.

She still had no idea what she would do. But unburdening had definitely made her feel lighter.

'And has being away given you space to think?' Elise looped her arm in Charlotte's once more as they set off again across the beach.

'Not enough to come to any conclusion yet,' Charlotte said, honestly. 'But it has given me a little perspective, especially since I met Emma and her grandmother, who are trying to make sense of much harder things . . .' She smiled mistily. 'I feel so confused.'

'Me, Theo and Jamie, we all love you so much,' Elise said, gently. 'And we love Dad too—though we are also angry with him, because how can't he see what he's doing to you?' Charlotte sighed but said nothing, and Elise went on, her voice quavering, 'We would be happy if you two could sort it out, and we would be sad if you broke up, but it wouldn't stop us loving you both. So you don't need to worry about us.'

Charlotte stopped. Wordlessly, she hugged her daughter and they held each other for quite a while before resuming their walk, their conversation turning now, by mutual, unspoken agreement, to lighter, happier things.

Nineteen

Before they'd left the garden the previous day, Arielle had told Daniel what lay behind the incident with the Grandiers at the flower market. It was important to her that he knew the full story. He'd listened, one arm around her, then said, 'If I can help you—if you want me to—I will. Whatever you need.' Hesitating for a moment, he'd added, 'I don't speak much with my mother—we don't exactly see eye to eye—but she is an excellent lawyer specialising in family matters, and if you feel at any stage that you need to go that route, I could put you in touch with her.'

Her heart swelling, she'd reached up to him and kissed him. 'I will ask you, definitely, if I need help. I won't be too proud to ask, Daniel. You can count on that.'

'Good,' he said, smiling, 'I am glad.'

Daniel had come home with them, he and Pauline had clicked at once, and they'd spent the rest of the afternoon talking, drinking tea, and later wine, and playing board games with Louis and Alice. He'd stayed for an early dinner of homemade pizza, soup and salad, and after he'd left, Pauline had turned to Arielle and said, 'As your older and wiser sister, I give you my full permission to keep seeing him.' She winked and added, 'And if you need me to babysit while you find a less crowded venue for a night of passion, I'm happy to oblige.'

Arielle blushed and hugged her. 'I'm so glad you like him.'

Now Daniel was perched on a stool beside her in the back room of the shop, as they shared an early lunch of savoury *pan bagnats*—a delicious concoction, which with its tuna, tomatoes, herbs, artichokes, olives and boiled egg, is basically a *salade niçoise* sandwiched in bread which has been marinated in vinaigrette and crushed anchovies. Coming from Provence herself, Arielle loved *pan bagnat*, and she was touched that Daniel had chosen to buy that.

They had so much in common, she thought, despite their differences. For a start, neither of them had been brought up in Paris, but both of them loved the city that had now become their true home. And both had a vocation—something they felt that they had been born to do—in his case, a love of history as expressed through humanity's long relations with plants; in hers, a love and understanding of the gifts that flowers bring to human lives. And though their differences of background were great—her happy childhood in the south-east, in the midst of sunny lavender fields; his lonely one in the north-west, in earshot of pounding Atlantic waves; his long solitary restlessness travelling the world before he found his true home; her finding love and the place where she wanted to be at a young age—these only served to heighten their commonalities.

It was something Arielle had not felt with Ludo. Her surface differences with him hadn't been as great but they'd assumed quite an importance, and it wasn't only about the relationship with his parents. Ludo had never really understood her passion for her work, for instance. She'd even wondered, recently, what would have happened if she'd discovered the catastrophic extent of his debts when he was still alive. Would their marriage have survived the shock of it? She hoped so but wasn't sure.

'Daniel,' she said, 'can I ask you a question?'

'You can ask me as many as you like,' he said, smiling. 'Any time.'

'That's a dangerous thing to say,' she said, smiling back at him. 'You don't know what I'm going to ask.'

'It doesn't matter. But I'll tell you if it's something I *can't* answer.' He took her hand and held it in his for a moment. 'Is that all right?'

She nodded. 'It is what I hope,' she said. 'For there to be real trust and honesty between us. Which includes the knowledge that we *don't* have to answer every question.' She paused, then went on, 'You're not working today, are you?'

He blinked. Clearly it wasn't a question he'd been expecting. 'That's right.'

'Would you like to help me?'

He stared at her. 'Here?'

It had been an impulse to ask him, now she felt it was a ridiculous idea. 'Don't worry,' she said, 'I know that even when you're not at the museum, you have things to do, it was just that I—'

'I would love to help,' he said, interrupting her. His eyes were shining. 'If you think Monsieur Renan won't mind.'

'I'll ask him right now,' she said cheerfully, 'to put your mind at rest.' A moment later she turned back to him, smiling. 'He says it's about time you made yourself useful, instead of hanging around getting in the way.'

Daniel laughed, that happy sound that had so warmed her yesterday in the garden. 'We'd better not delay then as the boss has spoken!'

She reached up to him and they kissed tenderly. It was such a simple, even banal thing they had agreed to and yet it felt huge. And romantic in a most unexpected way.

⁓

Daniel proved to be surprisingly quick at understanding what needed to be done—or maybe it was that he *had* spent quite a bit of time observing how things were done. And it was just as well that he *was* helping out, for a big group of British garden club members arrived moments after ten and most of them were keen to ask questions but spoke not a word of French. Arielle's few phrases of English were not up to their queries and their guide had vanished. But Daniel was able to easily interpret and the tourists left happily clutching various purchases and promising to recommend Arielle's stand to their friends. One of them also confided to Daniel that before this, they had thought of putting up a bad review on Tripadvisor about the flower market, due to the appalling rudeness of a stand owner who had treated them as if they were fools and tried to sell them stuff they didn't want. And what's more, the woman said, she was sure he'd been muttering rude things in French under his breath as they browsed.

Arielle was not in the least bit surprised to hear that the man in question was Vella. After the garden club people had gone, she caught him furtively glancing at their stand, his gaze flicking from Daniel to her. He'd have something to say about this unusual state of affairs, she knew. And sure enough, taking advantage of a time when the crowd had thinned and Daniel had absented himself to buy them some coffee, Vella strolled over to the stand and gave Arielle a sleazy grin.

'Arielle my dear, you look radiant today,' he announced. 'Is it the influence of that handsome new assistant perhaps?'

Arielle ignored him, but he persisted. 'Strange, I thought he was a customer before. Is Monsieur Renan aware that he has switched roles?'

'Monsieur Renan is fully aware.' Arielle kept her tone clipped and cold.

'Very good,' he said, with a hypocritical nod. 'But let us hope all is in order, because if not it could cause Monsieur Renan trouble with the market authorities. I do so hope that doesn't happen.'

Arielle stiffened. 'Thank you for your concern,' she said, keeping her voice light, though she longed to fling the contents of the compost bucket at his smug face. 'I hope as well that the video a very nice English lady showed us, which she made of her group's visit to your stand, doesn't go any further. She didn't understand French, but I certainly do. And I think our market authorities would be most interested to hear the kinds of things you say about your customers when you think they won't understand.'

She was bluffing about the video's existence, but Vella didn't know that, and his reaction, as his face went from florid pink to mottled grey, proved that she had struck a nerve. He shot her a look of pure venom but said, with a forced smile, 'I was joking, you know, letting off steam on a very busy day. I have nothing against our neighbours from across the Channel, or indeed anyone else from any other country, quite the contrary.'

'I am sure of that,' said Arielle, coolly, 'just as I am sure that like me you would never cause any problems for your fellow stand owners. I so admire and honour that spirit of camaraderie in our market, don't you?'

'Oh yes,' he stammered, 'it is indeed a very admirable thing. Well, Arielle, I had better leave you to get on with it, no rest for us hard-working folk, is there?' And with a bob of the head, he scuttled off.

When Daniel came back, she told him what Vella had said, and he looked worried. 'Maybe I should leave,' he said, 'I don't want to cause you or Monsieur Renan any problems.'

'You're not the one causing problems, he is,' she said, tartly.

'But you have enough to be concerned about without him as well. Would you like me to go and have a word?'

'No,' she said, more sharply than she'd intended, and saw him wince. 'I'm sorry, Daniel. I didn't mean to snap. But please don't worry. He really is the least of my concerns right now.'

Vella had never tried to directly threaten her before, she thought, uneasily remembering that look of hatred in his eyes. But she had dealt with it, and she was pretty sure he wouldn't try anything like that again. Anyway, beside the much greater worry about the Grandiers, Vella's antics were mere pinpricks.

Twenty

Emma arrived at the hotel ten minutes before the appointed time, but Liz Flynn, complete with white hat, was already waiting. Emma had expected someone dowdy, maybe mousy and old-fashioned, someone who you could imagine being afraid of venturing into Parisian streets on her own. But what she found was a tall, smiley woman in jeans and blue cotton jumper under a light waterproof jacket, the white hat—a nifty cotton bucket hat—pulled over grey-blonde chin-length hair. With her blue eyes sparkling behind round wire-framed glasses, she reminded Emma at once of Susie, her favourite of Paddy's sisters, and that impression was compounded by Liz's cheerful manner as she shook hands with Emma and admitted that she really hadn't expected to do much with her last day in Paris. 'But that Mark A can really twist your arm,' she added, and it took Emma an instant to realise, with a twist of amusement, that by 'Mark A' she meant Marc-Antoine.

She grinned, saying that she hadn't exactly expected to do this either. 'But add my grandmother to the arm-twisting, and what chance did we have?'

'None at all, clearly,' said Liz, 'but since the double arm-twisting worked and we're both here, tell me, Emma, is this something you really want to do?'

Emma hadn't been sure, till that instant, but now she was. 'Absolutely. Actually, I can't think of a better way to spend a sunny day in Paris.'

'Me neither,' said Liz, a flicker of relief washing over her face. Emma realised the other woman had in fact been looking forward to it, but wasn't sure if she was imposing on Emma, and she liked her even better for that. Marc-Antoine had been right, then. That would have annoyed her even a few hours ago. Not now. Now, she was just—well, ready to admit she might have been wrong about him.

Reaching into her backpack, she pulled out the stiff A3 cardboard wallet that held the map Mattie had drawn for them. 'My grandmother is Parisian born and bred and being married to my garden-mad grandfather means she's familiar with pretty much every garden of note in Paris.' Taking the map carefully out of the wallet, she showed it to Liz. 'So she took it upon herself to draw this map for us, creating the route we'll take today.'

'Oh wow. May I?' breathed Liz, reaching for it. 'So beautiful. Oh, will you look at it!' And she traced a finger around the curve of the map, with the river flowing through it, and all the gardens Mattie had recommended, each marked by its name, and a charming sketch: a little dog, a dancing statue, a rosebush with a star hanging among the flowers, a waterfall, and more... She had put in a hint of colour on each sketch, and drawn the features of the map—the streets, the bridges, the islands, the river—in flowing black ink, with the route they might take in blue.

'Yes, it's pretty special, isn't it?' Emma herself had been stunned not only by the loveliness of her grandmother's map, but also the speed with which she'd created it, and the way in which she'd seemed to have those places in her head. 'My grandmother worked as a commercial artist for a long time,' she went on.

'And she drew this just for our trip today?' Liz asked, shaking her head wonderingly. 'She didn't want to come with us as well?'

'No,' Emma said. 'Mattie—my grandmother—she's in her early eighties, and though she's pretty active most of the time, she's got a couple of health issues that mean a whole day out like this would tire her out too much. And yes, it was a spur of the moment thing—she said she'd thought of making a list for us but that a map would be much more useful.'

'I'll say. And isn't this so much nicer than relying on Google Maps! Not that you can actually rely on the bloody thing,' Liz said. Emma hid a smile, remembering what Marc-Antoine had said. But Liz was right, this was much, much nicer.

'So, if you're ready, shall we start?' she said. 'And would you like to be our navigator?'

Liz's eyes lit up. 'Wouldn't I just! Okay, so our first stop from here looks pretty close, it's er—Hotel de Sully—I'm probably mangling that, but you know what I mean, right? It's got a sketch of a little door with what looks like an old-school moneybag on it.'

Emma smiled. 'That's right. The moneybag is because this garden is in the grounds of an old mansion that used to belong to the Duke de Sully, who had once been the finance minister of one of France's greatest kings, Henri the Fourth, back in the early seventeenth century. He was quite a character, by all accounts, like his boss.' While Mattie had been making the map, Emma had looked up every garden that would be on it, finding interesting details about each one, and noting them down on her phone. 'And here's the door.'

She led the way to a corner of the square and a discreetly positioned door. 'Mattie chose the gardens on this map for two main reasons,' she said. 'The first is that they've all got stories. And the second is that they are mostly hidden or secret gardens.'

'Secret garden? Like in the book?' Liz asked.

Emma smiled. 'Exactly! So here is our first secret garden, whose existence you don't suspect until'—and she opened the door—'suddenly, there it is.'

'Ooh,' said Liz as they stepped into a small quiet garden that was so much like an extension of the garden at the centre of the Place des Vosges that it was disorienting, like stepping into a mirror world, especially as the beautiful mansion in whose grounds it was in was from the same era as those that lined the Place. They strolled around in the timeless peace, feet crunching on gravelled paths bordered with formal green squares of trimmed box, with a splendid evergreen holm oak tree in the corner.

And then they were off again, meandering along the picturesque streets of the Marais till they reached the next stop, in the Rue des Rosiers. This garden, tucked away behind buildings, was marked on the map by the rosebush with the star. 'This area was home to many immigrant Jews from Eastern Europe before World War Two,' Emma explained, 'and the garden we're going to see is named after a teacher called Joseph Migneret who taught in a primary school in the Marais. Many of his students were Jewish, and during the Nazi occupation of Paris, Joseph dedicated himself to saving as many of his students and former students and their families as he could, sheltering some in his home, and supplying forged papers to others so they could escape to Spain.'

As she spoke, they reached the grilled entrance that led into the hidden garden. Away from the bustle of the Rue des Rosiers, it was a calm mix of park, community garden and rose haven, about as different from the Sully garden as it was possible to be. 'I like this one better than the first one,' said Liz, and Emma agreed: though the restrained elegance of the other garden was admirable, this one was more beguiling, intimate, and filled with birdsong. And it was moving, as well, to reflect that this lovely tranquil space had been chosen to commemorate the bravery and compassion of a man who had risked his life more than once to try and save other people, at a time of such horror and cruelty. They spent quite a bit of time there, Liz walking around the different sections taking photos and pointing out flowers and other plants she had in her garden in County Wexford, Ireland. This led to a discussion of what Emma herself was doing in her grandfather's garden, and

Liz seemed genuinely interested. 'You know, I love my garden dearly, and it's in wonderful shape—but I can definitely see the appeal of something you can coax back to life! So tell me, what are your plans?'

Talking about Emma's plans for the garden took up much of the longish walk to the next stop, the Jardin des Arts Albert Schweitzer, newly created from the previously separate gardens of three local squares, to form a green haven that was supposed to be the largest garden opened in Paris for decades. 'Mattie said it was Paris's newest garden, in a manner of speaking,' Emma said, as they walked past green lawn, an ivy-covered wall and beds full of beautiful flowers, including, surprisingly, a bottlebrush bush covered in bright red flower spikes, 'and she says that she wishes Alain—my grandfather—could have seen it. He would have been so happy to know it could still happen, there could still be new gardens in Paris . . .'

This garden had been marked by Mattie with a sketch of a frolicking dog—it's the perfect garden for them, she'd said—and sure enough, they saw a particularly appealing character with a fluffy white coat and black button eyes, which was busily running around a laughing couple who were clearly its owners, ignoring their cries of 'Here, Nina!'

'It's a Bichon Frisé,' Liz informed Emma. 'They're very playful,' she added, with a wistful look back at the little creature, 'but Marty prefers the bigger breeds, and Rudi is gorgeous. Rudi's a German Shepherd,' she explained.

'Can't you have one of the others too?' Emma asked, 'I mean your place in Ireland looks pretty big'—Liz had shown her some pictures on her phone—'so surely you don't have to have only one dog.' She didn't say, *Why should your husband have the right to lay the law down about it?* but she certainly thought it.

Liz's eyes twinkled behind her glasses. 'Oh Emma, I know, but it's early days in our married life, and well, Rudi's been literally top dog for years, he wouldn't take well to a newcomer, he was already not so thrilled about me! So you know, I'm keeping my powder dry for the moment, but when the right time comes, I'll strike.'

Emma felt a bit foolish. Liz was clearly not the sort of woman to meekly accept some spousal stricture and what she said made sense. Animals could get jealous, just like people. *Like me with Marc-Antoine*, she thought, uncomfortably. Firmly dismissing the thought, she said, 'How did you and Martin meet?'

'In a garden, believe it or not! Well, if you're stretching a point, that is—it was actually Hyde Park in London. My office in London at the time was very near the park and I used to go for a walk there at lunchtime, if the weather was fine. Anyway, this particular day I managed to trip on something and twisted my ankle. Marty happened to be walking by, he came to my rescue, helped me to a bench, we got talking, and well, it went on from there. Romantic, eh?' Her face was lit up with a beautiful smile.

'Absolutely,' said Emma, smiling back. 'And now I know why you *really* love gardens.'

'Get on with you,' said Liz, flapping a hand at her. 'I've loved gardens since I was a kid. But now I've told you about my romance, I want to hear about yours.'

Emma stared. 'I don't have one—I mean, I'm not in a relationship, at the moment.'

'Oh. Sorry.' Liz's expression was a comical mix of dismay and surprise. 'It's just that the way he was talking about you, I thought that . . .'

'No,' Emma snapped, her colour rising. She didn't have to ask who Liz was referring to. 'He—we hardly know each other. And we're practically related. Well, not really. I mean, it's complicated . . .' She trailed off.

'Complicated. I see.' Liz shot her an unreadable glance. 'Well, it's my mistake, Emma. Me and my big mouth. Forget I said anything. Now, where are we headed to next?'

Emma remembered the warm tone of Marc-Antoine's voice this morning on the phone. Had that warmth been more than . . . No. Surely not. He was simply relieved she'd agreed to his crazy plan. And his text message had been friendly, but no more, Liz was imagining things. Emma looked down at the map, and, trying to keep her voice steady, she said, 'Well, it's across the Marie bridge here—' pointing to a line with 'Pont Marie' above it, 'over to the Île Saint-Louis, where I thought we could take a break from gardens and have some lunch in a bistro, and then an ice cream at the famous Bertillon stand, and then we can stroll across the Saint-Louis bridge, to get to the Île de la Cité and the flower market. We'll have a good look at that. And then—'

'Okay, okay,' said Liz, laughing, 'let's leave the *and then* for later, right? Onwards to the bridges and lunch. I'm famished!'

They had a very good seafood lunch—a superb scallop risotto for Emma and a big bowl of bouillabaisse for Liz—and by two o'clock the pair were threading through the crowds in the flower market, heading for Arielle's stand. The surly man from the other day gave them a sour look as they went past his shop without stopping, but Emma took no notice, her attention all on Arielle's magnificent display of pink and blue flowers. Beside her, she heard Liz breathe, 'Wow. I've never seen anything like it.'

Arielle, who was talking with a man as they approached, saw them and smiled in welcome. 'Hello, Emma. It is nice to see you again.'

'And you too,' said Emma. She introduced Liz, who said a few words in very hesitant French, and then Arielle introduced the man beside her as her friend Daniel, who worked in the Cluny Museum as a botanical historian. That interested Liz, who asked a couple of rapid questions which Daniel answered in English. Then Liz said, gesturing to the display, 'And this is amazing! Does it have a theme?'

'Thank you. Yes, it does,' Arielle said, beaming. 'It's about the beauty of May, expressed in pink and blue.' And she talked about the flowers, as Emma translated. There was borage with its bright blue star-shaped edible flowers; bleeding-heart plants with their hot pink and white bell blooms; the pale pink of impatiens next to the pale blue of flax flowers; the deep pink of rose campion with their velvety, silvery leaves; the trumpet-shaped sapphire-blue flowers of gentians, and the homely pink and blue glory of hydrangeas.

'Incredible,' Liz said, shaking her head. 'I'd never have thought to combine those particular flowers together, but they look perfect. Do you mind if I take a photo?'

'Not at all. Please go ahead.'

'Thank you. Emma, would you mind standing in front of the flowers for a moment?' Liz said. 'Just to give some perspective,' she added, seeing Emma's expression.

'It should be Arielle, it's her display,' Emma protested, but Arielle smilingly shook her head. She gestured at Emma's dusty-pink knee-length dress and pale green sandals. 'You are better colour coordinated than I am,' she said.

Thankfully, Liz wanted only a couple of photos with Emma in them, so she was glad to be able to duck away again as Liz continued taking photos from every conceivable angle. As they stood there watching her, Arielle said to Emma, in an undertone, 'This very *sympa* lady, is she a member of your family?'

'Oh no—she's a friend of a friend.' Not wanting to explain who the 'friend' was, she hurried on, 'I'm her guide for the day. She's Australian. She doesn't care for monuments but loves plants and gardens and so I've been taking her around the most interesting places: my grandmother made a map for us, and of course the flower market is on it—see here . . .' And she showed the map to Arielle, who drew in a breath, saying, '*Absolument ravissant!*' Absolutely gorgeous!

Daniel, who had been silent till now, leaned over to look and his eyes widened. 'Superb,' he agreed, in English, 'what wonderful detail! A garden map is such a wonderful idea.'

'Yes, exactly,' said Liz, and she and Daniel began an animated conversation about maps, while Arielle asked Emma about her garden project. Arielle was clearly taken with Emma's enthusiastic description so when she asked, rather hesitantly, 'Might you come and look at it one day and see what you think? I'd happily pay you for your time.' Arielle smiled, said she'd be delighted, and they exchanged numbers.

Shortly after, Emma and Liz left the flower market, taking the Metro to the station closest to the Champs-Élysées and the Tuileries Gardens. Not that they were visiting either today, but the station was near the hidden oasis known by two names: the Garden of the Swiss Valley *and* the Garden of New France. The first, older name, had come about because the garden had once been part of the grounds of the charming Swiss pavilion in the 1900 Universal Exposition of Paris; the second, official name, given long after the pavilion had been pulled down, was in honour of the early history of French Canada, once known as New France. On Mattie's map, it was marked with the waterfall sketch and, in tiny script, another name of her own invention: *le jardin des escaliers poétiques*, the garden of the poetic steps.

That was because the garden could only be reached by a set of worn, uneven stone steps, tucked in close to the unusual marble sculpture of the great poet Alfred de Musset. The steps wound down into a hidden beauty, as the busy, noisy boulevards above seemed to disappear completely, and you found yourself in a peaceful emerald world where the only sounds were birdsong, bee buzz, the occasional soft voice or footfall of a fellow walker, and the trickle of water.

Emma and Liz walked among deeply shaded paths, near inviting benches where they might rest a while in contemplation, past replica Greek ruins and statues of the early navigators and mappers of New France, passing stone archways and a carved wooden footbridge as they headed towards the alluring sound of water to reach a small stream with its own miniature waterfall cascading over rocks. The water was overhung with big trees that, at this time of year, were in full glorious leaf.

As they walked, Emma told Liz a bit about the area's origins in the time of Marie de Medici, who'd reigned for seven years as regent of France after the shocking assassination of her husband, the swashbuckling king Henri IV, the same one who'd employed the Duke de Sully as his finance minister. It was Marie who'd first created gardens here as a refuge, as well as being involved in the design of the Luxembourg Garden on the other side of the river. 'The garden of the poetic steps' had changed since her day, but it retained a feeling of another time; a tiny green sliver of what had once been a very different and smaller city, with fields and woods outside its now-vanished walls.

The two women stopped to rest on a bench, gazing at the water, drinking in the birdsong and talking softly about their conversation with Arielle and Daniel in the flower market. Emma had ended up buying a pretty enamel pin of a hydrangea blossom for her grandmother, but Liz had come away with a more substantial haul for her home in Ireland: three small garden ornaments in the shape of birds and several packets of seeds. Plus an open invitation to come back to the stand whenever she was in Paris. Which, she told Emma as they sat resting their feet before heading off to the river ferry, she was definitely going to do. 'Today has opened my eyes to a whole new way of seeing this city,' she said. 'If ever you decide to do more tours like this, I know plenty of people who would be interested. You're absolutely brilliant at it.'

'Thanks,' Emma said, a little embarrassed but very pleased. 'It was Mattie's map that did it really. I found it so inspirational.'

'You should go into business together then,' said Liz, stretching luxuriously before getting to her feet. 'A gorgeous tour and a gorgeous souvenir map. What could be better for a unique experience of Paris? People would line up for it!'

Emma laughed. 'There speaks a true entrepreneur,' she said.

'Well, why not, girl? Dare to dream and the world will dream with you!' Liz said cheerfully. 'What's next?'

'The last stop on our tour—the Luxembourg Garden,' Emma said. 'It's not a hidden garden, but it's a very special one, and it has its own secrets. Have you been there before?'

'Never,' said Liz, 'but I'm looking forward to it.' She pointed to it on the map. 'The dancing statue, right?'

Emma smiled. 'And soon you'll see why.'

A short time later, as they sat on the Batobus, gliding along the river towards the Left Bank, Emma thought again of what Liz had said about the garden tours. It had probably been a throwaway comment because she'd enjoyed the day, but with her marketing brain switched on, Emma could see that it wasn't a bad idea. Once she'd finished restoring the garden, maybe she could think of doing it. After all, among the tourists there would be many people who loved gardens, and gardens in Paris were especially appealing. And how wonderful would it be to work with her grandmother? But would Mattie even want to? She was in her eighties after all. *And could I really do it*, she wondered. *I don't really know enough about gardens. I can't pretend to give practical information because that would make me an impostor. Charlotte could do that. Or Arielle. But not me. The only thing I can do properly is tell stories.*

Just then, her phone buzzed with an incoming call. Mattie. 'Hello, sweetheart,' she said, when Emma answered. 'How is it going? Where are you now?'

'We've been having such a lovely day! And we'll be at the Luxembourg in twenty minutes or so.'

'I thought I could meet you there. What do you think?'

'That would be wonderful! I know Liz would be delighted to meet you. She adores your map.' She lowered her voice. 'And I think she'd love to hear your story of the dancing faun!'

There was a smile in Mattie's voice as she said, 'Then I will see you very soon, at the foot of the dancing faun. Oh, and Marc-Antoine is taking us to a restaurant by the river this evening with your lady and her husband, isn't that lovely? I am so looking forward to it.' She sounded almost girlishly excited. 'I haven't been out at night for quite a while, not even to walk on the quays.

Alain and I used to do that quite often, but it feels too lonely on my own.'

What could Emma say to that? That she didn't feel like going out after spending all day tramping around? That she could have taken Mattie for a night out by the river before this, rather than having to wait for Marc-Antoine to do it? And that she was ridiculously, stupidly nervous about seeing him again? 'That sounds lovely, Mattie,' she said, as the Batobus stopped, and they got out. 'I'm looking forward to it too.'

Twenty-one

The previous day, after the emotions of the morning, Charlotte and Elise had spent a good day in Étretat, not quite recreating what they'd done the first time they'd been there, but close. They had visited the Lupin museum, which was even better than they remembered, browsed in the shops, and took a long walk on the cliffs. Today, after taking it easy in the hotel before checking out, they went for lunch in a nearby restaurant. There, they had a traditional Norman meal, accompanied by excellent local wines. They shared mussels to start, then chicken in a cream and Calvados sauce for Elise, and rabbit in a cider and mushroom sauce for Charlotte, followed by a shared green salad and a plate of local cheeses, among them the most famous local creation of them all: Camembert. This particular one was divine, with a creamy distinctiveness that Elise said perfectly reflected the fragrance of the flowery Norman meadows where the cows had grazed. She'd turned into quite the foodie, Charlotte thought, amused and touched, watching her daughter's bright face as she waxed lyrical about provenance and terroir and regional character.

The cheese was followed by caramelised apples cooked in butter and Calvados, and a Bénédictine liqueur finished everything off nicely. Afterwards, needing to walk, they headed out to the beach again. The wind had got up a bit and it ruffled the calm water into silver frills of waves, but it didn't feel too cold.

They didn't talk about Tom, or any sort of difficult subject. Instead, somewhat to Charlotte's surprise, Elise asked about her work. None of her children had ever shown much interest in gardening, but Elise had been very impressed by Arielle's stand the other day, and it appeared to have triggered a new interest in her mother's own experiences. Perhaps she had only raised the subject to distract her mother from her troubles, but if so, Charlotte thought, as she happily answered her daughter's questions and recounted funny anecdotes—including Mrs Browning's flamingo bath—it was certainly working.

They had just turned back to go to the station when Charlotte's phone pinged with a text. It was from Gilles Auvert, telling her that due to an issue with his planned episode he'd be slotting in her interview instead, as it was edited and ready to go. It would go live at 8 pm.

Charlotte was somewhat stunned, not having expected it to come up so soon, but Elise was very excited. 'That's so great, Marm! I'm going to tell Theo and Jamie and we can make an occasion of it, all of us—we can have a group call via my phone and we can listen together on your phone! We'll get a bottle of champagne and a few snacks too . . .' and without listening to her mother's admittedly feeble protestations, she texted her brothers. They responded just as enthusiastically and Charlotte's phone pinged with *Way to go, Mum! Can't wait to hear it!* and she felt her heart swelling with love for them all, her three beautiful children who were the light of her life, and always would be, no matter what happened . . .

Charlotte and Elise caught the fast train back to Paris, and by 7.30, half an hour before the episode was about to start, they were sitting at Juliette's kitchen table, facing Elise's phone, a platter of snacks—charcuterie, olives, tomatoes and bread—by their elbows, as well as a bottle of champagne. Elise filled up their glasses and started the video call, and Charlotte saw her sons were together in one room too, each with a filled glass in hand and big smiles on their faces. Elise called for a toast to Charlotte, who couldn't stop smiling, even if tears also pricked at her eyes. Everyone started talking at once, the young people's cheerful banter chasing away the momentary twist of sadness their mother felt about the fact her husband wasn't on the call. Elise hadn't suggested it. She had too much tact for that.

At half a minute to eight, Charlotte switched her phone to the radio, and everyone fell silent as Gilles Auvert's cultured, mellow voice welcomed his listeners, burbling on a bit about what people had said about previous episodes. Charlotte hardly heard any of it, she was feeling much too nervous. The seconds ticked by agonisingly slowly till finally Auvert said, 'And now I'm very happy to present a special guest, an expert contemporary designer whose work combines the best of French and English ideas about gardens, rooted in the traditions of both cultures but also in the imagination of its creator. I've known this lady for quite a long time, from when I was a TV journalist working on garden shows, and I know how highly her work is regarded, but also how despite the accolades, there's not a sign of a swollen ego to be seen. A big welcome then to Charlotte Marigny, Parisian by birth and Londoner by residence. It's a real pleasure to have you on my show.'

'It's a real pleasure to be here, Gilles, and thank you so much for inviting me.' Charlotte was nervous. She and Gilles had talked for quite a long time and she was a bit hazy about all they'd said. Would she come out with things that might make her children cringe?

She needn't have worried. Auvert was a skilled interviewer and he'd guided her through a series of questions that had been designed to allow her the space to expand on particular topics—such as inspiration and ideas—and soft pedal others, such as commentary on other people's work. He did ask a few personal questions—such as asking her to recount how she'd started, with a holiday internship at the Lost Gardens of Heligan in Cornwall, which was where she'd conceived the idea for the business, but had also met Tom, whose parents lived near there. She had even managed to keep her voice steady when she'd said that, but as she listened back to it, she felt her throat tightening, and Elise silently took her hand and squeezed it. Then the interview went on to other things, to the challenges she'd faced when she was starting out, to how she'd created her first designs—including Juliette's garden. To herself, she sounded a little tentative, but as the children said afterwards, to others she sounded warm, engaging, smooth enough to be easy to listen to, but not so smooth that it sounded cheesy or insincere. 'In fact, Mum,' Theo said, 'I'd say you made it sound like anyone could do what you'd done and yet anyone listening would want to hire you on the spot to make over their garden!'

'Hundred per cent,' said Jamie. 'Hell, Mum, I'd get you over here in an instant to turn our horrible patch of cracked concrete and weeds into a Garden of Eden!'

'I think I might need to pack a magic wand along with the rest of my tools,' Charlotte said, and they all laughed. That sad bit of concrete at the back of the student house Jamie shared with three other guys could hardly be described as a yard, let alone a garden.

They chatted for a while longer before ending the call. Charlotte suddenly felt totally exhausted, the adrenaline having left her system. Elise saw it and got up to clear the table, but before she did, she hugged her mother tightly, saying, 'You were totally brilliant, Marm. We're so very proud of you.' Charlotte hugged her back, wordlessly, heart full. It was her children who were brilliant, she thought. She and Tom had not got that wrong, at least.

Twenty-two

Daniel had had to go to a brief appointment after lunch that day, but he'd come back just in time to meet Emma and Liz when they'd arrived at the stand. Arielle was glad he'd been there. Not because there was anything awkward about speaking with the two women, quite the contrary, but because she'd hoped that Daniel hadn't felt hurt by her snapping at him earlier about Vella. It wasn't like her to be so short-tempered, and he certainly hadn't deserved it. The business with the Grandiers had already rattled her, and Vella's stupid attempt at intimidation had simply made the cup of stress overflow. And poor Daniel had been there when it splashed out. But when she tried to excuse herself again after he returned from his appointment, he just smiled and said, 'It's quite okay. I completely understand.' She could see that he absolutely meant it.

Vella left them strictly alone for the rest of the day, not even casting a glance towards them. He'd been cowed all right, but for how long, Arielle didn't know and didn't particularly care right now. A few more customers came, mostly French tourists this time, but it was during a lull in the crowd that Emma and Liz had appeared. Arielle had thought the young woman was particularly lovely that day. Silhouetted against the pink and blue flowers, in her simple pink dress, with that beautiful wave of ash-brown hair, its soft gold sheen picked out by sunlight, and her almost periwinkle-blue eyes, Emma looked, Arielle thought, like an Impressionist painting of May herself, and she wasn't surprised when Liz asked to take her photo against the display. 'I can send it to you afterwards,' the older woman told Arielle, via Daniel. 'For your social media. You have Instagram or something, right?' She didn't raise an eyebrow or look surprised when Arielle told her it was the boss's daughter who maintained the account. Instead she said, 'What a great arrangement! She feels important, and you don't have to do the tedious work but can concentrate on what's really important.'

'Yes, exactly,' said Arielle, smiling.

'I'll post it then, and tag your stand, so your boss's daughter can access it,' Liz said, and later Arielle saw she'd been as good as her word, and that Romaine had wasted no time in reposting the photo.

Yes, it had been an enjoyable conversation with them, and though she hadn't angled for an invitation to the garden to meet the creator of that lovely map, she was certainly happy that

Emma had offered. After the two women had left, Daniel stayed on, helping with the rest of the afternoon's customers, who weren't anything as entertaining as Emma and Liz, but nevertheless were pleasant enough. By 5 pm, the trickle of customers had ebbed away completely and they were able to pack up early and close up bang on time. To her surprise, when Arielle glanced at Vella's stand, it was already closed. Yet he liked to claim that he was almost always the very last person to shut up shop, as if that was some kind of special achievement.

Daniel saw her frown and asked, 'What's up?'

She was going to say nothing was up but changed her mind and told him.

'It's a change in pattern, that's what you mean?' he said.

She nodded. 'It's out of character. He likes to feel important, and being the last to leave is a way of saying nobody works harder than him.'

'Perhaps you had more of an impact on him than you thought,' Daniel said, 'and he felt ashamed so decided to skulk off home.'

'Maybe,' she said, unconvinced. She hadn't thought Vella capable of shame. Embarrassment and annoyance at being caught out, yes. 'Anyway, let's not waste another instant's thought on that man. How about we go and have that drink you suggested before I have to head off home?' She'd already told Pauline she might be a bit late.

Daniel's eyes lit up. 'Absolutely. Let me introduce you to my favourite bar.'

It wasn't on the island, but across the bridge, on the Right Bank, not far from a Metro station with a line that would take her to her stop without having to change. Arielle suspected that it wasn't his favourite bar, but that he'd chosen it so it would make it easier for her to make her way home afterwards. He was such a thoughtful man.

They had seated themselves and ordered a couple of drinks—a mojito for her, a red wine for him—when he said, 'I got a message from Franck, that beekeeper in the Chevreuse who I mentioned in my talk at Cluny the other day, you remember?'

She nodded. 'The one who was going to set up his apiary based on what you'd gleaned from medieval texts.'

He smiled. 'The very same. Anyway, he's invited me to visit him on Wednesday to see the results of his endeavours, and I wondered if you might like to come too.'

'Oh, I'd love to! But I've already got the day off tomorrow'—she'd explained earlier that it was the anniversary of Ludo's death and that they always marked it with a special outing in his memory—'and I can't ask for the next day off as well.'

He looked sheepish. 'But this wouldn't be during the day. It would be after work as I can't get away before 5 pm either. And Franck's going away on Thursday.'

'Okay. But how far is this place?' she asked.

'That's the thing,' he said. 'The farm is about an hour and a half from Paris. And Franck will want to give the grand tour, so it might be quite late when it finishes. Plus, driving at night isn't my favourite thing. So I was thinking of staying overnight in a nearby village, there's a great hotel there, and coming back to Paris early in the morning, to be back in time for work.'

Arielle liked the sound of the bee farm, but it was the thought of spending a night alone with Daniel in a charming country hotel that sent her pulse racing. She longed to say yes. But what about the children? If she told Pauline, her sister would say that Arielle must go, that she herself could look after the children overnight no problem, that it was more than time that she had some fun as a woman, not just as a mother. All of that was true. And yet, with the menace of the Grandiers still hovering, Arielle couldn't help hesitating.

Daniel saw her expression. 'No need to decide now, Arielle,' he said, gently. 'Let me know on Wednesday morning. And don't worry about upsetting me if you decide you can't come. I promise I will not be offended one iota. I would completely understand, and we could always go together there another time, when Franck returns.'

'How long will he be away?'

'Two or three weeks, I believe. Some long-delayed family holiday. His neighbours will be looking after the bees.' He looked directly into her eyes 'But don't worry, Arielle. Let me know when you are ready. I've waited a long time for you,' he added, softly. 'I can wait a little longer.'

Arielle's body tingled. *But I don't know if I can wait*, came the unbidden words welling up from her heart, though she didn't voice them. *I want you soon, very soon. Two or three weeks! That feels like an eternity right now.* Aloud, she said, 'Thank you for giving me the space to think, Daniel.' She reached for his hand and kissed it. 'I promise I won't keep you in suspense for too long.'

Twenty-three

Very soon after Emma and Liz had arrived at the spot in the Luxembourg where the dancing faun capered on his pedestal against a background of spring flowers and trees in full leaf, Mattie appeared. She looked wonderful, dressed in a deep green calf-length velvet dress, with a dark loose jacket printed with poppies over it. Her thick silver hair was up in a becoming roll, and she wore red drop earrings and a touch of dark red lipstick.

Emma made the introductions, and despite the language barrier, her grandmother and Liz seemed to hit it off at once. At Liz's urging, Mattie began telling the dancing faun story, with Emma translating.

When night comes, the humans are all gone and the gates of the gardens are closed. Look! The dancing faun jumps off his pedestal and plays his merry tune, and all the other statues in the garden jump off their pedestals too, and join him in a dance around the garden. The flowers sway with them, and the night birds applaud. And if you are very quiet, and very still, you can lie in your bed and hear, faintly, on the air, the sound of the faun's flute as he leads the dance.

As a child, Emma had listened for the flute every night after Mattie had told her the story. She was sure she'd heard it, faintly, on the air, and it had filled her with wonder. Even when she was back home in Australia, she'd thought she could hear it, more than once, in the weeks after they had returned. Performing it now with her grandmother felt so special.

Afterwards, the three of them walked to the Grand Bassin and Liz challenged both Emma and Mattie to a yacht-sailing competition, which Mattie duly won. 'Well, I've sailed boats here since I was a child,' she said with a twinkle in her eye, 'and as I'm so much older than you two girls, I've had a lot more practice!'

Presently, Liz left them to go back to her hotel for a rest before dinner, but Emma and Mattie stayed in the Luxembourg, sitting companionably on green metal chairs under the trees. Mattie didn't want to go back to the house before the restaurant, so after a while Emma left her and went back to freshen up. She had a quick shower and changed into a dress she'd found in a Melbourne vintage shop but not worn yet here. It was a flattering full-skirted 1950s number in lilac-coloured chiffon, and she paired it with another op shop find, a beaded cream cardigan, as well as dark ballet flats and a simple gold locket she'd inherited from her mother. A touch-up of mascara, a dusting of bronze on her eyelids, a bit of lip gloss and a quick spray of Mademoiselle, the Chanel perfume her grandmother had given her for a late birthday present, and she was ready to go.

She found Mattie still sitting in the same spot, sketching. Emma glanced over her shoulder—in a few quick pencil lines Mattie had captured so much of the garden and its people. And in the middle, directing it all, was the dancing faun. 'Of course he has to be at the centre,' Mattie said, 'because he reminds us that in letting go, in trusting to the moment, we open ourselves to the gift of joy.' Then she glanced at Emma and added, 'And you, my darling, look absolutely ravishing, like the gift of joy in person.'

The restaurant Marc-Antoine had chosen wasn't, as Emma had assumed, a high-end place, but an unpretentious bistro with a classic French menu. It had a lovely view over the river and was only a kilometre from the Luxembourg. Mattie wouldn't hear of taking the Metro—*it's much too fine an evening to waste any of it underground*, she said—so they slowly meandered through the quieter, narrower streets, stopping to look in shop windows, pausing at landmarks, and Emma took pictures of the places, and of Mattie, who was so glowing and animated in her spring finery, happily recounting tales from long ago. This area had been where Alain had had his shop, back in the sixties, and as Emma listened, it seemed that she could *see* the shop, shoehorned into a tiny space but filled with unexpected treasures. And she could see her grandfather looking up from his work and seeing a beautiful black-haired young woman, clutching a sketchbook with a confident smile.

Mattie pointed to a street they were passing. 'In the cellar of that building over there was a jazz club where we went on weekend nights. It was a smoky, dim place, but you heard some amazing music.' She took Emma's arm as they kept walking. 'This is where our little Corinne loved to watch the boats going by when she was around five or six; she loved to count them, and wanted to know what each of them was for. We told her all kinds of stories about them, some of them rather fanciful. See that man over there on the quay, taking out his violin from the case? That's where Alain and I danced, on more than one warm evening, whether there was music or not.' There was something so lovely, so special, about Mattie tonight, an inward light that made you catch your breath, and Emma felt as though she could have walked with her for hours.

But they were at the restaurant, and there, outside, waiting, was Marc-Antoine, effortlessly stylish in a caramel-coloured three-quarter-length coat over a simple white shirt and dark chinos. He gave Mattie a warm hug and glanced at Emma enquiringly. She knew he was waiting for her cue. So, trying to sound as casual as she could, she said, 'I think we probably know each other well enough now to do *la bise*, don't you?'

'I think so too,' he said, and then they kissed each other lightly on both cheeks. And that did it. *He smells good, oh God, he smells so good*, Emma thought, in a daze, *and his skin is so soft and fresh where he's recently shaved, and his eyes on mine, that expression in them . . . if I let myself breathe him in one millisecond longer, I am going to be lost. And that can't happen. It can't.*

She stepped away, trying to regain her composure, trying also to ignore the speculative spark that had appeared in her grandmother's eyes. Mattie might be dreamily childlike at times, but she didn't miss much. She just took Marc-Antoine's arm, saying, 'So, my dear boy, shall we go in?'

They went in to where Liz and her husband, Martin—a tall, rangy man with iron-grey hair, a slow smile and a lovely Irish lilt— were having a drink at the bar. The couple raised their glasses when they saw them coming. Greetings and introductions, getting more drinks, settling at a table by the window all helped calm Emma, so she was able to chat normally. And when the Kir Royale she'd ordered came, she sipped at it gratefully, glad to have something to do with her hands rather than fidget. Especially as Marc-Antoine sat directly opposite and his legs were long so she had to concentrate on keeping her own legs well back in case they touched by accident. The thought of it made her skin tingle. *No, no, no!* She had to stop this. Okay, so he was seriously hot and that look in his eyes . . . But it was a bad idea. Wasn't it?

She started. Mattie, who was sitting beside her, had gently pulled at her sleeve. 'Sweetheart, have you decided?'

Emma looked wildly at her, unsure exactly what her grandmother meant. Then she saw the menu in front of her and smiled awkwardly. 'Sorry.' Ignoring Liz's wry expression, she quickly chose her food. She began to feel light-headed as she downed a glass of white and then another, hardly noticing what she was eating—which was nevertheless delicious, artichoke mousse followed by an excellent *steak frites*—and struggling to keep up with the conversation that ebbed and flowed around her. She didn't have to translate for Mattie because Marc-Antoine was doing a good job of that, so she could relax. Well, yeah, *nah*.

Finally, the evening wound down. Coffees were ordered, and liqueurs, and there was some more chat, and then Liz and Marty got up, saying regretfully that they had an early flight the next day and they'd better get going back to their hotel on the other side of the river. *La bise* was exchanged all round, promises to keep in touch were made, and then Liz and Marty left. 'I'll call a cab and see you both home,' Marc-Antoine said to Mattie, helping her up very gently. She swayed and Emma noticed for the first time that her grandmother looked tired. But Mattie said, 'No cabs, not yet, this has been such a nice evening, I don't want it to end yet. I want to have a walk by the river, see the lights on the water, and watch the people, like Alain and I used to do.' She looked at each of them in turn. 'And would you two young people come with me?'

They went out of the restaurant, into the still lovely but cooler night, and Mattie held out her arms for each of them to take one. 'It's a bit chilly, and that will keep me a little warmer,' she said, 'you know how *frileuse* I am.' She declined Marc-Antoine's offer of his coat. 'I will swim in that,' she said, smiling, 'but you can hold my bag if you like.'

Arms linked, they walked together beside the Seine, where the river flowed in black and silver silence under the moon. Even on a Monday evening, there were still quite a few people around—lovers entwined, friends chatting over late-night picnics, a young couple trying to get a baby in a sling to sleep, a man walking his frisky dog. Everyone nodded and said, *Bonsoir*. They had to walk slowly, because of Mattie, so every step was measured, and that felt good. Emma's nerves stopped fizzing, her head cleared, and she felt much calmer. Mattie had been right to suggest this.

They sat for a short while on a bench so Mattie could rest, and she took one of each of their hands in hers, murmuring, 'What a beautiful evening, thank you, my darlings.' Then she fell silent, watching the river, her hands still in theirs, while Emma and Marc-Antoine's eyes met over her head for a moment. But they didn't speak.

Presently, Mattie said, 'Let's keep going,' and they helped her to her feet and kept walking. But they had not got very far when Mattie stumbled and gave a choking gasp. Then she was sagging, crumpling between them, her eyes rolling back, and they only just managed to catch her before she fell.

Later, Emma wasn't sure how it had happened, but suddenly she was sharply in control, any lingering trace of confusion leaving her. Paddy had told her what could happen to someone with her grandmother's heart condition, and he'd shown her what to do. A very pale Marc-Antoine did exactly as Emma told him, helping to lower Mattie to the ground and calling the paramedics, telling them they needed to bring a defibrillator, while Emma kneeled beside her unconscious grandmother who lay with Marc-Antoine's coat under her head. She checked if Mattie was breathing—she was—and felt for her pulse. It was still there, but faint and slow.

Emma knew she couldn't do CPR as that would inflict more damage on someone who was still breathing, so all they could do was wait, and pray . . .

Thank God it was Paris. Thank God it was the centre. Thank God that an ambulance happened to be cruising very close by. The paramedics were there in just over a minute—the longest in Emma's life—and got Mattie's heart rate stable enough to put her in the ambulance. They wouldn't let Emma and Marc-Antoine accompany Mattie in the vehicle but told them which hospital they would take her to. They'd only be able to see her after the doctor had checked her out completely, which could take many hours.

Mattie looked so small and fragile on the stretcher as the paramedics hurried her away that Emma felt a terrible fear hit her. Her grandmother was on her way to hospital, but what if she never woke up? She was old. Her heart was already damaged. And she'd exerted herself too much this evening. What if she had a seizure on the way to the hospital, or if they couldn't keep her pulse rate and blood pressure stable? What if she . . .

'We have to go!' she cried, 'We have to follow them, right now! It doesn't matter how.' The strange calm control had left her completely, the shock of what had happened only hitting her now. She couldn't stop shivering.

Marc-Antoine draped his coat around her, and picked up Mattie's discarded bag before coaxing Emma up the stairs. 'It's okay, Emma, I've called a cab, they're coming. I've got you.'

In the cab, he arranged the coat on her like a blanket, and held her hand. She was grateful for the warmth and his nearness and comforted by the absolute certainty that he also loved Mattie and understood what Emma felt for her, because he felt it too.

The hospital emergency department was full of lights, rushing and noise but also quiet, echoing with unspoken fear, hollow with waiting. Waiting, waiting . . . Mattie was with the doctor, they were told. Her heart rate had stabilised but she was still unconscious and they were running tests to evaluate her condition. No, they couldn't see her. No, they didn't know when there would be more information. It was good they had known what to do when it happened, good she had been brought in so quickly, but there was a little way to go yet. Best to go home, they were told. Leave your contact details. We'll call you. But they *couldn't* go. They sat close together on plastic chairs and drank terrible coffee and picked up ancient magazines then put them down again. They leafed through Mattie's visual diary, which was still in her bag, delighting in the lovely drawings she'd created, not only the Luxembourg sketch but lively studies of people—including Emma and Marc-Antoine—and scenes of daily life in Paris. And most of all they talked, in low voices, in fragments. About Mattie. About Alain. About the house and the garden.

Emma learned a good deal in that strange, suspended time about the special bond between this man sitting beside her and her grandparents. They had taken a bewildered little boy and his frail mother into their hearts and helped them to find some peace and stability. She no longer felt any trace of jealousy or resentment, only loving admiration for what Mattie and Pappy had done. And a deep gratitude that Marc-Antoine had been in their lives, when she herself had been so distant, so unreachable . . .

Finally, well past midnight, a brisk nurse came out and told them that Mattie had been transferred from intensive care to a recovery ward. She was still unconscious but was definitely out of danger, although she still needed close observation. 'You can go in for a few minutes,' the nurse replied to Marc-Antoine's question, 'but you'll have to leave as soon as we tell you.'

They followed her to a dimly lit, hushed room down the corridor, and there was Mattie, lying still and very pale, hooked up to tubes and monitors. Emma stopped abruptly, the sight jolting her back to another hospital room, and her mother, lying unconscious after the stroke from which she'd never awoken. Marc-Antoine took her hand, saying gently, 'It's okay, Emma. You don't have to go in.'

'I—I want to,' she murmured, clutching his hand tightly as they went in.

Once they were sitting side by side on two padded chairs close to the bed, their eyes on Mattie, listening to her soft breath and the hum of the monitors, Emma felt calmer. After a moment, she found herself telling Marc-Antoine about her own childhood, of Paddy, who'd loved her as his own, and her mother, loving but complicated. She spoke about her childhood visit to her grandparents' house, and her recent attempts to find out the secrets of Corinne's past. 'Although right now that seems of such little importance,' she murmured. She asked him about his mother, who like hers had died too young. Emma learned then why he hadn't been at Alain's funeral two and a half years ago—because he'd been at his mother's final bedside. He spoke lovingly of how she'd raised him alone after his father abandoned them when he was just a baby, only to try to sue for custody in a bruising legal battle years later; how they had lived in Italy with his grandmother Vivienne until she died when he was six, and they'd returned to France, which was when Mattie and Alain had come into his life . . .

They fell silent for a moment, watching Mattie, until a nurse came in and told them they had to leave. 'And don't worry,' he added kindly. 'She's stable and safe as she can be right now, but she won't wake up for quite some time. So go home and get some rest. We will call you when she wakes.'

As they walked out of the hospital into the dark reaches of very early morning, Marc-Antoine said hesitantly, 'I'll call a cab and drop you off at the house and we can meet back here later. Or maybe I can book another room at the hotel for you, I know it will be hard going back to the empty house—'

Emma shook her head. 'No. I want to go home. But—' she looked at him, 'I don't want to be alone. Do you mind . . .' She swallowed, unable to finish.

He nodded, 'I can sleep in the spare room.' He called a cab.

In the car, the lingering effects of shock began to hit Emma hard and by the time they got to the house, she could barely stand. Marc-Antoine helped her up the stairs to her bedroom, where he drew back the bedclothes, helped her lie down, still in her chiffon dress, and covered her with the duvet, then went to close the curtains. But as he was about to leave, she whispered, 'No, Marc-Antoine. Stay. Please.' He stilled, his face turned towards her, unreadable. 'Please,' she said. 'I don't want to be on my own. And neither, I think, do you.'

'No, I don't,' he whispered. Then he was sitting on the bed, taking off his shoes, but not his clothes, and slipping in beside her. She felt a great peace envelop her then. 'Thank you,' she said, and was about to say more, but instead fell asleep so suddenly and deeply that she didn't even know she had.

She awoke hours later to the sunlight filtering through the curtains. Memories of the night before surfaced and her throat constricted. She looked over to where Marc-Antoine was still sleeping, one shirt-sleeved arm out of the duvet, face pressed against the pillow. It was an intimate sight, yet she knew all they had both done was sleep, and the thought sent an odd surge of warmth through her.

Getting up quietly, she picked up her phone from the bedside table and went to the window. It was 7 am. They had slept five hours. The phone was almost out of battery, but she managed to check messages and calls. There were none from the hospital. Putting the almost-dead phone down, she breathed a sigh of relief. So no call meant there was no change, that Mattie was okay. Then Marc-Antoine's voice behind her said, 'I checked my phone too. No word from the hospital.'

She turned and smiled at him. 'I suppose that's good news, right?'

He nodded. 'I think so. Are you okay, Emma?'

'Yes,' she said softly, 'in a way.'

'I know what you mean.' Yesterday at the restaurant, he had been immaculately stunning. Now his dark hair was messy, his elegant clothes seriously wrinkled and overnight stubble was beginning to pepper his chin, but she thought he had never looked so gorgeous, and her heart lurched. Then 'Oh!' he said, on a rising note of surprise, and Emma turned back to the window to see what he had seen.

'It's Monsieur Leroux!' she exclaimed in pure delight. 'Isn't he beautiful!' Down below, the squirrel was scampering about, a flash of red tail in the morning light. 'He's lived here for a while,' she went on, 'I've seen him a couple of times. I think he approves of what I'm doing in the garden—will you look at him!'

'Will you just,' said Marc-Antoine, with that wonderful smile in his voice. And somehow, as they both watched the lovely little animal, they found themselves in each other's arms, and when the squirrel vanished as quickly as it had come, they didn't let go, but reached for each other, kissing and kissing and kissing. 'I want,' Emma whispered, 'oh, Marc-Antoine, I want so much . . . Do you?' And he breathed, 'Oh yes, Emma, so do I.'

Then they were undressing each other, tumbling onto the bed, skin to skin, lips to lips, limbs entwined, before coming together in a wild unstoppable rush that had both of them gasping at the end, laughing, kissing, then content for a while in each other's arms before it all began again, tenderly this time, exquisitely slowly.

It was quite a bit later that they lay sprawled across the bed, spent, happy, astonished, smiling into each other's eyes.

'Before yesterday I thought you hated me,' Marc-Antoine said, tracing the line of her face with a finger. 'And that was a blow because I'd fallen for you at first sight, standing there so lovely and unexpected in the hall, in your bare feet and your hair all over the place.'

'Love at first sight,' Emma said, unable to stop looking at his beautiful face, his gorgeous body, her every sense prickling with desire. 'Ha! I don't believe in it.' But of course she did. And she knew that intense reaction she'd had on first meeting him—the instant prejudice—might well have been a cover not only for jealousy but for another powerful emotion that she'd been afraid of. 'And I didn't hate you,' she added mischievously, 'I thought that you were arrogant, patronising and entitled.'

He laughed. 'That's quite a hit list.' He held her tight, whispering, as his caressing hands sent thrilling tingles through her skin, 'And what do you think of me now, Ms Emma Taylor?'

She looked at him, the breath catching in her throat. 'Marc-Antoine—I feel you are . . .'

'Yes?' he said, smiling.

'It scares me. I'm not sure.'

He waited, the expression in those beautiful eyes unwavering yet she could see, deep in them, a hint of something like sadness that made her say in a bold, defiant, heart-filled rush, so he could have no doubt at all what she felt, 'It's just that I am not sure I can ever get enough of you.'

She heard his indrawn breath as he said, his lips on her hair, his hands travelling down her body, 'Then you won't have to. Because I *know* I can never get enough of you.'

It was a while before they finally came apart and laughingly decided it was time they really *must* get up, shower, and have breakfast. Marc-Antoine called his secretary to say a family emergency meant he wouldn't be in today, so there was no need for them to rush. They felt too lazy to go to the *boulangerie*, so Emma said they could grill the remains of yesterday's bread and have it as toast, with butter and jam, but Marc-Antoine said he'd make crepes. And to her delight that's what he did, from scratch, cracking eggs, whipping up the batter, letting it rest while they had their first cup of coffee, then tipping it into the pan and tossing the crepes with practised ease while she laughed and told him that he was such a show-off and it was very sexy watching a man who knew how to cook. He laughed back at her, retorting that she was such a critic and if she kept looking at him like that then he'd have to let the crepes fend for themselves. It was sensual and silly, and the crepes were delicious, crisp around the edges and of a melting texture in the middle. 'I cooked quite a bit at home from the age of twelve,' Marc-Antoine explained, as they polished the crepes off in record time, 'because my mother was often unwell by then. But crepes are something Mattie taught me to make when I was seven or eight. We had such fun doing it.'

At that moment, Marc-Antoine's phone buzzed loudly. It was a call from the hospital.

Twenty-four

It was early in the morning, not long before Elise left to go back to London, when Charlotte received a call from Gilles Auvert.

'Did you hear your interview yesterday, Charlotte?' he asked.

'Yes, I did. So did my family.'

'And?'

'They loved it. It was great, Gilles. I mean, you do such a great interview.'

'Well, it's easy, when you've got a good interviewee,' he said, sounding very pleased. 'Anyway, I wanted to let you know I've already received some really nice comments about it.'

'That's great,' she began, but before she could say more, he went on, 'One of them was an email from someone who said he heard the interview, enjoyed it, but also remembered you as someone he used to know. He said he'd like to be in touch with you again and gave me his number, asking if I could pass it on.'

'Okay.' Charlotte was wary. 'What's his name?'

'Wait a moment.' She heard the rustle of paper, then the click of a mouse. 'Ah. Yes. Here's the email. Name's Lamartine. Pascal Lamartine. He said you'd know him from St Jean.'

Charlotte stiffened. '*What* did you say?'

'Lamartine, Pascal,' Auvert repeated, uncertainly, 'from St Jean, wherever that might be. Do I take it you know this person then?'

Charlotte exhaled. 'Yes. I certainly do. But we haven't been in touch for quite a while.'

'I see. So do you want to er—to have his number?'

'Yes please, if you can text it to me.'

'No problem,' he said, obviously trying to keep any hint of curiosity from his voice, but Charlotte thought there was no reason to keep at least an edited version from him, so she said, 'Pascal's an old friend from school days, and another friend has been asking after him, so it would be great to be in touch.'

'That's excellent,' he said, warmly. 'It's always good to reconnect with old friends.'

'It is indeed, Gilles. It was lovely to see you again and thank you so much for the great interview. I'm really happy with it.'

'As am I,' he said. 'Will send you that number now.'

When the text came through, Charlotte saw at once that Pascal's number wasn't a French one. She had to look up the country code to discover it was Hungary. But by now, Elise was getting ready to go, and Charlotte had no time to call Pascal, or Emma.

It was a couple of hours later that she managed to phone Emma to tell her about Pascal but the call went straight to voicemail so instead she left a brief message to say she had new information. Half an hour passed and there was still no response, so she decided to write a text to Pascal. That way she might have more to tell Emma when she eventually rang back.

Hello, Pascal, it's Charlotte Marigny. Gilles Auvert gave me your number. It's been a long time. But I'm glad you got in touch. This is my number. Speak soon? Cordially, Charlotte.

Now it was up to him.

But she felt on edge. Yesterday, after the radio segment, she'd felt happy, almost as though her troubles were over. But now . . .

Stop it, Charlotte, she told herself, sternly. *And don't just sit here brooding.* Suiting the action to the thought, she'd left the house and was walking along the riverside quays when her phone buzzed in her pocket. The call was from Pascal's number.

'Hello. Charlotte Marigny here.'

'Charlotte, it's Pascal.' The voice was instantly familiar, yet also changed, slightly, in intonation. 'It's good to hear from you.'

'You too, Pascal,' she said, and to her surprise, realised she meant it. 'So I believe you heard my interview?'

'Yes. It was great! You might find this funny, but I've really got into gardening in recent years. Just as an amateur, not professionally like you. I was so pleased to hear that you are doing so well.'

His words sounded genuine, and she was touched. 'I've been fortunate.'

'I'm sure hard work was very much involved too,' he said. 'How long have you been based in London?'

'Since I was twenty.'

'Don't you miss Paris?'

'I do. But I still go there a lot. I'm there now, as it happens.'

'Really?' His voice rose a notch. 'So am I.'

'But your number—it's Hungarian.'

'I can't be bothered changing sims for a short trip like this,' he said. 'I've come for Papa's eightieth birthday tomorrow. It's going to be a big party, my stepmother doesn't do things by halves.' Anticipating her question, he added, 'My parents divorced years ago and left the Morvan. Papa and his new wife have been living in Paris for a while. Anyway, I'd very much like to catch up in person if you have time. I'm going home Friday morning.'

'Where are you now?' she asked, making a sudden decision.

'I'm about to head to Galeries Lafayette to buy some presents to take back home. Where are *you*?'

'I'm roughly near the Place de la Concorde. It's not far to the Galeries Lafayette from here. I can meet you there if you like, in their cafeteria, in twenty minutes or so?'

'Perfect.' There was a smile in his voice. 'See you soon, Charlotte.'

Reaching the store, she took the escalator up to the cafeteria. It wasn't as busy as it would be later, for lunch. But there were a few people seated at the tables, most of whom were in couples, and two or three singles, including a man sitting alone at a table by one of the windows that had a panoramic view over the city's roofs. He had his back to her, staring out. But she was sure it was Pascal, from the set of his shoulders and the bright blond of his hair.

As if he was aware of her gaze, he turned and got up, a smile spreading over his face. 'Charlotte. It's so good to see you. You haven't changed much.'

'Pascal.' She shook his proffered hand, noticing he wore a wedding ring. 'Neither have you.' That was a polite lie, and Pascal's wry smile showed that he knew but wasn't offended.

He was tall and broad still but he had put on quite a bit of weight, his beautiful golden hair had thinned, while his face showed the telltale signs of a life lived a bit too hard. 'Sorry, I skipped breakfast, so I was hungry.' He indicated the half-eaten ham and cheese sandwich in front of him. 'But what about you? Coffee? Something to eat?'

'Coffee, yes, but I had a late breakfast, so no food. Thanks.'

'Won't be long,' he said, and was as good as his word, returning quickly with two steaming cups. Sitting down, he looked at her across the table. 'It's been a while, hasn't it?'

'It certainly has.' This could have been the lead-in she needed, but it didn't feel quite right. Instead, she asked, 'How are you, Pascal?'

'Surprisingly well. Happy.' He picked at his sandwich, sipped his coffee. 'And that's the biggest surprise of all.' The very blue eyes, which were the only thing about him that hadn't changed at all, were filled with an expression of wonder that touched her.

'I'm so glad,' she said, really meaning it. 'You have a family?'

His eyes lit up. 'I do. Two little boys, six and four. And Anna, my wonderful wife, who I don't deserve.'

She reached across the table and touched his hand lightly. 'I'm sure she would say otherwise.'

'She probably would,' he said, smiling. 'But still I have to remind myself it's happened. A family, a home—I never imagined, in the years when I hit rock bottom . . . but enough about me. What about you?'

'Three children, like you heard in the interview, but all grown up now. It's taken a bit of adjusting to, but it's a different pleasure seeing the lovely adults they've become. But I do miss that sweet small stage—like the age your children are at.' She hoped he wouldn't ask anything about her husband, because there was no way she could tell him about it, but a lie would also choke her right now.

He'd lived in Hungary for the last eleven years. He had a job in a hotel, something he'd managed to hold onto when he'd beaten the bottle—he was quite upfront about being a recovered alcoholic. He'd met his wife in Hungary, nine years ago.

Charlotte listened, thinking wryly that, as a teenager, she'd imagined Pascal to be the kind of guy who would cruise into the adult world without a care, and now she realised that she'd been quite wrong. There had been serious tensions in his family and a fragility to Pascal she hadn't seen or understood at the time.

After a while, he looked at her and said, 'Forgive me. It must be tedious listening to a virtual stranger going on about people you don't know.'

She shook her head. 'Not at all. I'm so glad things have worked out for you. And I don't feel we're strangers.' A pause. 'I remember that summer we met really well. It was a good time.'

'It was,' he said. 'At least . . .' He stopped, then went on, 'Do you still hear from Corinne?'

It was the opening she'd been hoping for. 'She moved to Australia and very recently, I learned that she'd—' She swallowed. 'She died.'

Pascal's eyes widened. 'But she was only . . .'

'Our age, I know. It was cancer. Her daughter told me,' she added.

He ran a hand through his thinning hair. 'Her daughter?'

'She contacted me. She wants to know more about her mother's life in France. Corinne didn't tell her much.'

He smiled ruefully. 'That doesn't surprise me.'

Their eyes met. 'No,' she said. 'Did you ever see Corinne again, after that summer?'

'Yes,' he said, surprising her. 'Very briefly and by chance.' He saw her expression and went on, 'It was about two years after that summer, maybe a bit longer than that. I was at university in Tours, but not doing much studying, I'd got into a bit of a scene, and well . . . Anyway, a bunch of us had gone up to Paris for the weekend, we were going from bistro to bistro and it was then that I saw them in the street.'

'Them?' Charlotte echoed.

'Corinne and this guy. I recognised her immediately—she was so striking. Once seen, never forgotten.' He gave another wry smile. 'But I *had* forgotten her, or more accurately, put her at the back of my mind, because I knew I'd behaved badly towards her.' He rubbed at his face.

'Did you speak to her?' Charlotte prompted.

'Yes. I called out and she turned around and saw me. She didn't look pleased, but she didn't walk away either. I went up to them, and it was only when I saw them up close that I recognised *him*.' He looked up at her. 'You remember my friend Eric, who hung out with us sometimes?'

Charlotte stared at him. 'She was with *Eric*?'

'Yep. He'd grown taller, broader, not weedy like before. He'd cut his long hair and it looked thicker. And his face seemed—I don't know, more defined, somehow. He wasn't a skinny kid anymore, but a man. But his eyes were the same. You know, that stare of his that made you think he saw things you didn't.'

His words suddenly conjured up a sharp picture of Eric's face in Charlotte's mind, and she nodded. 'I know what you mean. But back in that summer we met, Corinne never showed any interest in him.'

'I'd never imagined it before either,' Pascal said, with a faint smile. 'But they were definitely a couple, when I saw them. Holding hands, looking at each other a lot, clearly besotted. And thinking about it afterwards, I realised it wasn't so strange. They were both intense, unusual people.'

'So what happened then?' she asked.

'We chatted for a few moments. Apparently they'd met up again in Normandy, where they'd both gone, separately, for some kind of seasonal job earlier that year. They asked about what I was doing, too. Our conversation didn't last long, though, just a couple of minutes, it was all a bit awkward and my friends were getting impatient, so we said goodbye and went our separate ways.'

'Did you ever see or hear from either of them again?' Charlotte asked.

He shook his head. 'But a few months after that my mother told me that Eric's father had been sent to prison for a long stretch, for fraud and extortion.' He saw her expression. 'Old man Dubois was a dodgy character, always into schemes. But this was a particularly nasty one, conning vulnerable old ladies. People were ready to lynch him. You can imagine what it must have done to his family. Especially his wife, who was, I believe, rather fragile. Eric was very protective of her.'

'Do you know what happened to them after Dubois was arrested?'

'They left the Morvan because the case had been national news and they'd been harassed. But that's all I know. I never saw or heard from Eric again . . . Or Corinne, for that matter.'

Eric must have taken that happy, laughing photo of Corinne in the meadow, Charlotte thought, trying to process everything she'd heard. Maybe in Normandy, where Pascal had said they'd met again. Or maybe in the Morvan, later. But what had happened after Eric's father went to prison and he and his mother left the area? Had the couple continued seeing each other, or had it all gone to pieces? The answer to that might determine if Eric was Emma's father. But if he was, why had Corinne taken off to Australia, alone?

'Corinne's daughter will want to know what you've told me,' she said. 'Is it all right if I tell her?'

'Of course. But maybe she should remember her mother as she was with her. If those are good memories.'

'I'm pretty sure they are,' said Charlotte. She got up. 'I've got to go now, Pascal. Sorry for taking up so much of your time, but it has been really good to see you.'

He got up to farewell her. 'You too, Charlotte. And I hope—' He took his wallet out and extracted a card which he handed to her. 'You have my number, but here's my address. Maybe one day you might consider a Hungarian holiday?'

'Maybe I might,' she said, smiling, extracting her own card from her wallet and handing it to him. 'Or you could visit us in London. In any case, let's stay in touch.'

'Absolutely. And give Corinne's daughter my best wishes,' he said, smiling.

As Charlotte walked away, her mind was whirling with what Pascal had revealed. Corinne and Eric! The idea took some getting used to. She tried to remember instances when the pair of them had interacted that long-ago summer they were all together, but nothing really came to mind that might explain the later attraction between them. Still, there it was. Two years or more after that Morvan summer, they had definitely been a couple . . .

She *had* to speak to Emma, as soon as possible. In person.

Twenty-five

Arielle stood under the shower, trying to wake herself up properly. She hadn't slept at all well, taking ages to drop off with her mind buzzing so much with everything that had been going on, and sleeping only fitfully afterwards. What on earth had possessed her to suggest last night that they get to the Luxembourg early, when the gates opened at 7.30? She could have done with a much slower start. But there was no way now she could change the schedule. The twins were too excited, chattering about the day's activities, and Pauline, bright-eyed and brisk, had already packed everything they needed.

It wasn't only thoughts of the Grandiers and Vella that had kept her awake last night. She had to give Daniel an answer about the trip to the bee farm. She'd wanted so much to say yes when he'd asked her. But something had held her back. Was it really because of the children? Or because she was afraid of taking the next step with him? She'd never been able to think of sex as something simple, something that you could take lightly and class with the ordinary things of life, and now it was even more so . . .

She'd come out of the shower and was getting dressed when her phone pinged. Glancing at the screen, she stiffened. It was a text from Thierry Grandier. Heart thumping, she fumbled the message open and stared at the words. *In Ludo's memory, please consider.*

No greeting, no sign-off, just those enigmatic words. She couldn't decide if they were conciliatory, menacing, or plain sad. He knew, of course, that it was Ludo's birthday, and that they'd be marking it with a special outing. The Grandiers had never come with them; in their view, the decent place to remember someone was by their graveside. Virginie especially had made no secret of the fact that she thought the memorial outings were strange. Grotesque, actually, she'd called it.

But they'd never contacted her before, on one of those days. And she knew what Pauline would say, if she told her—that it was meant as a threat and that she must on no account reply; that she should take up Daniel's offer and have him call his lawyer mother. Perhaps she should. But she didn't know what to think. She looked down at the message, rereading it carefully, but still came to no conclusion. Maybe she would, later . . . In the meantime, she'd keep quiet about it.

'Maman!' The twins were banging on the door. 'Breakfast is ready! We have to go soon!'

'Coming!' she called, putting away the phone and hurrying out of the room.

Forty minutes later, the four of them were standing at the gilded gates of the Luxembourg. There was already a small group of people waiting, but as the gates opened, the twins were the first to race in. They were on a mission: spotting as many statues as they could in five minutes. As the Luxembourg is home to more than a hundred statues, there were plenty around to choose from!

'Remember the rules. No running, only walking,' said Arielle, mock-sternly.

'And no cheating,' said Pauline, in the same fake-grave tone. 'No counting statues twice!'

Arielle and Pauline set the timers on their phones, the two teams—Arielle with Alice, Pauline with Louis—took off in opposite directions, and the race was on.

Alice had just counted the first four statues in their tally when Arielle's phone rang. *Thierry*, she thought, at once, her heart clenching. The text hadn't been enough, now he was calling. She took her phone out and checked it. The number pulsating wasn't Thierry's. It was Romaine. She frowned. Because a clashing commitment meant Coralie couldn't cover Arielle's shift today, Monsieur Renan asked Romaine to step in, and she'd agreed. They both knew how much these annual outings meant to Arielle and her family. So why was Romaine calling? Surely she hadn't changed her mind . . .

'Maman, they're going to beat us if we don't hurry!' Alice's reproachful voice called her back to the task at hand. Shoving the phone back in her pocket, she smiled and said, 'Sorry. Let's go!'

Minutes later, the timer announced the end of the race, and they hurried back to the start, where Pauline and Louis were waiting for them. 'We found ten statues!' Alice announced, proudly. 'Well, we found eleven, so we won!' Louis retorted, and Alice instantly said, 'That's not fair!'

'It is so,' said Louis. 'We got one more than you!'

'We would have got more than you,' Alice shouted, 'only Maman had to stop!' And she glared at her mother, who snapped, 'That's enough, Alice! Someone's got to win and it doesn't always have to be you.'

Pauline raised an eyebrow. Normally it was her who said tough things like that. 'Never mind,' she soothed, as the little girl's lower lip trembled, 'both you and Louis did very well. Now, how about we go and have our second breakfast, and you two can tell Maman and me which were your favourite statues.'

'Oh yes, let's do that,' said Arielle, ashamed of her outburst. It was the second time in as many days that she had lashed out at those close to her. 'Alice found so many interesting statues, didn't you, darling?' she went on, putting a gentle hand on her shoulder. The child didn't answer, but at least she didn't flinch.

They made their way to a patch of grass, sat down, and spread out their feast—fresh brioche and *pain au chocolat* from the local *boulangerie*, and hot chocolate and coffee from thermoses. With the help of the double chocolate hit, Alice recovered very quickly, and she was soon chatting away about her favourite statues, while Louis, still glowing from his unexpected win, but thoughtfully not rubbing it in, was just as talkative. But Arielle still felt bad, and the coffee and brioche didn't give her the same pleasure as usual.

They had finished when Arielle's phone buzzed once more. She glanced at the screen. 'Sorry,' she said, 'but I'm going to have to take this. It's Romaine, and she's already rung once.'

'Dear God, can't the woman do one shift without bothering you on your day off?' Pauline grumbled. Arielle shrugged, walked a short distance away, and swiped up to reply. 'Hello, Romaine. What's up?'

As she listened to the panicky blurting on the other end, her stomach dropped. 'He's lying,' she said, tightly, when Romaine drew to a halt, 'but don't worry, give me fifteen minutes and I'll be there, okay?'

Going back to Pauline, she said, in an undertone, 'I'm going to have to go to the stand for a little while, there's a bit of a situation,' and quickly recounted what Romaine had told her. Pauline's eyes widened, but all she said was, 'Go, don't worry about us, we'll be fine, and we'll see you when you get back.'

Hurrying out of the park towards the Metro station, Arielle called Daniel. 'Listen, I know it's a lot to ask, but this is what's happened . . .' She filled him in rapidly, and after she'd finished, he simply said, 'I'm on my way.'

She reached the flower market in the promised fifteen minutes. It was just before opening time. Arielle approached Monsieur Renan's stand from the far end of the pavilion, so she'd not have to run the gauntlet past Vella's stand, where a small knot of people had gathered.

Romaine was hovering anxiously at the back of the stand, out of sight behind some tall plants, but when she saw Arielle, her face brightened. 'Thank God you're here. He says he's going to call the police. Oh my God, when Papa finds out . . .' She'd told Arielle that she hadn't said anything to her father yet, not wanting to worry him. Arielle thought Monsieur Renan would have coped better than his daughter, but she didn't say that.

'It's okay,' she soothed. 'We'll sort this out in no time. Besides, I'm sure the police have better things to do than investigate a few broken pots and a rude note. Now tell me again exactly what happened.'

'I got here early, at about quarter past seven,' Romaine said, 'because I was worried that I wouldn't be able to get everything ready before opening time, despite those very helpful instructions you left. There was hardly anyone else here when I arrived and I had been here about twenty minutes when Monsieur Vella arrived, opened up his shutters and yelled very loudly. Like others, I ran over to see what had happened and that's when we saw that his stand had been vandalised, there were broken pots and dirt and crushed plants everywhere. And on top of the mess was a sheet of paper, with words computer-printed in bold: **Casse-toi, con.**' Break yourself, dickhead, literally; idiomatically, Piss off, dickhead.

How many times have I longed to say that to him, Arielle thought, *and I'm not the only one.* Vella was not a popular man. Aloud, she said, 'And that's when he accused me and Daniel of doing it?'

Romaine nodded, miserably. 'He was very angry, wanted to know where you were, and when I said you had the day off, he said,

How very convenient! Then he claimed that you'd had a heated argument with him yesterday, that you threatened him and that it wasn't the first time you'd threatened people, there was some situation the other day with some other people, Daniel was involved in that too, Vella seems to think it's part of a pattern of aggression . . .'

Fury rose in Arielle. He had not only accused her, but he was also dragging Daniel into it, *and* trying to make Romaine suspect there was something to what he'd said. 'He's twisted everything, Romaine,' she snapped. 'I'm going to talk to that bastard, right now.'

'But he'll only say that you are trying to intimidate him again . . .'

Arielle didn't answer. Turning on her heel, she headed to Vella's stand. The people had dispersed now, apart from a man Arielle knew vaguely, a fellow market trader called Olivier, who was trying to coax Vella up from the chair where he sat slumped, looking the very picture of misery, Arielle thought, sarcastically.

When Olivier saw her, he shook his head, slightly, in a gesture that cheered Arielle, for though it was advising her to keep away, there was no condemnation in his eyes. He was a decent man, she knew that. Then Vella looked up and saw her and immediately jumped up, shrieking, 'Keep her away from me!' And he actually stood behind Olivier's broad back, as if seeking protection. Well, overacting was clearly one of his skills.

It didn't play well with Olivier, who looked uncomfortable. 'For God's sake, Jacques,' he said, 'she's half your size. What do you think she's going to do to you?'

'You saw what she did!' Vella wailed, throwing his arms around in a dramatic gesture. 'Hundreds of euros worth of damage! And what about the note? It's not simply telling me to get lost, I think it's threatening to break my limbs, just like the pots!'

The renewed commotion was attracting attention, not only from other market traders now, but from the first customers of the day, who had started trickling in. Arielle knew that although most of the other stallholders would be on her side, a few would only see the possible damage to their trade. And with the ubiquity of mobile phones, the fracas could quickly find its way onto social media via tourists' posts, attracting scandal and speculation as well as the ire of market authorities. She had to stop this in its tracks, right now. Forcing herself to speak calmly, she said, 'May I enquire why you think it was me, Monsieur Vella?'

'Who else could it be?' he sneered.

'How could I have got into your stand, Monsieur Vella, when it was locked?'

'Well—you see, I was so shaken yesterday after she threatened me—' and he looked piteously at Olivier—'that I forgot to lock up, and that's how she managed to . . .'

Arielle remembered how she'd noticed Vella's stand had closed earlier than usual yesterday afternoon. She had a sudden vision of him crouching in his stand, behind the closed shutters, waiting till everyone had gone and he could go about the business of breaking pots and leaving stupid notes. It seemed utterly crazy. But the alternative, that he really had left his stand unlocked and an opportunistic vandal had taken the chance to wreak havoc, with a taunting note as a bonus, was, to say the least, very unlikely. 'What do the cameras show?' she asked Olivier.

He shrugged. 'Jacques hasn't had time to ask.'

'He does now,' said Daniel, appearing at that moment, followed by Romaine. 'Monsieur Vella, shall we accompany you and this other gentleman to the market office and ask to see the footage from last night? I am sure that in the circumstances they would agree.' His tone was polite but steely, and Vella blinked.

'I know what I know,' he snapped, 'I don't need cameras to prove it. She threatened me and you know it.' He gave Daniel a hard stare. 'And if it wasn't her, it was you.'

'Jacques,' Olivier protested, 'come on, that's enough. You know vandals have caused problems here before and you certainly can't accuse people, let alone fellow traders, without proof. What this gentleman says is perfectly reasonable. Let's go together to check the cameras . . .'

'Oh, *casse-toi, pauvre con*,' spat Vella.

The moment he said it, he must have realised what he'd done, but too late. Olivier gave him a look of utter contempt, then turned to Arielle, saying, 'I'll leave him to you. But no one believes him. We all know what he's like.' And he walked away.

Vella stared defiantly at Arielle and Daniel. 'Whatever that fool says, I know what I know, and I'm going to report you for this.'

'That's your choice, Monsieur Vella,' said Arielle, grimly, 'but I really wouldn't advise it.'

'Legal action is very expensive,' Daniel chimed in, 'and I think there will be no shortage of witnesses to your unacceptable behaviour not only recently but over time.'

'Including my father and myself,' Romaine added, unexpectedly. 'And you know how well regarded my father is here, Monsieur Vella.'

'He's an old has-been,' growled Vella, 'who cares what he says?'

'I think you'll find the Mairie de Paris cares, Monsieur Vella,' she retorted, head high, eyes cold as ice. 'And that's where I work. Reviewing market trading permits, as it happens.'

Arielle smiled inwardly. Romaine really *was* her father's daughter!

Vella had gone chalky white. 'I'm sorry, Madame Vinier, I didn't mean to—you understand—it's simply that I've been shaken by—'

'Yes,' said Romaine, still in that coldly confident tone, 'I do understand. And I'm sure this has all been a misunderstanding. If you apologise for your intemperate accusations at a time of stress, perhaps Madame Lunel and Monsieur Auban will accept that and it will go no further.'

Vella glanced at them. In a choked voice, he said, 'I was only—it was just such a shock—I am sure you can understand—but if I have caused offence, I regret it.'

Arielle felt like throwing the so-called apology back in his lying face, but galling as it was, she knew she had to accept it. Insisting on an investigation would take time and cause too much trouble. Besides, gossip about what had happened would fly around the market like lightning and Vella's reputation, such as it was, would be shot for good. It wouldn't merely be contempt he'd meet with; it would be ridicule, and for a man like him, that was worse. To cap it all off he could hardly dare to claim for the damage on his insurance or risk facing questions about the supposed vandals. So he'd have to cover the costs himself.

Yes, he'd be punished enough, she decided. And fittingly, it would be by his own stupidly malicious hand.

'Very well, Monsieur Vella,' she said, coolly, 'we will speak no more of it.'

'Indeed,' Daniel agreed, adding silkily, 'for I am sure you deeply regret your actions.'

You could almost hear Vella grinding his teeth as he muttered something in agreement. And so they left him there, looking at the mess he'd have to clear up on his own now, for no one would be willing to help him.

Twenty-six

All the way to the hospital, Emma had hardly dared believe that the news was as good as the doctor had told them. Rationally, she knew they wouldn't say Mattie was okay if she wasn't. But a nagging worry persisted in her, so seeing a smiling Mattie sitting up in bed, looking *so* much better, with just one canula attached to her, had been a wonderful relief. After kissing her and depositing their gifts—a box of handmade chocolates and a bag of fresh cherries—on the bedside table, Emma asked if there was any more news from the doctor.

Mattie shrugged, 'The tests didn't show anything sinister, but I'm going to need a pacemaker before they let me leave. Such a nuisance!'

'Now then, Mattie, you know your doctor's been advising that for a while,' Marc-Antoine said smiling.

'Yes, I know. I'm a stubborn old woman,' she said, cheerfully, 'but I suppose this time I'd better listen.'

She looked from one to the other with a mischievous smile and said, 'And now, my dears, I think you may have news for *me*.'

'Don't be coy, dearest Mattie,' Marc-Antoine said, putting an arm around a blushing Emma. 'You've known it from the moment we walked in.'

'Well, it's written all over your lovely faces,' said Mattie, biting into a chocolate. 'I'm simply a bit surprised it took you that long to fall into each other's arms.'

'Mattie!' they said, in slightly shocked unison, and she laughed.

'I'm not so old that I can't see when two people have that spark between them, even if they won't admit it at first.' Her tone changed, and she said, with a smile that lit up her whole face, 'I can't even begin to describe how happy this makes me.'

They stayed by her side for over an hour, talking, eating cherries and chocolates, and posing for Mattie, who had declared she wanted to draw them, to mark the occasion. So they sat together on one of the armchairs, a little shy at first, but soon at ease under the gentle patter that Mattie kept up throughout, and which Emma had come to realise was her way of making sure her subjects didn't feel awkward. When a nurse appeared and exclaimed, with a disapproving glance at the sketchbook, and a frown at Emma and Marc-Antoine, that Madame Lenoir really shouldn't tire herself, Mattie said sweetly, 'This is the best rest I could have because nothing soothes me like drawing.'

The nurse harrumphed, but after checking Mattie's blood pressure and pulse, she pronounced them satisfactory. 'You will still have to rest in the usual way, Madame Lenoir,' she said tartly, as she turned to go out. 'We want you to be in good shape tomorrow for the pacemaker fitting, don't forget.'

After a while, Mattie did start to look tired, and Emma and Marc-Antoine left, promising to come back the next day. Picking up a Moroccan takeaway for lunch, they went straight back to Mattie's house.

Back home they only managed to close the front door behind them and stumble to the living room, arms around each other, kissing passionately, before falling onto the sofa, hands all over one another, so frantic to touch that next thing they knew, they were actually falling off the sofa and onto the floor, laughing. Marc-Antoine sat up then, his back against the sofa, and pulled her onto his lap. Emma leaned into him, breathing hard, wrapping her legs around him as he moved into her, and it was so fast and hot that very soon she was crying out and he was too. Afterwards, Emma nestled in his arms, as he said, a smile in his voice, 'Just as well these old walls are thick, hey?'

'Or we'd scandalise the neighbours,' she said.

'This is France,' he replied. 'They'd be more likely to cheer us on. Or be jealous.'

'Well, those stickybeaks do have something to cheer and be jealous about, *cher Monsieur Hugo*.'

He kissed her, encircling her again in his arms. 'I do so agree, dear Ms Taylor.'

After a time, they got up, recovered their discarded clothes, straightened the sofa and made their way to the kitchen where Marc-Antoine heated up the takeaway lamb tagine and set out plates and cutlery while Emma poured them both tall glasses of Breton cider from a bottle she'd found in the fridge. They toasted each other and Mattie, and Emma thought she had never been so happy in her whole life. She couldn't stop smiling, looking at him, so beautiful, so outrageously desirable. He saw her expression and said, with a catch in his voice, 'Hey, we really do need to eat, so stop looking at me like that!'

'Like how exactly?' she replied teasingly, and he laughed and caught her up into his arms, and they kissed so deeply that she felt almost dizzy with it.

'Now sit,' he said, disengaging himself with an obvious effort, 'let's have this tagine, and then . . .'

'And then what?' she breathed, watching his every move as he took the tagine off the stove and dished up the meal.

He kissed her playfully on the top of her head before sitting down, 'Then we'll see, won't we?'

The tagine was as delicious as it smelled, and Emma wolfed down a large plateful, washed down with cider. They followed that up with a couple of *cornes de gazelle*, traditional Maghreb almond paste and orange flower pastries. Emma had never had them before, but Marc-Antoine's mother had been very fond of them, he said, and he'd tried to learn how to make them. 'But I wasn't very successful.' He smiled. 'But Maman still said mine were the best she'd ever tasted. Not that I really believed her. Mothers tend to praise their children, don't they?'

'*My* mother would probably have said I needed to try harder,' Emma said. 'She could be tough sometimes, and didn't always find it easy to give praise, but when she did, you knew she really meant it. And that made it all the more precious.' Her eyes prickled with sudden tears. She tried to blink them back. 'Sorry. I didn't mean to . . .'

'Don't be sorry,' he said, taking her hand across the table. 'I still miss my mother, and she's been gone for two and a half years. But for you, it's still so very raw.'

She nodded, unable to speak for a moment. He had spoken with such understanding and empathy, and that almost made the tears fall. Finally, she managed to say, in a rush, 'My mother kept so much back from me, Marc-Antoine. Sometimes, I feel angry about it; sometimes I feel sad. But mostly, I miss her, you know? Yes, she could be tough, but she was a lovely mother, too. And she could be so much fun! I remember her making up such good games when I was little, teaching me songs, making me costumes for the school concert, and introducing me to Tintin and Asterix in French. And after I left home, she was always so happy when I came back for visits . . . I loved her dearly and I know she loved me too, deeply. I just wish she'd opened up to me more about herself, about her past, before it was too late. And I really hoped I would begin to understand her, coming here. But—'

'But it hasn't happened yet,' he said, his hand warm on hers, his eyes never leaving her face.

'Seeing Mattie's face light up when we walked into that ward made me think how Maman could have made her parents happy, too, like she made Paddy and me. But she chose not to.'

'I'm not sure if she *chose* it,' he replied. 'Maybe she didn't know how to make things better.'

Emma looked at him. 'That's what Paddy says. He says she just froze up. But that can be an excuse for not trying.'

'That kind of emotional paralysis can be so deep-seated that it's almost impossible for people to move beyond it,' he said gently. 'Your mother was complicated, that's very clear—but you, Paddy and Mattie all loved her, and I know Alain did too. And that, to me, means she was someone worth loving.'

Her heart swelled. 'You are so right! She absolutely was. But I wish she could have seen how much happier she might have been, if she'd trusted more.' She looked at him. 'Oh, Marc-Antoine, I hope we can always be as open with each other as we are now. I can't possibly live like my mother, with secrets and silences and frozen feelings.'

'And neither can I, darling Emma,' he whispered, picking up her hand and kissing it.

At that moment, the door buzzer sounded, making them both jump. 'Are you in, Emma?' came Charlotte's voice, over the speaker. 'I have some news and I think you are really going to want to hear it.'

Twenty-seven

When Emma opened the door, Charlotte was struck by how radiant she looked. Wondering what had happened, Charlotte kissed her on both cheeks, and followed her into the kitchen, where she was surprised to see not Mattie, but Marc-Antoine, in a rather rumpled T-shirt and jeans, setting up a tray with cups, a teapot, and some nice-looking *cornes de gazelle*. He looked up when they came in and greeted a somewhat bemused Charlotte. What was going on?

Emma must have seen her expression, because she said, 'We've just been to see Mattie in the hospital.' And she explained, rapidly.

'Oh my goodness,' Charlotte said, eyes widening. 'What a shock that must have been! I'm so glad she's all right. Please give her my best.' When Emma nodded, Charlotte went on, 'I tried to call you earlier, but you must have been at the hospital, I suppose.'

'I'm afraid I forgot my phone and left it here,' Emma said, and Charlotte saw the look that passed between her and Marc-Antoine. She knew at once that something had changed between these two. You could almost *see* it—a supercharged atmosphere of intimacy. A twist of pain shot through her as she thought that once, she and Tom had looked at each other like that.

'Shall we head out into the garden?' Emma said. 'It's such a lovely afternoon.' Charlotte nodded, and Emma led the way into the garden, picking up an old blanket from a laundry shelf as she went.

As Emma spread it out on the grass, Charlotte glanced around, taking in the changes. Her first impression was of the light. Before, it had been buried deep within the mass of rampant weeds, like a treasure held so tightly that you didn't even know it was there. Now there was light everywhere, picking out the re-emerging shapes and patterns of twigs and branches and showcasing a palette of soft new colour: pale purple flowers on the old wisteria, yellow rose buds beginning to unfurl on a bush, and a panoply of all shades of greens on leaves and stems and the fuzz of new grass starting to spread on bare patches of earth. She could hear the melodious song of a blackbird in one of the trees and smell the scent of newly turned over soil, the fragrance of wisteria blossom, and faintly, the emerging perfume of the rosebuds. The new life of this garden had really begun and that made Charlotte's heart lift. She always loved seeing the rebirth of a neglected garden.

'You've done a really good job,' she said.

Emma beamed. 'Thank you. I know there's still a lot to do, but...'

'There's always a lot to do,' Charlotte smiled back. 'But it's a great start.'

At that moment, Marc-Antoine came into the garden with the laden tray. As they sat down and he began pouring out the tea, Charlotte said, 'So, my news: I've just come from a meeting with Pascal.'

'Oh my God!' Emma's hand flew to her mouth. 'How did that happen? What did he say? Did he and Mum . . . Sorry—I don't mean to babble but I'm a bit overwhelmed—' She broke off, and Marc-Antoine took her hand, a small but telling gesture of tenderness that brought a lump to Charlotte's throat.

Quickly, she explained what had happened. When she'd finished, there was a pause before Emma said, blankly, 'It was *Eric* with her? But I thought from what you said before that they barely knew each other.'

'That was probably true that summer. But, as Pascal said, they met again in Normandy and that's when they—'

'Fell in love,' Emma cut in quietly.

Charlotte took a deep breath. 'Pascal saw them together two or maybe two and a half years after we'd all been in the Morvan. So, while it's significant, it's not absolutely conclusive as far as . . .' She broke off awkwardly.

'As far as him being my father,' Emma said. Her tone was flat.

Charlotte felt a pang for her. 'Look,' she said, 'it might not be easy to track him down, Dubois isn't exactly an uncommon surname, and we have no idea where he lives now.' Or even, she thought but didn't say, if he's still alive. 'But I can give you the contact details of someone I know who works in a private investigation agency in London. That might help speed things up.'

'I—I have to think,' Emma said. A shadow had come into her eyes. A few days ago she'd insisted that she *had* to know because she thought that's what her dying mother had wanted to tell her, but now she was clearly not sure about taking the next step.

'I understand,' Charlotte said, lightly touching Emma's hand. 'Just let me know if you want that number.'

An hour later, as she made her way back to the Metro station, Charlotte's thoughts returned to that long-ago summer in the Morvan. It had once connected the four of them—herself, Corinne, Pascal, Eric. Four very different people, four very different backgrounds, four very different fates. And now, decades later, here they were again. Corinne had gone from this life but her secrets had brought her daughter from the other side of the world, and Charlotte and Pascal plunging back into their common past. But Eric remained hazy, an enigma like Corinne, even if in a very different way.

What would I do, if I was Emma? Charlotte thought. *Would I walk away and get on with my life, or would I run towards this new knowledge, no matter where it might lead? I have no idea,* she decided, then stopped abruptly as an uncomfortable thought struck her hard. Of course she had no idea, because this was pretty much the dilemma she faced with her marriage. Go for good, or stay and fight? A dilemma she had to resolve sooner rather than later.

Twenty-eight

It was very early and Arielle was sitting up in bed, rereading the text she had just written to Thierry Grandier. *It wasn't a big house or the latest car or designer clothes that made Ludo truly happy but sharing joyful moments in places like this with us, in a city he loved. This is what I can give our children, this is how he can always be with them. In memory of Ludo, consider.* She attached a photo, of the twins sailing toy yachts yesterday across the Grand Bassin in the Luxembourg Garden, and hit send. Now the die was cast, and she'd deal with whatever came from it. For she was no longer afraid. Not of them, not of Vella, not even of her own doubts.

It had been the confrontation with Vella that had triggered her new resolve. His act of bastardry had actually been absurd self-sabotage, and now he was worse off than before. And she could see that could also be said of the Grandiers. If they'd wanted to build a closer relationship with the twins, all they had to do was speak with Arielle, discuss it like normal people. Instead, they'd gone in for all-out assault in an attempt to seize control. How could they be so deluded? They'd made things so much harder for themselves. 'In a court, you would absolutely win against them,' Daniel had told her, as he accompanied her back to the Luxembourg Garden, after they'd left a relieved Romaine back in charge of the stand. 'Just as you would against that bastard Vella, if you wanted to.'

She didn't want to take Vella to court, she just wanted him gone from her life. Daniel said he wouldn't be surprised if the man put up his stand for sale—there was a lot of feeling against him in the market now—and certainly he'd closed his stand hours early today. She didn't want to take the Grandiers to court either. But she couldn't wish them away. Despite everything, they were still the children's grandparents, and she had to give them one last chance.

Picking up her phone again, she tapped out another message. To Daniel this time.

I don't expect you to answer this as you are probably still sleeping, but I am so looking forward to this evening. That had been another result of the events at the flower market. She had known then that the time for hesitation was over.

His answer came almost immediately. *Me too. I don't know how I'll get through the next however many hours it is till we meet.*

She sent him a heart emoji and sank back on the pillow, closing her eyes, happiness filling her. She hadn't even realised she'd fallen asleep again till the children knocked on the door. As they came in,

Louis was very carefully holding a cup of coffee while Alice carried a plate with a fresh croissant on it. 'What's this?' Arielle said, sitting up and smiling at them. 'It's not Mother's Day or my birthday, is it?'

'Of course not,' said Alice, in a somewhat scornful tone.

'Tati Pauline said she wasn't sure if you'd wake up in time to have a proper breakfast, so we thought we'd help.' Louis placed the coffee on the bedside table.

Arielle picked up her phone and checked the time. It was indeed later than her usual waking-up time, and if she didn't get a move on, she'd miss her train. But she said, 'Come, sit with me while I have your delicious breakfast. You've had yours, haven't you?'

'Ages ago,' said Alice, but she looked longingly at the croissant. Arielle smiled and broke it into three pieces. She gave two to the twins, who took them with alacrity. 'Now, my darlings, you are going to be okay tonight, aren't you?' she asked, gulping down her coffee, which, fortunately, was only just warm.

'We're going to have a lot of fun,' said Louis. 'After Tati Pauline picks us up from school, she's going to take us to see the ducks in that park we go to sometimes.'

'And she's going to buy us an ice cream,' said ever-hungry Alice.

'So you must not worry about us, Maman,' Louis added seriously.

Arielle hugged them both tightly. 'I'm not worried, sweetheart,' she said. 'I know you will have the loveliest time with Tati Pauline. You can tell me all about it tomorrow, and I'll tell you all about the bee farm where I'm going.'

Carrying her overnight bag, she made her train with seconds to spare and got to the stand in good time to open up. There was no sign of Vella at all, and his stand stayed closed throughout the day. Maybe Daniel's prediction would come true sooner rather than later. The morning passed quickly, with quite a crowd of tourists, and she was kept so busy she barely had time to think. Then, not long after lunch, Charlotte came by, and they had a brief chat. She seemed very interested in the bee farm and asked Arielle to send her photos, which she happily agreed to.

As the afternoon wore on and the crowds began to thin, Arielle's impatience to be gone turned into nervousness and when the time crept towards 5 pm, she was almost jittery with anticipation.

Daniel arrived as she was locking up the stand. Carrying a backpack, he was dressed in jeans and a rather unexpected flower-patterned short-sleeved shirt. He looked fresh and happy. 'Hello,' he said, smiling, 'are you ready?'

She smiled back at him, the jitters vanishing at once. 'I certainly am. Shall we go?'

Twenty-nine

*E*mma had spent a quiet but not inactive morning on her own as Marc-Antoine had had to go to his office. First she'd headed to the market to buy supplies, then worked for an hour or so in the garden, pulling up the last of the stray weeds, her mind on what Charlotte had told her. She had briefly looked up the name 'Eric Dubois' in the online telephone directory, but Charlotte was right, there were far too many of them, and she'd given up almost immediately. Was that a sign she should give up altogether? Or should she call Charlotte and ask about the PI she'd mentioned? She still had no idea, even after talking it over with Marc-Antoine, who was very supportive but couldn't decide for her. Finally, after vengefully pulling up the last weed, she'd decided she would talk to Mattie about it when she went to see her later that day.

Over a cup of coffee, she caught up with her messages, first sending an email to Paddy to tell him what had happened to Mattie, but stressing all was well. There was an email from her contact at Thornton's, telling her how much everyone had loved her new series, and a lovely email from Liz, sending her fabulous photos of their garden day together, with an unexpected PS. *I mentioned your wonderful tour to Fran Reilly, a friend of mine who's visiting us at the moment. She has an agency in Sydney specialising in bespoke tours. She was really interested, and said she'd love to have a chat about it with you. Hope you don't mind me opening my big mouth!*

Emma was delighted and wrote back to Liz thanking her.

Closing down her laptop, she made and ate a simple lunch of a half-baguette filled with the succulent Paris-style cooked ham, adding some soft lettuce and fresh tomatoes that she'd bought from the market. Then she picked the most advanced of the newly blooming yellow roses from the garden and set off for the hospital.

Mattie's pacemaker was to be implanted at 3 pm, but Marc-Antoine couldn't be at the hospital before 4.30. The procedure was just an hour under local anaesthetic, but Emma wanted to be with her grandmother beforehand.

She found Mattie sitting up watching TV, but she turned it off as soon as Emma came in. 'Will you look at that,' she said wonderingly, her eyes fastening on the rose. 'Is that beauty from our garden, by any chance?'

Warmed by the simple words 'our garden', Emma nodded and handed over the rose. Mattie held the golden flower to her nose and sniffed deeply, her eyes misty. 'My darling, you couldn't have brought me a better gift!'

Emma filled a glass with water to put the rose in. 'Marc-Antoine can't come until after the operation's over, but I'm staying here till you're out of surgery. And no arguing,' she said, seeing her grandmother's expression. 'There's nothing else I'd rather do.'

Mattie smiled. 'You win. Now, why don't you tell me what you've been up to since yesterday, you and Marc-Antoine.'

Emma felt heat rising up her neck at the mischievous glint in her grandmother's eyes but answered steadily enough. 'This morning I went to the market—everyone there said to give you their best wishes—and then I worked in the garden.' She told Mattie about Liz's email and showed her the photos from the tour. Mattie agreed the pictures were great. Then she added, 'But I fancy you are turning around the pot, as my mother used to say. What is it that you *really* want to talk to me about, my little Emma?'

Emma took a deep breath. 'Charlotte came to see us. She'd been talking to Pascal.' She told Mattie what Charlotte had reported, and Mattie listened in silence. When Emma drew to a halt, Mattie asked, 'What are you going to do, my darling?'

'I don't know.'

Mattie took her hand. 'If you don't do anything, it won't go away. You won't be rid of it, even if's just a nagging feeling of *what if*. But if you decide to look further and you do find him, what he tells you may prove he can't be your father, and then maybe you can put it completely from your mind. And if it becomes clear that he *is* your father, then you will need to decide if you want to take that final step and tell him. Because I am sure he has no idea you exist.'

'I know,' Emma cried, 'it's hard. Whichever way I turn, there are difficult things that I'm not sure I want to face.'

'But deep inside,' Mattie said, 'you know what you really want, what you need to do, don't you?'

Their eyes met. Emma said, slowly at first, then in a rush, 'That photo of Maman . . . I am sure that she had it out because he was the one who took it, and she was going to tell me about it. And I feel there was so much love expressed in that picture, so much happiness . . . And so I want to understand why that wasn't enough, why my mother went alone to Australia.' She choked a little, before adding, 'She loved Paddy, she loved me, she loved her life in Australia, she never showed any sign of regret.'

'And yet she kept the photo,' Mattie finished.

Emma nodded. 'So you think I should try to find him?'

'I do.'

Thirty

Charlotte had been struggling to write an article that a garden design magazine had asked her to contribute. She usually refused such requests because she wasn't a natural writer. Words that flowed naturally from her lips seemed to stiffen up on the page. But this issue of the magazine was a tribute to one of her mentors and she really wanted to do it. She'd written draft after draft and still it wasn't right, so she'd taken herself for a long walk, ending up at the flower market.

She chatted for a while with Arielle about the bee farm in the Chevreuse Valley, and after she left the market, it occurred to her that what the other woman had said, about how bees were perceived in the Middle Ages, could be something she could adapt for the beginning of her magazine piece. She could say that the nectar of flowers, carried back to the hive to transform into honey, could be likened to the wisdom of mentors. You needed the right flowers for the bees to gather nectar, or your honey wouldn't taste right, just as you needed the right mentors to gather wisdom from if you were to transform their insights into something new. It sounded like a good metaphor to her, and she had pulled out her phone to make a note when it buzzed with an incoming call. It was Emma, asking for the contact details of the detective agency that Charlotte had mentioned. Now all they had to do was wait.

She was back at Juliette's and about to start work again on the article when her phone rang once more. Elise, this time.

'Marm—' Her daughter sounded agitated. 'Have you heard from Dad?'

Charlotte's stomach dropped. 'No. Why?'

'I—oh bugger,' Elise's voice was wobbling, as if she was close to tears. 'I didn't think. I was so angry!'

Charlotte felt a wave of cold engulf her. With an effort, she said, 'It's all right, sweetheart. Calm down. Tell me what happened.'

'I went round to see Dad yesterday evening,' Elise said shakily. 'I'd been thinking about how unhappy you've been, how you've had to put up with so much shit, how Dad's been so bloody selfish and unfair, shutting us all out, not letting anyone help him, and I—well, I guess it got to me. *Somebody* had to make him see sense, to make him realise what he was doing, and it might as well be me.'

Charlotte heard her swallow. Of all the children, Elise had been the closest to Tom, always able to elicit a smile from him, even when he was cranky. 'So I went round there,' Elise continued. 'He didn't look great, and I almost relented, but then he . . .' She broke off, and Charlotte suppressed an urge to shout, *What happened?*

'I told him I'd been to Paris to see you,' Elise said, 'and that I was worried about you.'

'Oh, Elise.'

'He just looked at me, nodded, then started asking me how I was doing at uni. I lost it then, I'm afraid. I told him everything I felt about how he was behaving, and he, well—' She swallowed again. 'He stood there and said nothing. I couldn't bear it, so I left.'

Charlotte couldn't bring herself to speak because the scene Elise had described was all too vivid in her mind. Then she said, 'I'm so sorry you had to go through that on my account, but thank you,' her voice cracked, 'for trying.'

'That isn't all.' Elise took a deep breath. 'This morning, I woke up and I kept thinking of the look on his face as I was ranting away at him. I tried to call but the phone went straight to voicemail. I called him at work, but they said he hadn't come in. I went round to the house just now, but he didn't answer my knock, and I was worried, so I used my key and went in and I saw . . .'

Charlotte felt as though she could scarcely breathe, her mind filling with awful images. 'What did you see?' she cried.

'His laptop was on the kitchen bench. When I popped it open the screen sprang to life.' Her voice changed tone. 'He'd been looking at Eurostar timetables. And his passport's missing—I saw that when I looked in the drawer he usually keeps it in. I'm afraid he's probably heading to Paris.'

The relief that he was okay hit Charlotte at the same time as a new anxiety flooded over her. If Tom was heading here, then there was no time left. She had to decide what it was she really wanted. *But I'm not ready*, she thought, wildly. *Not yet!*

'Marm? Are you still there?' The stress was clear in Elise's voice.

'It's okay, darling,' she said as steadily as she could. 'It's probably a good thing he's coming. Try not to worry. Everything will be all right.'

After Elise had rung off, Charlotte sat staring into space, heart thumping, thoughts whirling wildly. Part of her wanted to run away at once and hole up in a hotel where Tom wouldn't find her so the showdown would be staved off once more. But another part knew she could no longer avoid it. Then a thought struck her. Was he *really* coming? He might have bottled it at the last minute.

She brought up his number on her phone, her finger hovering over the call symbol, then retreating. She couldn't speak to him. Not on the phone. Instead, she tapped out a terse text. *Where are you?*

She didn't really expect an answer. And none came. She sent another message. *I might not be here when you arrive.*

A beat of time, then a reply. Only one word. *Please.*

She stared at it for a long moment, her eyes smarting, her chest constricting with such a painful mix of emotions that she felt like she could barely breathe. Then she tapped out a final text. Just one word, too. *Okay.*

Thirty-one

In common with many other Parisians, neither Daniel nor Arielle owned a car. It wasn't a problem as you couldn't drive into much of central Paris anyway, and the public transport was excellent. But outside of Paris it was a different story and there were lots of places you couldn't get to without a car. The bee farm was one of them.

After work, they'd taken a train to a station on the outskirts of Paris where Daniel had arranged for a hire car. Now, as they left the last reminders of the city behind, driving deeper into the countryside, it felt to Arielle as though they were entering another world. The Chevreuse Valley might be close to Paris but it was encompassed by a large national park that had helped protect it from the encroachment of modern suburbia.

Unlike Daniel, Arielle had never been to the region before and was absolutely enchanted as they left the main road and drove slowly along green lanes, past tranquil meadows where cows grazed, detouring to look at charming villages that time appeared to have forgotten, and seeing the occasional castle appear on the brow of a hill. She couldn't stop exclaiming about it all, snapping photos through the open window. Daniel smiled at her enthusiasm. 'It looks so quiet now,' he said, 'but back in the Middle Ages, it would have hummed and bustled with people.' He gestured towards a field they were passing, where a tractor was working. 'Today you need hardly any people to work the land, but back then pretty much everyone depended on it. It's fertile ground and had to be protected from raiding parties. But people still found the time to make gardens—not only to eat out of or make medicine from, but also for the sheer pleasure of it.'

Arielle could vividly imagine it: men and women working in the field, sowing, planting; travellers on horseback bringing news of distant events; the bustle of castle keeps and kitchens, the peaceful beauty of their walled gardens; the monasteries and convents where the work of prayer and devotion continued alongside the production of exquisite manuscripts, as well as liqueurs, honey and healing tonics and ointments.

She usually didn't have time to sit back like this, relaxing, and it felt like she was on holiday. Glancing at Daniel as he drove steadily, telling stories, she thought with an inward smile that he actually *looked* like he was on holiday, in that unexpected shirt. And then she thought of what it would be like tonight, when they were alone in their hotel room, and another kind of feeling took hold of her.

She had to look out of the window before she did something to distract him from the road.

They arrived at the turn to the bee farm, and bumped down a long dirt track, on either side of which was a lush meadow where about a dozen cows grazed. Daniel told her that Franck leased that part of the property to a local farmer because grazing encouraged clover to grow in the pasture, and bees loved clover flowers. He'd kept a few acres behind the house specifically for the hives and planted that with other kinds of flowers and grasses.

They arrived at the farmhouse, an attractive long low building with cream stone walls and pale blue shutters, and walked around the side to where a smaller outbuilding stood, overlooking a large sweep of lovely meadow, its rich green starred with yellow, blue and white wildflowers. At one end of the meadow were a couple of *merisiers*, or wild cherry trees, and just in front of the trees was a cluster of tall wooden beehives. In the peace and soft light of the early evening, with no sound of cars or machines, only birdsong, the faint buzzing of bees, the occasional rooster call and the lowing of cows, it felt to Arielle as if they'd stepped into one of those illuminated manuscript pages and that at any moment someone in medieval dress might appear.

But it was a short, stocky man in modern black jeans and a khaki shirt who came out of the building and approached them. Despite the flecks of premature grey at his temples, his face looked young and Arielle guessed he was in his early thirties. 'Hello, Daniel,' he said, holding out a hand. 'Sorry, I didn't hear you coming,' he added as his glance flicked over Arielle.

'We're a bit early,' Daniel said. 'This is my friend Arielle, who knows a good deal more about flowers than I do.'

'Don't you believe that,' she said to Franck as they shook hands.

He laughed. 'Clearly you are well matched as neither of you sing your own praises!' Gesturing towards the meadow he went on, 'So, what do you think?'

'It's absolutely amazing,' Daniel said. 'The meadow is glorious. And those hives look medieval but I'm sure they've been adapted for modern beekeeping.'

Franck beamed. 'The ones in the manuscripts you showed me would have been too impractical, so we worked on a different design. These are made of beech wood like back then, but all the working parts inside follow modern practice. I bought the frames from an apiary supplier, but a local guy made the hive bodies for me. He works as a guide in the national park, but he's also a brilliant woodworker. And he's married to Marie-Madeleine Perrin, you remember her?'

'Sure I do,' Daniel said, 'she owns the cows in your meadow and makes that amazing cheese you served me last time!'

Franck grinned. 'That cheese is getting so popular! There was even a Parisian cheesemonger came up to check it out recently, Max I think his name was, he's put in an order for his market stall.'

On and on he rambled, but Arielle's attention wandered to the flowers she could see in the bee meadow: she could spot cornflowers, dandelions, mignonettes, daisies and clover, among others. They were all wildflowers known to attract bees, as were the wild cherry trees and the bushes of rosemary and thyme growing close to the building. She took out her phone and snapped some photos. When Franck finally paused to draw breath, she said, 'I am sure your bees feel they are in paradise here!'

Franck looked pleased. 'I like to think so,' he said, as he led the way into the building. The first room was a small office, crammed with stuff: a desk on which reposed a closed laptop, a calculator, and an untidy pile of papers; a filing cabinet, a cork board covered in photographs, a shelf which contained a few books, as well as an unusual wooden sculpture of a dancer, which Franck said had also been made by the hive-man. Taking down a scrapbook, he began to show them photos of the farm as it came together, talking all the while.

'This is when you came here the first time, Daniel—and there we are, with my neighbours, quite a few of them came to help—and here's me and Perrin, with one of the first hives he built for me—and here's when we put them in place—and oh yes, the drama of the bee moving—' Franck went on in this vein for some time and Daniel asked a question or two when he could get a word in, while Arielle took pictures of everything to keep herself engaged.

Finally, Franck ran out of things to say and led them down to the hives, where the bees had already retired for the night. The hives were beautiful, made of pale wood decorated with an exquisitely carved tracery of bees and flowers. They looked stunning in the setting, framed under the cherry trees, in a sea of meadow grass and delicate wildflowers.

At last, Daniel managed to remind Franck that it was getting late and that they still had to check into their hotel. The beekeeper wasn't quite ready to let them go, though, and insisted on taking them back to the house for a glass of the mead that he'd made from a previous batch of honey. So it was getting close to nine o'clock by the time they managed to make their escape, clutching two jars of clover honey as a last-minute gift.

As they drove away from the farm, Arielle exploded in giggles. 'Oh my God, he is such a nice man and his place is so lovely, but I thought my ears were going to drop off!'

Daniel laughed and said he'd felt the same then he added, 'That's what too much solitude does to you, I guess. I talk too much about my own subject too.'

'You don't,' Arielle reassured him, touching his knee.

His face was alight with an expression that made her pulse beat faster, and a tingle started under her skin. But she didn't feel nervous at all.

The hotel kitchen was about to close when they finally arrived, but the cook kindly agreed to whip them up a quick chive and cheese omelette and a salad of lettuce, sorrel and mint, with a tangy vinaigrette, thick-cut slices of bread, a carafe of house white, and a bowl of deliciously sweet, juicy cherries to follow. It was exactly what they needed, and they ate it downstairs in the deserted hotel restaurant, unhurried yet full of anticipation.

After they finished they climbed the stairs to the bedrooms above, holding hands. Daniel unlocked the door and they stepped into a simple but appealing room, with a blue and yellow colour scheme, polished wooden floorboards and country-style furniture, including a wide and inviting-looking bed.

'Will this do, Arielle?' Daniel said happily. To answer, she put her arms around his neck and kissed him, long and deeply.

They took their time, undressing each other, tenderly tracing the contours of each other's bodies, looking into each other's eyes, kissing and stroking, in a beautiful slow build-up that made every cell in Arielle's body ripple with longing before they were joined at last.

Afterwards, raising herself on one elbow, she looked at Daniel as he lay there smiling up at her, and felt her heart constrict. She wanted to say something but couldn't find the words. He held out his arms to her and she slipped back into his embrace, the beat of his heart under her ear. And that's when the tears started.

At first, he was troubled, asking what was wrong, thinking maybe that she regretted this. But she smiled through her tears and kissed him, saying that nothing was wrong, she was simply weeping from sheer gratitude that they had found each other.

Thirty-two

The procedure to implant Mattie's pacemaker had gone very well, and by the time Marc-Antoine arrived at the hospital, she was back in her room, cheerfully joking with Emma about being able to run marathons in the future.

If felt like the right moment for Emma to speak about the idea for the garden tours. 'It started off as Liz's suggestion after I took her around the gardens,' she explained, 'but it's really grown on me.' She took her grandmother's hand. 'It's something we can do together, Mattie. To start out, we could have our secret garden tour, and plot out another two, each with their own unique map and theme, but with the common thread of a stop at the flower market, at Arielle's stand. And maybe,' she looked at Marc-Antoine, 'if you don't mind, we can walk the tours together first to check they work.'

'I'll be in for that, definitely, in fact I can't wait to help with your market research.' The look in his eyes made Emma catch her breath.

Turning quickly to her grandmother, Emma said, 'I know there'll be a fair bit of work to do, but what do you think, Mattie?'

Mattie's whole face was alight. 'It's a marvellous idea! But are you sure that my maps are good enough to—'

'Your maps are essential,' interrupted Emma firmly, 'the tours won't work without them.'

Mattie shook her head, her eyes sparkling. 'Then it doesn't sound like I can refuse, does it?'

They stayed with her for another hour, until the doctor came on his rounds and confirmed that Mattie could go home the next day. After the doctor left, Mattie turned to Marc-Antoine and told him that he should cancel his hotel booking and stay at the house instead. That is, she added with a smile, as long as Emma was okay with that. Emma, refusing to blush, but with her heart beating fast, said tartly that she didn't mind how long he stayed as long as he did his share of the chores. Marc-Antoine laughed and took Emma's hand, saying he didn't think he'd have any problem keeping to that, as long as she did *her* share. And Mattie shook her head, saying sadly but with a twinkle in her eye that romance really wasn't what it used to be if lovers just wanted to talk about household chores.

Back at the house, Emma and Marc-Antoine took a glass of wine and some olives out into the garden and sat on the grass in the mellow golden light of early evening, talking softly.

'How about you give me a little tour right here?' Marc-Antoine said, suddenly.

The laughter bubbled up in her. 'Why not?' So they got up and she took him around, pointing out the peony plants and the hydrangea, the bed where she'd found the pendant, and the hollow tree where Monsieur Leroux lived. What started as a bit of silly fun soon turned into something else as she began weaving stories and images of what it might become, with a wooden bench under the wisteria—she'd seen a very nice one, painted a faded blue, in the online catalogue of a local store—some dwarf fruit trees in pots along the southern wall, with tomatoes and herbs in a small bed at their feet, and a winding path leading from the back of the house.

Occasionally, Marc-Antoine made an observation, but mostly he was quiet, listening to her. When she drew to a halt, he put an arm around her. 'No wonder Liz wouldn't stop raving about your tour! You have taken this little bit of land and turned it into a whole world.'

Emma couldn't speak for a moment, her heart swelling with happiness and astonishment. Somehow the words had flowed out of her, creating a rich tapestry of stories she had never known were in her. 'It's this place,' she said. 'It has its own special magic.' She looked up at him, and in a different tone said, 'Maybe we should have a surprise ready to welcome Mattie home tomorrow. Not a party, but a homecoming. Something to do with the garden. What do you think?'

'I think that's perfect,' he said, eyes shining. 'And I suggest we start with your bench idea.'

'And maybe a small table to go with it.'

'With champagne,' he added.

'And strawberries. And the finest macarons, like those fancy ones you brought the first day we met.' Emma gave him a mischievous look.

'Sounds like a plan,' he said, drawing her to him, 'but perhaps before we start hitting the stores, there's something else we might want to do?'

'I'm sure I don't know what you are talking about, Monsieur,' Emma said, then promptly spoiled the prim and proper effect by reaching for the zipper of his jeans.

Thirty-three

Just before the light started to fade, unable to concentrate on anything and desperate to escape the urge to constantly check her phone, Charlotte had left the device on the table and gone out into Juliette's lovely garden, pacing around in an attempt to calm herself.

Like Alain's garden, but a larger version, it was a secret green world behind high walls, and felt like it was kilometres, rather than metres, away from the busy streets outside. But unlike Alain, Juliette had never done the gardening work herself. She had always employed people to keep it in perfect shape. That included a big mulberry tree, which was an absolutely superb specimen of its kind, like everything here. Strolling around, Charlotte thought about how all those years ago, Juliette had entrusted the design of the garden to her. And it had worked so well that Juliette had entered it for an award, without telling her niece. To Charlotte's complete astonishment, it had won, setting her business on the road to success. Those had been happy times, when everything seemed so new, so promising, so exciting . . .

The sudden thought came to her, then: *How long has it been since I was happy? I mean properly happy, rather than not unhappy?* And the answer came, unbidden, unwelcome even, but ringing with truth—it was before Tom went into a funk, before things changed between them. It had begun happening in subtle ways before that. Why? She wasn't sure. Maybe it was because she had achieved what she thought she wanted in her work, and now it was just a question of maintaining things rather than building them; the excitement gone along with the challenge. Or maybe it was because the hectic, heady years of building a family and raising children with Tom had gone. Or simply because two years ago she'd turned fifty and still felt unsettled about that. Or maybe it was none of those things. Or all of them. 'Because, you see,' Charlotte said, addressing the garden, 'the truth is that I haven't been wholeheartedly happy for quite a while. And I can't blame Tom for that.' With that thought, she headed back inside.

Hours passed. Still no word from Tom. The only messages were two from Elise, which she'd already answered. And one from Arielle, which she'd received a couple of hours ago but hadn't properly looked at, or replied to, as she could see it consisted mostly of pictures of the bee farm. She made herself some dinner from a tin of cassoulet she'd found in Juliette's pantry and drank several cups of coffee, determined to stay awake till Tom arrived or at least she heard something. She'd checked the Eurostar timetables and knew the last train from London would arrive at about 11.20 pm. Even allowing for delays, and even if you walked, it shouldn't take more than forty minutes to get to Juliette's house from the Gare du Nord terminus.

But at midnight there was still no sign of Tom, and no word from him either. A dozen times, she had wanted to message him and a dozen times she'd stopped herself. She could not sound as though she were pleading with him. She had to take charge. She had to be the one in control here, not him. But who was she kidding? Not even herself, she thought, morosely. She was very far from being in control of her emotions, let alone anything else.

Now, as the time ticked inexorably towards 12.30 and then 1 am, her nerves were so jangled by the coffee, a maelstrom of emotions and the long, anxious wait, that she would have grasped at anything to distract herself. And so she brought up the photos Arielle had taken. The place certainly looked pretty, with the golden-brown hives set against the cherry trees, the setting sun in the background, and the flowery meadow underfoot. She scrolled through the rest—the attractive but shabby farmhouse, two men chatting by another building: one of them a short, stocky figure who seemed to be the beekeeper, the other man, tall, angular-faced, and vaguely familiar to Charlotte. Her memory for faces was good, and in a moment it came to her—he'd been talking with Arielle that day Charlotte had first seen her at the flower market. She glanced at the final image briefly when something caught her eye. She stilled.

No. Surely it couldn't be. She zoomed in on the image, stared at it, trying to make sure. But there was no doubt at all.

She *had* to let Emma know. But it was much too late to call. And it would take too long to explain in a text. So she recorded a brief voice message and had only just sent it with the photo when the door buzzer rang, the sound startling her so much she jumped up, almost dropping the phone. Heart beating wildly, she stood frozen. *This is it. This is really it.*

The buzzer rang again. This time, a voice came through the speaker. 'Hello, Lottie.' Her familiar nickname, in Tom's familiar voice. She bit down on her lip but managed to say, 'Hi, Tom' as she pressed the button that released the door.

He looked exhausted, his sharp features drawn into deep lines, the lids of his blue-green eyes puffy, his chin and upper lip unshaven, his usually springy fair hair lying lank against his skull. He'd clearly dressed in a hurry, which gave her a shock because even lately he'd taken care to be well groomed, well dressed, as if that façade might be enough to convince everyone that everything was fine.

'I know it's late,' he said. 'I got in hours ago—but I couldn't—I was just—I was simply walking around.'

She swallowed. 'I couldn't sleep, anyway. Come to the kitchen. I'll make us some coffee.'

He followed her and, putting down his overnight bag, sat down in the chair she indicated. He glanced around. 'Where's Juliette?'

'Gallivanting around Europe with her fancy man,' she said lightly. 'I have the house to myself.' It felt surreal talking to him like this, as if they were having a normal conversation about normal things . . .

'Oh,' he said, putting his hands palms down on the table. Charlotte knew that gesture of old. He made it when he was about to say something he was nervous about but really wanted to say. He'd done it when he asked if she would go out with him; when he'd asked her to marry him; when he'd asked if she'd thought about them trying for a third child. To all those things she'd said yes; but now? What was trembling on his lips? Uneasily, she went over to the coffee machine, asking, 'Okay, so you want one?'

He nodded but didn't say anything, his hands flat on the table.

'For fuck's sake, Tom, you've come a bloody long way just to sit at that table,' she snapped, the tension finally exploding in her. 'What do you want to say?'

He looked at her, the hands twitching a little. Then he said quietly, 'I know this is probably far too late. But I'm so sorry, Lottie.'

The hollowness in his voice struck deep into her, but she could not let it show. She said, her tone quiet again, 'You are going to have to *tell* me, Tom. You know that, don't you?'

She saw his Adam's apple move up and down in his throat. He nodded and put his hands flat down on the table again. *Here it comes,* Charlotte thought, as reasons for his behaviour over the last couple of months flashed into her brain, each more heartbreaking than the next.

'I quit my job,' he said.

For a moment, she couldn't process it, could only gape at him.

'I've quit my job,' he repeated, adding, 'I called my boss from the Eurostar this afternoon.'

'This *afternoon*?' Her voice rose steeply. 'Tom, this—this shit of yours has been going on for months! So what the fuck does quitting your job *this afternoon* have to do with anything?'

He winced at her tone. *Good.*

'Everything,' he said. 'I—' Emotions ran across his face, and it made him look more like the Tom she knew. 'It's been quite a while since I've felt okay there. Much longer than months.'

'You never said,' she said, staring at him.

'How could I? I couldn't see the point of what I was doing anymore, it felt hollow, empty. But I was so embedded in the whole thing, I couldn't see a way out. And moaning about my privileged life, my brilliant career'—he gave a bitter laugh—'well, that would reveal me as a total loser in front of everyone. You, most especially, Lottie. You cope so well with everything—your work, our kids, life in general. Whereas I . . .' The words had come tumbling out, like floodwater over a dam wall, but now they ceased as abruptly as they'd started and he sat there, looking at her with such a desolate expression that it caught at her throat.

'No, Tom,' she said thickly. 'You know I'm not some kind of superwoman. You can't use that as an excuse for not telling me what you were going through. I would never have thought you a loser! You must know I would have tried to help if only you'd let me in. You have put me through absolute hell, and now you want to blame me for it? That's not fair.' Her eyes filled with tears, but she blinked them away. She wouldn't cry. Not now.

'Oh, Lottie,' he said sadly. 'I'm not blaming you. I know you tried to help but I couldn't bring myself to talk, let alone to act. And the longer it went on, the harder it became. Then, when you left, I thought we were finished. I'd driven you away and that was almost . . . a relief.' He put his head in his hands. 'I thought you'd do better without me—' He broke off and Charlotte almost jumped in to shout at him, but he lifted his head and looked into her eyes, halting her words. 'But when Elise came round and gave it to me with both barrels,' he went on, 'when she told me how unhappy you were, when she said how you'd tried so hard to soldier on, despite it all, then I saw clearly what a narcissistic self-pitying coward I was, throwing away everything that has ever meant anything to me. And for what?' His eyes were bright with unshed tears. 'For bloody stupid macho pride!'

Charlotte felt a strange sensation in her chest, as if something that had been squeezed tight was beginning to deflate. It hurt, but so had the pain that had been lodged deep inside for months. 'Oh Tom,' she said, sadly. 'We used to tell each other what we felt, even if it was hard. When did we stop?'

He looked at her, a question in his eyes. 'I don't know, Lottie. I suppose it just happened.'

She remembered her thoughts earlier, in the garden. 'It did, to both of us.'

There was a silence. Then Tom said hesitantly, 'I—really—I really don't want to lose you, Lottie, but I understand if you—if you can't forgive me for . . .'

He broke off and she touched his hand, very briefly, and the flicker of hope in his eyes wrung her heart. 'Let's not say any more right now,' she said. 'It's very late and we're both exhausted. In the morning, we can see better what things look like.' She pointed to his bag. 'Did you book into a hotel?'

He nodded. 'It's not far.'

'Forget it. Stay here tonight. In one of the spare rooms,' she added. 'You've stayed here before—I don't need to tell you where everything is.'

He nodded, the ghost of a smile on his face. 'Okay, Lottie.' And he picked up his bag and headed for the stairs.

Thirty-four

Arielle and Daniel had left the hotel early the next morning and were driving back to the station when Arielle's phone rang. Her heart jumped as she saw the name flashing up on the display, and she almost let it go to voicemail, but decided it was no good putting things off.

'Daniel,' she said, 'do you mind pulling over? I've got to take this call and I'd rather not do it while we're driving.'

He glanced at her, but didn't ask any questions, just nodded and pulled over into a layby. With an apologetic smile, she got out and walked a few steps away. 'Hello,' she said guardedly.

'I'm sorry if I've woken you,' Thierry said. His voice sounded odd, cracked, almost.

'It's okay, you haven't,' Arielle said automatically, but with sudden apprehension. 'What is it, Thierry? What's happened?'

'It's Virginie,' he said. 'She was hospitalised yesterday.'

Arielle was shocked but also wary. What was coming next? 'I'm sorry to hear that.'

'Thank you.' He was quiet for a moment, then he said, in a rush, 'Arielle, I wanted to tell you there will be no more talk of . . . you know. Your message touched me deeply and finally made me tell Virginie that enough was enough.'

She ought to be feeling relief as the import of his words sunk in, but all she felt was confusion.

As if he had read her thoughts, Thierry said, 'My wife has not coped well with our son's death, despite pretending to. These last few weeks, it all came to a head. Panic attacks, rages, unrealistic plans. It's been very difficult. And yesterday, after we had words, she collapsed.' His voice cracked again. 'I'm not telling you this as an excuse, I just wanted you to know.'

Arielle gulped as a wave of pity washed over her, and she found her voice at last. 'Thierry, I had no idea. I'm so sorry.'

'You have nothing to be sorry about.' Another pause. 'But I do. I am so very sorry for what we put you through.'

On the verge of tears, Arielle finally managed a whispered, 'Thank you.' Then she added, 'I hope she'll be okay, Thierry. Let me know, won't you?'

'I will,' he said.

It was over. It really was. There would be no more harassment. The relief was almost overwhelming, but alongside that was a deep pity. Never in a thousand years would she have picked the overbearing Virginie as someone who had such vulnerabilities. And yet, the signs had probably been there all along, if she'd cared to look. Images of Virginie's face flashed into her mind. The strange, fixed expression in her eyes that time at the flat; the way her hands shook; the hectic flush in her cheeks at the market; and the way Thierry was always trying to divert her. She'd thought it was because he was a coward. For an instant, a kind of shame filled her, that she hadn't seen the truth, but then she recovered herself. Why *should* she have known? They had never breathed a word of the pain they were feeling.

Squaring her shoulders, she took a deep breath and went back to the car. Slipping into the passenger seat, she looked at Daniel. 'There's something I need to tell you.'

It would take time, to sort out her feelings about the Grandiers. And even then it would probably always be a little awkward between her and them. But maybe it might be a *better* sort of awkward, Daniel said. He'd understood, as she'd known he would.

When they were on the train, she went out into the corridor and video-called Pauline to ask how the twins were. 'See for yourself,' said Pauline, gesturing to where Louis and Alice were buzzing around the kitchen. She managed to get a cheerful wave out of them before they disappeared, while Pauline told her they'd all had a lot of fun, but she had been absolutely shattered by the time she went to bed. 'I hope *you* weren't too tired, though,' she added, with a meaningful wink. Arielle blushed and said she certainly wasn't going to talk about that in public. 'Well, tonight, in private, then,' Pauline said, unabashed, 'and don't think you'll get out of it!'

Daniel went with her to the market stand, helped her open up, and fetched them both much-needed cups of coffee before he had to head off to work himself. So the day began, busy but not too hectic. Vella's stand was still closed and Olivier, who came over to say hello at one point, commented that he supposed the man couldn't face them all right now, after what had happened. 'Maybe a break from work will reset his brain,' he said. Arielle doubted that, but it didn't matter. Even if he came back, she wouldn't care. He couldn't affect her. Not anymore.

It was almost lunchtime when she looked up from an order of posies she was creating for a bridal party and saw Emma standing there. 'Hello,' she said brightly, 'how are you? And how's the garden?'

'It's going well,' said Emma, but her expression was distracted. 'But I've had to stop for a couple of days, because my grandmother took ill.'

'Oh, I'm sorry to hear that,' Arielle said. 'I hope she's okay.'

'Yes, but . . .' She hesitated, then blurted out, 'Arielle, there's something I need to ask you.'

Arielle's hands stilled briefly on the current posy before continuing her work. Whatever the other woman wanted to ask, from the expression on her face, it wasn't gardening advice.

'I got a voice message from Charlotte,' Emma said. 'She told me that you had sent her photos of a bee farm you visited with Daniel.'

Arielle stopped working and stared at Emma, but before she could speak, Emma went on rapidly, 'Sorry to be cryptic, but one of those photos shows a man both Charlotte and my mother knew, when they were young. Someone . . . someone I've been looking for. Charlotte said you'd know more.'

'Me?' Arielle said, completely flummoxed now. 'Why on earth would I know anything?'

For answer, Emma took out her phone and showed her a photo. It was one of Franck's scrapbook photos, showing him with the man who'd made his hives. Arielle looked up at Emma and frowned. 'If the beekeeper, Franck, met your mother, he must have been very young. A baby, even. He looks to be in his early thirties.'

'No, not him. The bearded one,' Emma said, pointing to the other man.

'That's Monsieur Perrin, he's a neighbour of Franck's.'

Emma interrupted sharply. '*Perrin*? Are you sure? Not Dubois?'

Arielle shook her head. 'Definitely Perrin.'

Emma looked crestfallen for an instant, then brightened. 'Did you meet him?'

Arielle shook her head. 'No, but Franck told us a bit about him. He's a guide in the Chevreuse national park, as well as being a woodworker. His wife is a dairy farmer, some of her cows are pastured on Franck's meadow.'

'His *wife*?' Emma repeated, her eyes wide, as if such a concept was the oddest thing in the world.

Arielle looked at her, suddenly understanding. 'This man you've been looking for—he was more than someone who knew your mother once, wasn't he?' she asked.

For a moment, it seemed as if Emma might not answer. Then she said, 'I think he might be my father.'

Thirty-five

Emma hadn't noticed Charlotte's voice message at first. Her phone had been on silent all night and because she and Marc-Antoine had got up late, unwilling to leave each other's arms, she hadn't checked her phone at all after she'd woken up. Right after Marc-Antoine had hurriedly left for the office, the delivery man had arrived, bringing the bench and table that they had ordered the day before. The bench was a simple wooden three-seater, painted in that lovely faded blue, the small round table was in the same colour, and they'd also ordered cream-coloured outdoor cushions to go on the bench. She got the man to take everything out into the garden and place it under the wisteria, then, when he'd gone, she sat on the bench and took a selfie, sending the picture to Marc-Antoine, with a caption: *I think Mattie is going to like our surprise, don't you?* She smiled as she saw his reply, *Looks like she might have to fight you for it!*

It was only then that she realised she'd missed a message. She'd seen the photo first but it had meant nothing to her until she'd listened to what Charlotte had said. *Emma, our friend Arielle from the flower market went to a bee farm in the Chevreuse yesterday, and she sent me some photos. The photo I sent you was one of them.* A pause, then, *You're not going to need the agency, Emma. We've found Eric. The man with the beard in the photo I sent you—I am certain it's him.* Another pause. *Ask Arielle, she can tell you more. And I'll speak to you when I can. Bisous.*

Stunned, Emma had looked at the photo again. It looked like it was a photo of a photo, from an album or a scrapbook, that showed two men standing by a beehive in a rather cluttered room. One of the men was older and bearded, the other younger and clean-shaven. The younger man was smiling, gesturing at the hive, but the bearded man was staring straight into the camera. The photo was in colour so you could see his close-cropped hair was mid-brown, his beard darker but with flecks of grey in it too. But it was his eyes that drew her attention. Not because of their blue colour, which was neither unusually pale nor bright, but because of the expression in them, a look Paddy called the thousand-yard stare, the kind that looked straight at you and straight through you. Emma remembered something Charlotte had said Pascal had told her: that even though Eric had changed, filled out, shot up, the expression in his eyes was the same, *as if he could see things you couldn't.*

Emma tried Charlotte's number, but it went straight to voicemail. She didn't leave a message. There was no point now, not until she'd spoken to Arielle. But she called Marc-Antoine first. After she told him, he said, 'Are you okay?'

'I think so,' Emma said uncertainly. 'A bit shocked, obviously. This man could be my father—he has the same colouring as me and he was in love with my mother, but lots of people have that colouring, and who's to know if they were together long enough to make me . . . and besides, he has a different life now so . . .'

'So it's complicated,' he finished for her.

Now, as she looked at Arielle, a thought struck her. The photo her mother had left her. Could it be . . . Bringing it up on her phone, she showed it to Arielle. 'I think that the man I'm looking for took this photo of my mother. Does it look at all like it was taken in the area that Monsieur Perrin'—the name felt strange in her mouth—'lives?'

Arielle considered, carefully examining the image. 'It *could* be,' she said, at last. 'There are meadows just like it, and with that castle in the distance . . .'

Emma had looked up the Chevreuse before coming here, wanting to have an idea of where this man, who might be her father, lived. The images had shown a green landscape, woods, castles, old villages. A setting right out of a fairy tale. Her throat tightening, she said, 'Arielle—you said that man in the photo was a neighbour of Franck, the beekeeper. Do you happen to know what his first name is?'

Arielle shook her head. 'Daniel probably does.' She turned away and spoke softly on the phone. After a moment, she returned to Emma. Even though he hadn't met Perrin in person, Arielle reported, Daniel had met his wife Marie-Madeleine and so knew his first name was Eric, and also that while his wife was a local girl, Eric was not from there originally, but had lived in the area for a long time. The couple had two children, both boys, both in their twenties. Daniel didn't have the Perrins' number, but he'd ask Franck right away.

Emma's thoughts were racing, a strange mix of feelings agitating in her. If Eric Perrin, who was married with two sons, was indeed her father, then she had a family she hadn't known even existed . . . But she had a family already. They were enough. And it would be hard on the Perrins too, so . . . what on earth should she do?

Arielle's phone pinged with a text. It was Daniel, sending three numbers, with a short explanation: *This is the Perrins' number, the landline for the farm, and then their mobiles, the first mobile number is Eric's.* Arielle forwarded the whole thing to Emma's phone, then looked at her and said, as if she could read Emma's thoughts, 'I don't know what I would do, either.'

Thirty-six

Charlotte had woken from a heavy but unrestful sleep to a sense of disorientation. For a moment her stupefied mind struggled to make sense of where she was and what had happened. Then she remembered and groaned. Last night, she had said they'd talk in the morning. Well, it was the morning, but she didn't feel like talking, though she knew they must. Dragging herself out of bed, she headed to the bathroom, which to her relief was empty, but she could hear someone moving about downstairs. Tom rarely got up before her but today he had. And that meant . . .

She couldn't go for a run to clear her head, so it had to be the next best thing. Stepping into the shower, she turned the cold water on full bore and, gasping, stood stoically under the jet of flesh-crimping chill. It was only a few seconds, but it made her mind sharper, clearer. Towelling herself off, she got dressed in a T-shirt and loose linen pants, brushed back her hair, slipped on some shoes, and went down to the kitchen.

Tom was standing with his back to the door, staring at the coffee machine as it ground and hissed and whirred its way towards producing a brew. On the table beside him, she could see things he'd laid out, which he had obviously found in Juliette's pantry—a packet of *biscottes*, the breakfast rusks that were popular in France, butter, and a pot of jam, as well as two plates and knives. He hadn't heard her over the noise of the machine, so she stood there for a moment, watching him, her chest constricting at the familiar yet strange sight of him, and then she went in, saying brightly, 'Seems like I've timed it well by the smell of that coffee.'

He started and turned around. He still looked tired but he'd washed his hair, shaved, and put on fresh clothes. 'I hope so,' he said, giving her a tentative smile. 'Not sure if I've worked out this machine properly.'

'It is a bit of a beast,' said Charlotte, seating herself at the table. 'Took me a while to work out myself.'

'Yes, they're all different,' Tom said, and she could hear the nervousness in his voice under the delaying tactic of small talk. She was sure hers sounded the same to him.

The coffee machine finished its work. Tom brought the full cups to the table. He sat down opposite her and gestured vaguely towards the breakfast things. 'This being Paris, I suppose we should really have fresh bread from the bakery, but . . .'

'This will be fine,' said Charlotte, his obvious nerves making her own recede. *Enough with delaying tactics!* She looked straight at him. 'I have to ask you upfront, Tom, even if we are now talking to each other, would you be willing to talk to someone professional, as well, back home?'

He glanced at her quickly. 'Yes,' he said, adding, after a beat of time, 'I know that I should have done that before it all went to pot and . . .' He didn't finish his sentence, but Charlotte didn't press him. She knew what an effort it had cost him to admit it, he who had previously only spoken of therapists with disdain. No use harping on it.

Buttering a *biscotte* and spreading it with jam, she said, 'How did your boss react to you resigning over the phone?'

He winced, and she wondered if she'd been too blunt. It had been intentional because she knew that if they were to properly repair things, they had to be honest with each other, not beat around the bush. 'Poor fellow,' he said, 'his ears are probably still ringing. I didn't give him a chance to respond before I hung up.' He saw Charlotte's expression, and added ruefully, 'I know. I have to call him, apologise, and resign properly when I'm back.'

She nodded. His words showed that he understood that it wasn't his boss's fault, nor the company's, that he'd been so out of joint with his work. It had been his own inability to move on. But she was also glad of something else: he hadn't got cold feet about resigning. He had taken a step towards the future.

She wasn't going to ask him what he planned to do next. That would come in time, when he had disentangled what he wanted from the stranglehold of what he thought he should do. And that made her say something that had come to her in the middle of the night. 'You know, Tom, I've realised something since I've been here. I was nervous about leaving Aidan in charge at work, never having been the world's best delegator'—Tom gave a faint smile at that—'but he's doing absolutely fine. I have no need to worry. I love my work, Tom, and I'm good at it, but being here has made me realise that the business won't fall apart just because I'm not there all the time, and actually I *need* not to be there all the time, but it took all this to make me understand . . .' She was about to say more, but the words somehow got choked in her throat.

Tom sighed. 'Jeez, Lottie, being a so-called mature adult isn't all it's cracked up to be, is it?'

She gave a surprised bark of laughter. 'You're right there!' Then she grew serious again. 'We might have made lots of mistakes, you and I, but one thing we did do really well—'

He broke in, finishing the sentence for her, 'Is our kids.'

'They've turned out to be beautiful adults,' she said, 'who are very much their own people but who love us and each other. Maybe we haven't truly grasped often enough what an amazing and wonderful thing that is.'

He drew in a breath. 'You know, as Elise was tearing strips off me, even in the midst of my shame, I was so proud of her, because she's not afraid to go straight to the heart of things, even when I was still messing about in a swamp of self-pity.'

Their eyes met. 'She is wiser than the two of us put together,' Charlotte said. 'It won't be easy. There are still things we have to face. But we'll get there, Tom. If it's what we want.' She drew in a breath. 'And I do want it.'

Reaching across the table, he took her hand, his touch warm and familiar, his eyes never leaving hers. 'So do I,' he said. 'We'll get there, Lottie. We will.'

Years ago, after a blow-up, that conversation would have ended with them in bed, making love. But this was more than a simple blow-up, and things were still raw. Here in Paris, on neutral ground, they had been able to take the first real steps, but it might not be smooth sailing back home. Old expectations and resentments might be lying dormant, ready to raise their ugly heads. But they had to risk it, they had to trust. Their marriage *was* worth saving, and they would put in all the time it needed.

And that was more than enough, for the moment, Charlotte thought, as they cleared away the breakfast things. Tom would be getting the Eurostar back to London in a couple of hours. With her full agreement, he had decided to return straight away, to go and see Elise, Theo and Jamie, to put in his formal resignation, and to make an appointment with a psychologist. Meanwhile, Charlotte would stay in Paris for another day or two, and then head back. There were things she still needed to do before she left, she told Tom, and he didn't argue, or ask for explanations.

༄

A little later, after Charlotte had farewelled Tom at the station, a call came from Emma, who told her what she'd learned about Eric from Arielle. 'I've decided I *have* to contact him,' she said.

'But how? I mean, should I call? Email? Write him a letter? Or just turn up on his doorstep?'

'I'm not sure,' said Charlotte thoughtfully, 'but I can come over a bit later if you like, and we can discuss it.'

Emma agreed at once. 'I'm about to head off to the hospital to bring Mattie home, but why don't you come round this afternoon, at around four o'clock? We'd all love to see you.'

'If you're sure it won't be too tiring for Mattie.'

'More likely she'll tire *us* out. It's amazing to see what a difference that pacemaker makes—she's well on the way to turning into the Energizer Bunny, if we're not careful!'

Charlotte was still laughing as she ended the call, a tingling fizz of what felt suspiciously like joy running in her veins, making her light-headed *and* light-hearted. She hadn't felt like that for such a long time! She didn't have her running gear or the earbuds keeping her in a bubble of her own devising, but she didn't care about the startled looks of passersby who stared at this middle-aged woman running like a reckless kid through the bright May morning, heading for the flower market.

It took Arielle a moment to recognise the sweaty, bright-faced woman who arrived in a rush at her stand as the elegant Charlotte Marigny. 'You look like you're in a hurry!' she finally said.

'I suppose I am,' said Charlotte, smiling and panting at the same time. 'In a hurry to catch the future after doing the *pied de grue*'—running on the spot—'for far too long.'

Arielle gave her a sharp glance. Something had definitely happened to Charlotte, something good. She wasn't so indiscreet as to pry, but said, 'I hope you catch the future you want.'

Charlotte laughed. 'So do I!' Then her expression changed. 'Emma came by, right?'

'An hour or so ago. She's gone to the hospital now to pick up her grandmother.' She looked at Charlotte. 'It was rather surprising to hear about Eric Perrin.'

'He was Eric Dubois when Corinne—Emma's mother—and I knew him.'

'Why would he change his name?'

Charlotte shrugged. 'I don't know.' Pascal had only said that Eric and his mother had left the Morvan. The name change must have come later, maybe even after Corinne had left. Which would make sense, because even if she'd tried to find him at some stage, the name change would have made it impossible.

'I hope Emma gets the answers she wants,' said Arielle. 'Eric Perrin sounds like a decent man, from what Daniel says, but . . .'

'I'm going to be talking to Emma about it later today,' Charlotte said, 'but I'm really not sure what to advise her. Being contacted by a stranger out of the blue with news like that . . .' She broke off.

An unexpected idea flashed into Arielle's mind. 'But what if it *isn't* a stranger?' she blurted out. 'What if it's someone he used to know who contacts him?'

Charlotte stared at her.

Arielle was about to apologise for giving gratuitous advice when Charlotte's face broke into a wide smile. 'That's a brilliant idea.

It would be much easier for me to speak to him first, to prepare the ground.'

Arielle smiled with relief.

'And now, Arielle, I wonder if you could put together one of your beautiful bouquets for me to take to Emma and her grandmother this afternoon. Something that might express wishes for recovery and good health, but also joy and new beginnings, and hope.' She grinned. 'It's rather a lot to pack into one bunch of flowers!'

'Not at all,' said Arielle, thinking how those feelings were strangely close to her own right now. Joy, new beginnings, hope, and even sincere wishes for recovery and renewed good health for Virginie. For, with the weight of worry lifted off her chest, she now felt only compassion for the Grandiers. Maybe this crisis would finally make them open their eyes and change. Thierry was already on the way to that, and maybe Virginie would be too, with his support. For it struck her now that he had spoken with genuine love and a touching understanding of his wife, a woman who other people found unpleasant, if not odious. Love was indeed mysterious.

Charlotte was looking at her quizzically.

'Sorry, I was far away. My suggestion would be for a mix of white and yellow flowers, with a surprise note of purple.' She pointed in turn to flowers on her display. 'We could have the calm simplicity of daisies and white hydrangea for a fast recovery and good health, the joyful notes of yellow tulips for hope, yellow irises for joy, and purple lilac in the middle for the heady scent of new beginnings.'

Charlotte shook her head, smiling. 'You've described the perfect bouquet for this occasion, combining both beauty and meaning. And you've done it off the top of your head! It's a rare gift.'

Arielle blushed as she pushed the boxes to one side and started to select the flowers for Charlotte. 'It's a small thing, really, something I've always been able to do instinctively, even as a child.' She smiled. 'I'm not like my friend Daniel, who knows the deep histories of plants in human culture, and I'm not like you, who can see a piece of unpromising bare land and turn it into something wonderful. I'm just someone who loves sharing the consolation and joy of flowers with other people.'

'Oh, Arielle! Didn't Paris teach you to forget about being modest? You *have* a rare gift, no question.' She watched for a moment as Arielle deftly started arranging the flowers into a pleasing shape. 'The other day, when we were in the Carnavalet gardens, you said you'd like to go to London one day. I have a proposal to put to you. Come to London and speak to a selection of my customers and suppliers about what you do.'

Arielle stopped what she was doing and stared at Charlotte, unable to say anything at first. Charlotte must have thought she disliked the idea, because she added quickly, 'It would be all expenses paid, plus a fee, and you could bring your family with you, we'd time it for your school holidays, maybe early July? And don't worry about not speaking English. I could translate for you. Or your sister could. You said she speaks English, right?'

Arielle finally managed to speak. 'It sounds absolutely wonderful. And I'm so grateful. But do you really think that important people in London would want to hear from someone like me?'

'You are just as important as they are,' said Charlotte, firmly, 'and they will lap up everything you say. In fact, I think you will be a star. And that will bring *me* kudos too, let me tell you.'

Arielle laughed shyly. 'You are very kind.'

'Not kind, realistic,' said Charlotte briskly. 'So?'

'I'd love to,' said Arielle, with a joyful catch in her voice.

Thirty-seven

Mattie had been excited about coming home and had chatted all the way in the cab and into the house, but she fell completely silent when she entered the garden and surveyed the tableau before her. In the sunlit, rejuvenating garden sat the pretty blue bench, with its welcoming cushions, under the flowering wisteria. Beside it was a table with three lovely flower-patterned teacups and small plates, which Marc-Antoine had found this morning in a second-hand shop around the corner from his office. The musical call of a wood pigeon provided a soft soundtrack to the scene.

'My darling children,' Mattie said at last, 'it is the most beautiful thing I have seen in a long time. You have made an old woman so very happy.' She held out her arms, embracing them both tightly. Releasing them after a moment, she said cheerfully, 'You do realise you are going to have trouble getting me to go back into the house now, don't you?'

Emma laughed. 'We can stay out here all afternoon if you like.'

And they did, sitting together on that very comfortable bench, eating divine strawberries and macarons, washed down with fragrant Lady Grey tea—the champagne, they'd decided, could wait for Charlotte—and talking about everything and nothing, while the wood pigeon kept up its nostalgic tune.

When Charlotte arrived a couple of hours later and was ushered by Marc-Antoine into the garden, she caught her breath, feeling as though she'd wandered into a painting. An unfinished one, yes, with ragged edges and brush strokes that weren't quite defined yet, but with a vitality that you could already see. The focus of this painting was the bench, and the two women sitting on it, their heads close together, completely absorbed in looking at a large old photograph album they held across their laps. Mattie's silver hair was loosely held back with a tortoiseshell clip, and beside her, Emma's hair was shining with mellow lights in the sun.

Charlotte almost felt reluctant to intrude, not wanting to break the spell of this lovely moment. She met Marc-Antoine's glance and saw that he was smiling. 'I daren't take a photo,' he whispered, 'but it's certainly worth one, isn't it?'

Mattie and Emma looked up, their eyes widening as they saw what Charlotte was holding. Then there were warm greetings, and happy exclamations over the flowers and what Arielle had said about them, before Marc-Antoine went to get a couple of chairs from the kitchen, as well as champagne, and a non-alcoholic sparkling wine for Mattie, who wasn't allowed alcohol just yet. 'Time for a toast,' he said, pouring the wine into four flute glasses, and handing one to each of them. Raising his own glass, he said, 'To good health!' and they toasted it.

'To joy!' said Emma, smiling, and they all clinked glasses again.

'To hope and new beginnings!' Charlotte said, her thoughts fizzing like the champagne, and they all drank to that.

Then Marc-Antoine said, firmly, 'We definitely need a photo,' and Emma and Charlotte arranged themselves behind Mattie on the bench while he put the timer on his camera phone.

'Another toast!' Emma said, as he scurried back to join them before the timer went off.

'To flowers and squirrels!' said Marc-Antoine, and they all laughed as they raised their glasses, so that the camera captured their faces filled with silly, wonderful merriment.

As they trickled back to their seats, Charlotte knew this was the right moment. 'Arielle made a suggestion,' she said, looking directly at Emma. 'What if I call Eric first? I knew him, long ago, and he knows I was Corinne's friend, so it might help to break the ice. I'll just say that you are Corinne's daughter. But I will tell him I met up with Pascal. He'll know then that I know he and your mother were together once upon a time. What do you think?'

Emma held her breath. She could read in Mattie and Marc-Antoine's expressions that they thought it was a good idea. But they wouldn't make the decision for her. She had to take that final leap herself. And suddenly, she knew she was ready. Exhaling, she pulled out her phone and sent Charlotte the numbers.

Marc-Antoine put an arm around her, and Mattie took her hand, while Charlotte tapped out the first mobile number, putting the phone on speaker.

It rang, and rang, and rang. And then, just as they thought it would ring out altogether, a voice spoke. 'Hello. Eric Perrin here. Who is this?'

His voice was deep, mellow, with a trace of some regional accent Emma couldn't place. Marc-Antoine's arm tightened around her as she gave an involuntary shiver.

'Hello, Eric,' said Charlotte.

How could she sound so composed, Emma thought, *my throat would have seized up!*

'This is Charlotte Marigny. I don't know if you remember me, but we met long ago, when we were kids, in the Morvan.'

There was a moment of silence before he said, 'Charlotte! I remember. You were Corinne's friend.'

Had his voice sounded different when he said her mother's name? Emma thought she'd heard an inflection, something . . . But he hadn't hesitated. He hadn't stammered. He hadn't been uncertain at all.

'That's right,' Charlotte said. She seemed a little uncertain herself now, as if she hadn't expected his directness or his lack of questions. 'A friend of mine showed me some photos of a visit she'd made to your neighbour's bee farm and I recognised you. So—well, she passed on your number, and here we are.'

There was the hint of a smile in his voice. 'Here we are.'

'How are you?'

'Well,' he said. 'You?'

'Very well.' Charlotte rushed on. 'Look, Eric, I know this is completely out of the blue, but Corinne's daughter is over from Australia, staying with her grandmother in Paris, and we've been talking about old times. I've been in touch with Pascal too, and—'

'Corinne's daughter is here?' Eric interrupted sharply, the tone of his voice changing. 'But what about Corinne?'

Charlotte hesitated. And in that moment, Emma knew that the time for delegation was over. She gestured to Charlotte to indicate she'd speak, then took a deep breath and said, 'Hello, Monsieur Perrin. I'm Emma, Corinne's daughter. And I'm very sorry to inform you that my—that my mother died a couple of months ago.'

'Oh my God.' The phrase was a whisper. A beat of time, then he said, 'I wish . . .' He broke off before going on, 'It was a long time ago, and everything is different now, but once we were very close. I am so very sorry to know she is gone.'

'Monsieur Perrin, may I perhaps come and visit you some day?'

The genuine depth of feeling in his voice had given Emma courage. She was turning the key and she would go through the door, no matter what she found when she was on the other side. 'I know you live in the Chevreuse. And I know that's not far from Paris, where I am at present. Of course, it's asking a lot but it would mean so much to me.'

'Come whenever you like,' he said. 'I would very much like to meet you, Corinne's daughter.'

This time she was sure that his voice had a different inflection when he spoke her mother's name. Was it regret, longing, sadness, or just fond memory? She didn't know. But she had to find out. 'Would tomorrow be too soon?' she asked.

He gave a little laugh then. 'You sound so like your mother. Patience was never her strong suit. No, tomorrow is not too soon. Catch the train to Saint Rémy-les-Chevreuse station, and I will pick you up from there. We can talk over lunch.' A pause. 'My wife knows about my past, so you don't need to feel awkward. Bring Charlotte too, if you like. It would be good to see her again.'

'You too, Eric,' said Charlotte into the speaker. 'But it will have to be for another time. I have to go home to London tomorrow.'

He didn't ask questions, simply said, 'Okay, then. Another time. You've got my number.'

'And you've got mine now too,' said Charlotte cheerfully.

'Forgive me, I have to go out now so I must say goodbye. But I will see you tomorrow, Emma. Text me the time of your train. And, Charlotte—I'll see you sometime soon, I hope.'

Charlotte was the first to speak after the call ended. 'What are you going to say to him tomorrow?'

Thirty-eight

When Emma got off the train at St-Rémy-les-Chevreuse the next day, Eric was already there. He was looking towards another carriage, so for an instant she had him in her gaze without him being aware of it. He was of medium height, plainly dressed in a dark blue jumper and grey pants and he carried himself with a natural confidence that matched his manner on the phone. His close-cropped hair was almost the same colour as hers, but a bit lighter, his short beard of a darker brown, scattered with spikes of silver, just as he'd appeared in the photo. When he finally turned and saw her what struck her most was not a 'thousand-yard stare' but the laughter lines around his eyes as he strode towards her.

'Emma?' he said, and suddenly she felt tongue-tied.

'Monsieur Perrin,' she managed as they shook hands.

'Eric, please,' he said, 'we are not formal here in the country.' He led her to his car, an old but immaculately kept Peugeot van, and opened the passenger door for her. 'I hope you don't mind dogs, because he insisted on coming with me.'

Sitting in the back was a beautiful cream Labrador who looked at her with friendly curiosity, wagging his tail and gazing at her with big dark eyes. 'This is Athos,' Eric said. 'Just like in *The Three Musketeers*,' he added, seeing her expression.

'He's lovely.' Emma held out a hand to the dog, who licked it enthusiastically. 'We had a Labrador when I was a child, and I loved her.'

'They are loveable dogs,' Eric agreed, the lines around his blue-grey eyes, the same colour as hers, crinkling with his smile.

This isn't a man haunted by a lost love or a dark secret, she thought, this is a contented man, at ease with himself and his life.

She gave the dog one last pat and settled herself into her seat. She glanced sideways at his profile as he drove. Did they look alike? She couldn't tell. His colouring was similar to hers, but so was Paddy's. An uncomfortable thought occurred to her: maybe her mother was first attracted to Paddy because he reminded her of this man. Quickly, she dismissed the thought, saying, 'It's beautiful here.'

'I never tire of it. I've lived here a long time, though I did leave for a few years after my mother died.' A shadow crossed his face. 'I tried to work this place out of my system by living in the city for a while, doing something completely different. But it tugs at you, this place. The pace of life, the ancient feel of it, the woods . . . I missed it too much.'

'So you came back?'

'And once I was back, I knew that I didn't have to run any longer. This was my place.'

'Those beehives you made—they are so beautiful . . . works of art, really. How did you learn to make such things?'

'I've always been good with my hands,' he said, smiling. 'And I've always loved working with wood. I whittled a lot when I was a little kid and when I grew up, I thought I might make a career of it.'

'As a carpenter or a cabinet maker?' she asked, but he shook his head. 'No, as a sculptor.'

This was unexpected, and she looked at him, frowning, her mind snagging on something she'd heard. And then she knew. 'Franck has one of your sculptures,' she said. 'I saw it in the photo. It's very good.'

He shrugged. 'It's from long ago. I don't do those anymore, but when I was living in the city, making them helped keep me sane and—' He broke off and looked at her. 'But you haven't come to talk to me about my woodworking, have you?'

She shook her head.

'Open the glove box, Emma,' he went on, quietly, 'there's something in there I want you to see.'

Inside was a collection of random stuff and an envelope that she took out, pulling out the photo inside. Immediately her breath caught. She looked at him with wide eyes.

'Your mother took it, not far from here. I'll show you.' He turned left and they were soon on a rutted track leading into the fields. When they got out, she found herself looking at a flowery meadow, with a beech tree in the near distance, and the pointy top of a castle tower in the far distance. She glanced at Eric, her heart beating fast. 'I have the exact same picture,' she managed to say, 'only it's her in it, not you.'

'Ah,' he said, with a long sigh.

She turned over his photo and saw *un jour de printemps* written on it, in her mother's firm script. She pulled her photo out of her bag, handed it to him and his expression changed.

'We gave them to each other,' he said. 'It was your mother's idea that she should have hers, and I have mine. She said it showed what we were to each other, through the eye of love.' He looked at her with a faint smile. 'She was like that, your mother. She had these unusual ideas . . . didn't like things to be obvious, easily understood.'

'Yes,' Emma sighed, 'that's absolutely true.'

'She kept it,' he said, with a wondering shake of the head. 'I wouldn't have thought that.'

'I never saw it until she died. She left it for me.'

She didn't want to say any more right now. Instead, she watched him put the two photos together, turning them into a kind of story. In his photo, a younger version of himself is looking up from making a daisy chain, his face alight as he glances towards the person behind the camera. And in the other photo, her mother is wearing the daisy chain . . . Emma looked at the two of them, captured in sunlight, and there was a lump in her throat as she asked, 'What happened?'

'Corinne didn't say anything?'

She shook her head.

'We were so young,' he said, 'but so much in love. For the first time in my life, I felt I had met someone who understood me. At home things were bad—my father in prison, my mother going to pieces, and me trying to keep it together—it was all I could do to keep my head above water. But Corinne had big plans. She didn't want to stay in France, she had her sights set on faraway places, and she wanted me to go with her. I was hesitant because I was hoping to go to art school, and because I was worried about my mother, who was still very unwell. And I didn't have the same urge as Corinne did, about wanting to get away. But for a time, none of that really mattered, we just loved being together. Then out of the blue I was offered a place in a great art school in Paris, a course that was for three years, and I accepted it without discussing it with Corinne first. I thought she'd understand, but she thought I was riding roughshod over her plans, all of which would all have to be put on hold. I understand that now, but I didn't then. I thought she was being selfish, and she thought the same about me. We had a massive fight, and she stormed off.' A pause. 'Two weeks later, I heard she'd gone to Australia. We never saw or spoke to each other again.'

'You didn't try to contact her?' Emma whispered.

He shook his head. 'I knew it was over. It was a horrible fight—it had started over a clash of dreams and expectations but spiralled into conflict over much more fundamental things, like family and home. We'd said terrible things to each other . . . it had broken something between us that couldn't ever be repaired.' He sighed.

'I never forgot her. But in time I met Marie-Madeleine and found happiness again.' He looked at Emma. 'I truly hope Corinne did, too.'

Emma exhaled. She hadn't even noticed she'd been holding her breath. 'She did.'

'Then I am glad,' he said, simply.

'Did you end up going to art school?' she hazarded.

'For a time. Then I had to return to nurse my mother. After she died, it was my turn to fall apart. I stayed in Paris, but I didn't go back to my course. I was in a bad place for a while. That was when I changed my name . . .' He took a deep breath. 'Sorry. That was probably more than you needed to know.'

'No, I am glad you told me.'

He gave a wry smile. 'Shall we keep going now?'

In the car, she thought about what he'd said. There had been no dark secret, no tragic separation of star-crossed lovers, as she'd imagined, occasionally, as a teenager, but a less dramatic yet sadder tale—a clash of dreams that had shown up fundamental differences. And two strong-willed young people so single-mindedly convinced of the rightness of their own position that they hadn't believed it was possible to negotiate.

Yet, despite all that, my mother chose to have me, Emma thought, overwhelmed for a moment by the idea. Knowing all she did now made it easier, yet harder, to ask him *the* question. Maybe she shouldn't. She thought of those two young people in the flowery meadow on that beautiful spring day long ago and knew with absolute certainty *that's* what her mother had wanted her to know. *That I was conceived there, that day or another like it*, she thought,

I was made in the love and joy of a perfect moment. And maybe knowing that is enough.

She sneaked a glance at Eric. He must have sensed it, because he turned his head and something changed in his eyes.

He pulled over to the side of the road and said, in a strange, choked sort of voice, 'How old are you, Emma?'

And she knew then that she had to tell him. Everything. 'The day before Maman died,' she began, her voice a little unsteady at first, 'I got a call from the hospital, telling me she needed to see me, to tell me something important. But I never got the chance to hear what it was.'

Hours later, when Marc-Antoine met her at the station in Paris, she was able to describe to him what happened after she finished her story: how Eric sat without a word for what seemed like a long time, and how the weight of his silence pressed on her like a stone; how she had almost decided to get out of the car and walk back to the station, but then he'd turned to her and said, flatly, 'I can understand her not telling me, at first. A baby at that stage was the last thing I would have wanted.' His voice hardened. 'But *never* to say anything—not to me, not to you . . . how *could* she do that?'

Emma's eyes were full of tears. 'You changed your name,' she managed to say. 'Even if she had tried to contact you, she wouldn't have found you.'

'But do you think she even tried?' he asked tightly.

'I don't know.' *Maybe she did try, maybe that was part of what she was going to tell me*, Emma thought. And that made her feel calmer and sadder at the same time. She looked straight at him and said, 'She was not always easy to understand. But she loved me, and I know she thought she was doing the right thing by not telling me. How was she to know how you would respond, anyway?' Her throat felt choked but she forced the last words out, hot and ragged, while he sat there in silence, staring at her. 'And at the end, she *was* going to tell me, I am certain of that. That photo was on her bedside cabinet. She had it out, ready to tell me the story. She was going to start with that—and that means something, don't you see? Only she never got the chance to say it.' She couldn't keep the tears back then; the grief filling her like a bitter brew. 'I'm sorry,' she managed to say, 'this was a terrible mistake. Please, could you take me back to the station?'

His expression changed. 'It is I who should be sorry. It was so brave of you to come to me. And what did I do but throw it back in your face? I'm so very sorry, Emma. Will you forgive me?'

She nodded, still choked with emotion, but with the bitterness easing. 'Yes,' she whispered, 'of course.'

∽

She was able to recount the exact words they had both used, describe the feelings that had risen in her, even evoke the way that Athos the dog had nudged his nose against the back of her neck, as if in reassurance. But she struggled to accurately depict the feeling that rose in her when Eric looked at her with his blue-grey eyes, those eyes that were so similar to hers, and said, 'Emma, I am so very sorry Corinne never had the chance to tell you. But I am glad her photo brought you to me. I can't ever take the place of the man who loved you from babyhood and raised you as his own. And nor do I want to. But I would very much like to get to know you better. If you are willing.'

Epilogue

NEW YEAR'S EVE

It had snowed earlier in the day and the streets and rooftops were still dusted with it; the bare branches of trees were decorated with delicate white traceries that turned silver under the light of streetlamps. Charlotte and Tom walked in companionable silence through the streets that led to Mattie's house, carrying paper bags of *traiteur* delights as their contribution to the party.

It had been more than a few years since Charlotte had celebrated New Year's Eve in Paris, and she wondered why she'd left it so long. Paris was always beautiful but on this in-between night there was a kind of magic in the air, made up of all that had been and all that was yet to happen. It was a grown-up magic, airbrushing away pain from the past year and offering healing and hope for the year to come.

They had come a long way, she and Tom, since he'd turned up haggard and unshaven at her aunt's house seven months ago. On his return to London, he'd immediately set about making a fresh start. As promised, he'd seen a psychologist, who had been of great help to him—and to Charlotte too, by extension. On the advice of his therapist, he'd explained to the kids and his parents what had happened and apologised for his behaviour. The kids had been warmly supportive, and his parents a little embarrassed but deeply relieved. And he'd sorted things out properly with his work. And then, in October, he had surprised everyone, except Charlotte, by getting a part-time position as a coordinator for community outreach programs, which he loved.

As for herself, everything was back on an even keel at work, but she had taken a step back from day-to-day operations, with Aidan promoted officially to general manager. With more free time to spend together, Charlotte and Tom had rediscovered what they had both missed and so very nearly lost—the warm intimacy of their long relationship. Only now that intimacy had been heightened because they didn't take it for granted anymore.

Charlotte glanced at her husband, this loving, complicated man she would grow old with. And she didn't even shy away from that last thought, either. Because growing old with the love of your life was an absolute privilege that so many people never had.

'Penny for yours,' said Tom, breaking into her thoughts.

'I was thinking how lucky we are,' she said. 'And what you'll be like as an old man,' she added, with an impish smile.

He laughed. 'Really? Oh dear. Probably grumpy and grouchy.'

'You wouldn't dare,' she said firmly, 'not while I'm around. Understood?'

He laughed again. 'Yes, ma'am! But we've got a bit of time before we grow old, right?' And then he stopped, took her hand, and said, 'This is what *I've* been thinking: how about, when we're back home, we head to Cornwall and renew our vows in the Lost Gardens of Heligan, where we first met?'

She stared at him, her breath catching. 'That's lovely—but . . .'

He looked anxious. 'Is it too soon? The wrong thing? Or you just don't want . . .'

'It's wonderful,' she cried, finding her voice again. 'But you can't simply rock up there and say you want to renew your vows, you have to organise it.'

He was smiling broadly now. 'You're not the only one who can organise things, my love, and the kids have been a great help in—'

'You've been plotting this with our children?' Charlotte pretended to look stern, even though she felt she might burst with joy.

'Sure we have,' said Tom, 'and even Mum and Dad have got in on the act, though I had to stop Mum from planning a full-on party in the village hall afterwards with a swing band and everything.'

It was Charlotte's turn to laugh. 'Why not? It could be a lot of fun.'

'So it's a yes, is it?' he said, deadpan.

Instead of answering, she put down her bags, flung her arms around him and kissed him right there in the street under the frosty lights of that magical evening.

Arielle and Daniel strolled through the Luxembourg Garden, still laughing about the busker who had entertained them in the Metro. Dressed in a fabulous seventies-style sparkly suit such as you used to see in variety shows on French TV, he'd crooned songs into a fake microphone, with exaggerated gestures and a schmaltzy throatiness that had most people in the carriage laughing and clapping. It was almost with reluctance that Arielle and Daniel had alighted at their stop.

They'd decided to walk through the Luxembourg Garden rather than go in a straight line to Mattie's house. And with the snow that had fallen still lying on the paths, on the branches of trees, and on the heads and shoulders of statues, the whole place assumed an air of stilled enchantment, as if holding its breath, waiting for the humans to leave so the garden's secret life could begin.

'What are you smiling about?' With his beanie pulled down firmly over his ears and his big puffer jacket, Daniel looked like a skinny version of a Michelin Man, and Arielle felt an irrepressible joy fizzing in her chest. 'Just an old story,' she said.

Daniel stopped, and putting down the dried-flower arrangement he was carrying, pulled her to him. 'Tell it to me,' he said, kissing her forehead under the faux-fur hat.

'So on New Year's Eve,' said Arielle solemnly, 'when the sun has gone down, the old year and the new year meet and look each other in the eye. Then, at the first stroke of midnight, they become one, till the clock has finished striking the twelfth chime.

And in those moments, till the twelfth stroke, there is a magic that touches everything, if only you have eyes to see it.'

'I've never heard that one before,' said Daniel, 'but it's lovely.'

'Monsieur Renan once told it to me,' she said. The old man had given them both a most unexpected Christmas present: a whole week's extra paid leave for Arielle, on top of the usual short Christmas break. And a bonus payment, to cap it all off. 'Romaine and Coralie and I will cover that extra week,' he said, 'and you and Daniel should take yourselves off somewhere nice and sunny!'

They *had* gone somewhere nice, and more or less sunny—down to Grasse, where Arielle and Pauline came from, and where their extended family still lived. With Pauline and the twins, they'd taken a *gite* in the middle of the countryside for a week and had spent a lovely Christmas there with all the relatives, and then Arielle and Daniel had come back to Paris two days after, leaving Pauline and the twins—who were delighted to be in the midst of cousins—to follow later.

It had been blissful, the two of them together, staying in Daniel's apartment in the 11th, making love and making plans, including the big decision that they would move in together, sometime in the new year. Not an apartment this time, but a house, where Pauline could also live if she wanted to. They'd even started looking at possible places in the 18th, because Arielle didn't want the children to have to move from a school and neighbourhood they liked, and Daniel was happy to live wherever she wanted.

She was looking forward to the party tonight. She hadn't seen Charlotte for a while but had wonderful memories of her visit to London, which had turned out very well, both professionally and as a family holiday. They'd even planned another event there for April. And over the last few months, she'd got to know Emma well as the pilot program for the garden tours was launched in July, with a few small groups that Liz's travel agent friend had put together. Arielle had taken part in all the tours, giving brief talks at the flower market with translations by Emma. Complete with Mattie's gorgeous maps, it had been a real success. The last tour had been before Christmas—winter gardens had their own charm—and now there would be a break before it started up again in February with full marketing as *Secrets of Paris Gardens*.

'I'm looking forward to celebrating with everyone,' Arielle said. 'I'm so glad for them all that everything has worked out.'

He kissed her. 'You are always glad to see other people's happiness, and that is only one of the many reasons why I love you.'

'And I love you too, Daniel Auban,' she said joyfully, 'but it's not just for other people's happiness that I am glad, it's for ours too.'

She could even feel happiness for the Grandiers. Things were still somewhat tentative between them, but progress had definitely been made. Virginie's crisis hadn't transformed her into a lovely person, but she was clearly making an effort, while Thierry had relaxed into a much nicer version of himself. And that was enough, for the moment.

'Can you guess what my wish for the new year will be?' Daniel asked.

'Yes,' said Arielle, on an indrawn breath. 'Because I think it's probably exactly the same as mine.'

Almost as if it had been deliberately targeted, the snow had fallen heavily on the 7th arrondissement of Paris, turning the garden at Mattie's into a miniature winter wonderland. The grass was blanketed in a soft cold duvet of snow, which had also painted the branches of trees and bushes in thick white brushstrokes. A few splashes of other colours remained among the sparkling white: the dark green and bright red of the holly bush, the pale blue of the bench and table under the wisteria, and glimpses of the brown-and-cream speckled pavers Marc-Antoine had laid in the summer to create a winding path from the laundry door to the back of the garden. It had been wonderful, in the warmer months, to plant things and see flowers blooming—including some rather beautiful pink peonies from that surviving clump—and to make their own homegrown tomato and basil salad, or to sit on the bench watching Mattie creating new drawings. Now pretty much everything except for the holly bush was asleep under the blanket of snow; there was no sign of the plants that had flourished so satisfyingly in the summer and autumn, and it was too cold to sit on the bench. But soon the cycle would begin again, starting with the snowdrops, those lovely winter-blossoming promises of spring.

Emma was supposed to be getting nibblies together for the aperitif that would precede the New Year's Eve festive meal, but she'd been distracted by the sight of the snowy garden. She'd spoken to Paddy a few minutes ago; he had been spending New Year's with his sisters and was still awake, so they'd raised a glass together, across the kilometres. He'd be here in person in a couple of months. Meanwhile, her grandmother and Marc-Antoine were in the dining room, finishing the setting of the table; Eric had phoned to say he and his family were on their way; and Charlotte and Arielle had messaged to say they were almost there. She couldn't wait to ring in the new year with them all and toast their new beginnings.

She'd seen Eric several times since that first extraordinary day in the Chevreuse, and they were slowly developing a relationship. At Christmas, he'd given her a superb wooden box he'd carved with a delicate flowery design, inlaid with enamel. 'For your seed packets,' he'd said.

Most important of all, Mattie had taken to him straight away, and Marc-Antoine had also got on well with him. His wife, Marie-Madeleine, had been welcoming and kind from the start, while their two boys had been wary but had gradually warmed up.

Soon the house would fill with the sound of happy, celebrating people; but right now, looking out at the garden, with the first rays of moonlight beginning to touch it with silver, Emma heard only a soft, waiting silence, and her mind filled with a vivid picture of a man and a child, happily throwing snowballs at each other on a night like this one.

'What's up, Emma?' Marc-Antoine said from behind her. He put his arms around her and she leaned back into them, the warmth of his body filling her with a sensual delight that never seemed to fade. 'Nothing's *up*, exactly. I was just seeing my grandfather and my mother out there, when she was young, playing in snow like this. And that makes me feel at peace.'

He kissed the top of her head. They were silent for a moment, before he said, 'Shall we join them?'

'But the others will . . .' she began, then stopped, and turned around to smile at him. 'Let's!'

They put on their coats and boots and stepped out bareheaded into the snowy garden. Emma took in a deep breath and blew out a plume of steam.

'It's cold,' Marc-Antoine said, laughing at her startled expression. He lifted her left hand, where the lovely antique emerald engagement ring he'd given her glowed, and kissed it. 'Snow does that, my little Australian.'

She stuck her tongue out at him. 'You're a smart arse,' she said to him, in English, 'and no one likes a smart arse.'

'And here's me thinking you liked this one just a bit,' he said, chuckling.

'I do,' she agreed, bending down and picking up a handful of snow, '*just* a bit.' She threw the snowball at him.

'You'll pay for that!' he shouted in mock outrage, picking up one in turn, which she managed to dodge, laughing, as Mattie's voice rang out cheerfully from the doorway, 'Time to stop playing, our guests are arriving!'

'Coming, Mattie,' they cried, in cheerful unison, heading back to the house.

As they were about to go inside, Emma saw a flash of red. Squirrels were supposed to hibernate all winter, but Monsieur Leroux clearly hadn't received the memo, for there he was, scampering about in the snow in a surprised kind of way, as if he couldn't quite believe his eyes, or the feeling in his paws. 'Oh!' she exclaimed, making Marc-Antoine and Mattie turn, their eyes widening.

For another squirrel had appeared, and the two little creatures darted together towards the nearby holly bush with its shiny red berries, looking for all the world as though they were about to gather provisions for their own party on this enchanted night in this snowy Paris garden.

Author's note and acknowledgements

Writing this novel took me on an extraordinary journey as I followed Emma, Charlotte and Arielle through the winding paths of their lives in Paris, against a background of that glorious green and flowery world that's such an integral part of the charm of the city. Over the years, I've visited most of the places my characters went to, but I discovered quite a few more in the process of researching and writing this novel, as well as some fascinating facts and anecdotes about Paris gardens.

I also came across wonderful resources, including the beautiful medieval manuscript Daniel showcases in his talk at the Cluny Museum, *Le Jardin de vertueuse consolation*. It's held in the French national library, the Bibliothèque Nationale, and you can see it online at their free digital archive, Gallica: gallica.bnf.fr

The snippets Daniel reads out, by the way, are my own translations of real passages in the manuscript. And the book that Emma finds, *Petit guide pratique du jardinage*, that becomes her guide for the restoration of her grandfather's garden, also really exists, complete with the touching dedicatory flyleaf to the young woman who used to own it, though in the novel I changed her name. The weird thing is that I'd decided there would be a dedicatory flyleaf in Emma's copy even before I got the real book from a French online second-hand bookshop. It was only once it was in my hands that I discovered the dedication on the flyleaf, though there had been no mention of it in the bookseller's listing! That was just a bit of the magic that seemed to follow the creation of this novel and made it such a delight to write.

I'd like to acknowledge the many people who have helped make this book such a lovely reality: many thanks to my wonderful agent, Margaret Connolly, for her encouragement, suggestions and support; to all the fantastic Ultimo Press team for their dedicated, thoughtful and inspired commitment to making this book the very best it could be; and to Cheryl Orsini for the gorgeous peony and fabulous map. Special thanks to my husband, David, gardener extraordinaire, for advice on plants and the restoration of overgrown gardens, and to my Paris-based sister Gabrielle and brother-in-law Bruno whose intimate knowledge of the city's gardens helped to greatly expand my repertoire. And to all my beautiful family in Australia, France and the UK, I am so very grateful for your loving support and encouragement, as always.

Finally, I'd like to thank all the wonderful readers who took my previous novel, *The Paris Cooking School*, so much to their hearts. I hope *A Secret Garden in Paris* gives you just as much pleasure.

Reading group questions

1. How many of the gardens of Paris depicted or mentioned in the novel had you heard of before reading the book? Have you visited any of them? And if so, which is your favourite?

2. Monsieur Leroux, the red squirrel, appears at various points in the narrative. What do you think he represents?

3. Mattie tells Emma that in France it's said that 'everyone has their secret garden'. She explains what it might mean—but can you think of other meanings? What is your own image of a 'secret garden' in the psychological sense?

4. Why do you think Corinne never told Emma about Marc-Antoine and his mother?

5. Charlotte went to Paris in order to escape a difficult atmosphere at home. Do you think that was a wise decision? Is there anything else she could have done?

6. Charlotte has made a home in London but she is still very Parisian, with a foot in both worlds. What differences between the two cultures—English and French—do you think she might have found challenging to navigate (aside from language)?

7. Tom found it impossible to be open with Charlotte or the rest of his family about his unhappiness at work. He says to Charlotte that it was 'bloody stupid macho pride'. But do you think that's the full story?

8. Arielle has an extraordinary understanding of flowers, but there is no indication she has had any special training for that. How do you think her talent might have developed?

9. The relationship between Arielle and her sister, Pauline, is very close: how does the author depict it? And who do you think is the stronger sister?

10. Daniel's talk about the medieval manuscript marks a turning point in the way he and Arielle interact. Why do you think that is?

11. Grief and consolation are important themes in *A Secret Garden in Paris*. How are these explored within the novel?

Sophie Beaumont is the pen name of Sophie Masson AM, who was born in Indonesia of French parents and was brought up in France and Australia. A bilingual French and English speaker, she has a master's degree in French and English literature and a PhD in creative practice. Sophie is the prolific and award-winning author of more than fifty novels for children, young adults and adults, many of which have been published internationally. Her first novel as Sophie Beaumont, *The Paris Cooking School*, was published by Ultimo Press in 2023.